# Praise

Maria has received many honors and awards for her work including the Readers' Choice Heart of Excellence Award, the Write Touch Readers Award, The NEST (National Excellence In Story Telling) Award, the Carolyn Award, The Stiletto Reader's Choice Award, Long & Short Reviews Book of the Month Award, and Still Moments Magazine Reader's Choice Award.

Praise for *The Blueberry Swirl Waltz*:
"This fast paced and easily readable story is a delight...By her talent in creating dialogue and voice, author Imbalzano's talents clearly extend to creating a setting which takes one back to a small riverside town...Ahh, the memories."
~*Kat Henry Doran, Wild Women Reviews*

"...a nostalgic, sweet romance I read in one sitting...a must-read."
~*N.N. Light's Book Heaven*
~*~

Praise for *Dancing In The Sand*:
"...an intense and emotional read...Ms. Imbalzano does an amazing job of defining the characters, and I feel like I knew them all intimately...a well-written story that twists and turns in all the right places."
~*LJT, NetGalley reviewer*
~*~

Praise for *Sworn to Forget* (The Sworn Sisters Series):
"Nicki and Dex have amazing chemistry and their heat is scorching, both in and out of the bedroom."
~*LJT, NetGalley reviewer*

# Island Detour

## by

## Maria Imbalzano

*The Sunrise Island Series*

**Island Detour**

Cover Art by *Diana Carlile*

The Wild Rose Press, Inc.
PO Box 708
Adams Basin, NY 14410-0708
Visit us at www.thewildrosepress.com

Publishing History
First Edition, 2024
Trade Paperback ISBN 978-1-5092-5364-7
Digital ISBN 978-1-5092-5365-4

*The Sunrise Island Series*
Published in the United States of America

## Dedication

To my husband Chris, who introduced me to the Florida
Keys a long time ago

Chapter One

Max Heaton paced the length of the school director's office, again attempting to sway his boss. But Andy Dalton leaned back in his chair, hands behind his head, sandaled feet up on his chaotic desk, looking ever so relaxed over Max's rant.

"Come on, Andy. You've got to put yourself out there. Sunrise Island School is unique. But no one knows about it. It's hidden down here in the Florida Keys. How do you expect it to grow?" He had repeated the same words dozens of times to no avail.

"I'm not ready to put funds into marketing yet. This school is only two years old. It needs to grow slowly, by word of mouth." Andy swung his feet off the desk and leaned forward. "You know as well as I do, Max, that once we go the social media route, the floodgates will open. As it is, I get hundreds of applications for only sixty-four spots every semester."

"That's why you should expand. More students mean more interest, which means more in grant money."

"You're the marine biology teacher here. Not the director of development."

Although Andy spoke with an edge, Max knew he wasn't angry over his persistence, so he pushed a little harder.

"Once you turn this environmental school of yours into a coveted experience for high school students around the country, I'll have a better chance of getting a grant to start my environmental research institute."

Andy sighed. "So we're back to that." He removed his glasses and rubbed his eyes, a movement that usually signified exasperation.

Max stopped pacing and slid into the chair in front of Andy's desk. "Come on, Andy. Think about how important this research institute will be to the school." Not to mention how important it would be to him—a living, breathing tribute to his brother.

"I know. By signing on, I'll be helping to save the ocean. A very admirable goal, and vital."

So Andy had heard him in the past. "I'm sure of its success. It will bring dozens of environmental scientists down here every summer to work on experiments. And the hands-on experience the students will gain during their semester here will be invaluable. I know it will work." Max hit the desk with his palm to make his point, then tossed out the ultimate carrot. "Sunrise Island School will become synonymous with the greatest high school teaching and research institute in the country. You'll be famous." He ventured a smile.

"What about you?" Andy arched an eyebrow.

"I don't care about fame. I just want to do this."

There was no other explanation. He was driven by an unknown force. Maybe his brother's spirit. Or his need to jump a hundred and fifty percent into a project he could call his own.

"I'll take your request into consideration." Andy stood and riffled through his telephone messages. While not a resounding yes, at least Andy would ponder his suggestion. That was something.

Andy looked up. "I have to go to the airport and pick

up our new English lit teacher."

"What new teacher?" Although Sara was on bed rest with five months still to go before she'd have her baby, Max hadn't heard of any new hires. "I thought you were covering for Sara this semester."

"I was going to. Then an old friend of mine from the Valen School called. She's on sabbatical this semester and had some free time. It worked out perfectly. She's brilliant and will be a great addition to our staff. You've probably heard of her. Everyone else has. Sophie Kearns. She runs the Summer Teaching Academy at Valen. Very prestigious. It's the leading educational program for teachers on the East Coast." Andy's brow furrowed. "I thought I told everyone at dinner Monday night."

"I was helping a few of the students with an experiment Monday night. I missed dinner."

"Well, you'll meet her tonight. See you later." Andy tossed the phone messages on his desk and headed for the door.

Sophie Kearns. The name sounded familiar. But not from the Summer Teaching Academy. Although he had heard of it. He slouched in his chair and stared off into space, rolling her name around his brain.

Until he remembered.

She was the one who had helped Andy with his grant applications to get Sunrise Island School started. She was much more than an English teacher. She'd been instrumental in making Andy's dream a reality. And now she was coming here.

A slow burn rose in his chest. This couldn't just be a coincidence. That she had a sabbatical at the same time Andy needed a literature teacher. There had to be something more to it. He let the wheels turn a little longer. Andy wouldn't be courting her to bring her Summer Teaching Academy here, would he? That would certainly put an end to any discussion of his research institute. Maybe that's why Andy kept putting him off. Why he consistently knocked down all his ideas. His jaw tightened as his concern rose.

"Damn." His curse bounced off the walls of Andy's office. What was he up to?

Andy ignoring his advice on marketing was bad enough—an indirect snub of his plan for a research institute. Did he have an ulterior motive? A motive that involved an old friend from Valen?

He rose from his chair and sprinted outside. "Wait up, Andy. I'll go get her. You have enough to do."

Andy frowned but tossed over the keys to the school Jeep. "Great. Thanks, Max."

This was his chance to find out, straight from Ms. Kearns' mouth, exactly what her and Andy's intentions were.

And do whatever he could to thwart them if they interfered with his own.

*****

She was alive!

Sophie breathed a huge sigh of relief. The ten-seat turbo-prop plane taxied to a stop in the middle of the island's tiny airfield. Her fingers unfurled their death-like grip on the ragged upholstery of the armrest, and she wiggled them to get the blood flowing again. The plane looked to be made out of tin—old tin—and the ripped Naugahyde seats testified to its age.

*Someone should be putting these planes out of commission.*

She exited down the wobbly stairs along with her

fellow passengers, none of whom seemed as worried as she. Once her feet touched solid ground, she sent up a prayer of gratitude and exhaled the pent-up fear she'd been holding.

The warm, humid breeze felt like heaven as it rushed to envelop her, and palm trees swayed and bent in a welcoming motion. The January sun of the Florida Keys nearly blinded her as it reflected off the white open-air building that purported to be the airport. At least that's what the sign said.

Following employees who moved the baggage from the plane to the floor inside the terminal, Sophie retrieved her two suitcases, with not a checker in sight. Apparently, no one on Sunrise Island was worried about security.

She strode outside, and before her stood a line of pastel-colored taxis, all driverless. Over to the left, a group of men chatting amiably sat on folding chairs around a crate, playing cards. *Interesting way of life.*

"Sophie Kearns?" An unfamiliar voice pulled her from her observations.

She turned and saw a very handsome man: classic Greek profile, hard-muscled body, chocolate-brown eyes. Definitely not her friend Andy, the stereotypical, nerdy biologist who had worked with her at the Valen School three years earlier.

His light-blue T-shirt gripped strong arms bronzed by the sun. A small logo for Sunrise Island School was stitched on his left pocket.

Sophie nodded. "That's me."

"I'm Max Heaton, the marine biology teacher at Sunrise Island School." He held out his hand, and a semi-smile inched over his mouth.

She shook his hand. "It's nice to meet you. I thought Andy would be picking me up."

"He was busy, so I offered. The school is only twenty minutes away. I'm sure he'll spend an hour or two with you this afternoon giving you the tour, getting you acclimated."

His eyes scanned her body, and she felt drab and overdressed in her gray, sensible traveling slacks and white, long-sleeved blouse.

Max grabbed the handle of one of her rolling suitcases and led her through the parking lot. The sun beat down on her head, and hot, heavy hair clung to her neck as she nearly sprinted to keep up with him.

They passed two teenaged girls in short shorts and bikini tops, and a flash of her younger self made her smile. Not that she was old, but no bikinis or cut-off shorts inhabited her luggage. She had become unquestionably cautious over the past seven years—at least with her wardrobe. Knee-covering skirts, button-down blouses, and a blazer now and then made up her uniform of sorts for the conservative, preppy type she had become. Fitting in with her colleagues at Valen and being one with them had been a major goal.

When she refocused on her route, Max was two rows ahead, standing at a beat-up, green Jeep also sporting the school's logo. "Are you coming?" A hint of annoyance tracked his words.

She ignored it and smiled, hoping to disarm his irritation. "It must be nice to work in paradise."

"It is beautiful." He looked around as if to confirm his statement. "But don't let your surroundings fool you into believing you're on vacation. Our new batch of students arrived last week, and in just four months we have to teach them about ways to protect the marine environment. In addition to their regular studies." He opened the trunk and heaved her two suitcases over the tailgate. "It's an exhausting job—six days a week, sometimes sixteen hours a day."

She hoped for a chuckle from him to signify his inflation of daily life on the island, but he soldiered on.

"When you're not teaching or helping students with their school work, you'll be going on marine trips with them or camping in the pines."

Maybe the others, but surely, he couldn't mean her.

"I hope you're up for it." A taunting chuckle accompanied his statement.

She slid into the passenger seat and glanced over at him. "Sure," she said, giving the appropriate answer for the time being.

What had she gotten herself into? She was used to working either in classrooms, her office, or the library— her head in the books and rarely on the outdoors. Although Valen was set on a beautiful campus in Princeton, with picturesque landscaping, ivy-covered buildings, and hundred-year-old oak trees standing sentry on winding pathways, enjoying her physical environment had not been on her agenda.

Easing out of the parking lot and onto the main road, Max relaxed into his apparent driving mode—one hand on the steering wheel, the other arm resting on the doorframe. Sophie gathered her long hair in her fist, attempting to keep it out of her face and off her perspiring neck as hot air blew through the open car windows. Either Andy didn't believe in air conditioning, or he didn't want to spend the money on an added feature that, to most people, was standard in an automobile.

Given Max's frightening tutorial of life as a teacher at Andy's esteemed school, Sophie focused on the scenery instead of anticipating the worst. To the left was the Atlantic Ocean, with its shades of light aqua to deep teal—much calmer than up north. The white masts of sailboats dotted its surface intermittently, and a speedboat pulled a multicolored parasail in the distance.

"The beach is so narrow here," she commented, changing the subject to minimize her angst.

"On this stretch of the island, it's made up of shells and stones. Not very comfortable. But a little farther down the coast, there are more sandy beaches."

Before long, Max pointed out the favored spot. Dozens of umbrellas staked out their owners' little patch of sand, and palm trees aided those without artificial shade. A row of food trucks parked nose to trunk along the curb, hawking everything from hot dogs and hamburgers to souvlaki and water ice. If it hadn't been January, Sophie would have thought she'd been deposited in the middle of spring break.

"Doesn't anybody work around here?"

"Tourism is the number one industry. Most residents work for hotels and restaurants or on fishing boats or adventure-type tours. Those are all vacationers."

"Do you ever get bored living on an island? Especially one this small?" She'd read it was approximately one mile wide and two miles long. There couldn't be much in the way of cultural activity.

"No. I love it. And, of course, I love the school. But it's not for everyone." He glanced over at her, again assessing her. "You don't seem like the outdoorsy type."

An understatement if she'd ever heard one. But she couldn't—no, wouldn't—admit to it. It might skew

Max's opinion of her before she even started. And her goal was to fit in, not point out her differences.

"What brings you here, if not the lure of water sports and working in a marine environment?"

She considered her answer, keeping the real reason to herself. "Andy needed a literature teacher for a semester. He's been trying to get me down here for a while now to see his school. I'm glad it all worked out."

"He asked you to work here before?" His tone was inquisitive but had an edge. What was that all about?

"Not in those specific words." But on several occasions, he'd suggested she come down and see the school for herself, with the intimation that she'd love it and never want to go back north again.

"In what specific words, exactly?"

Before she could respond, Max slammed on the brakes at a red light, and she grabbed the dashboard to avoid hitting her head on the window.

"Sorry," he said with no apparent sympathy in his voice. "This light is in the middle of nowhere."

From that point on, Max stopped talking, hopefully to concentrate more on his driving and not because he had something against her being here. She didn't mind the quiet. She'd be safer and not have to hear more about her sporting adventures to come. Sliding back into sightseeing mode, she gazed out the window as the Jeep veered away from the water and snaked through narrow streets of small but well-maintained houses. Everyone seemed to have a flower garden of brilliant, tropical blooms winding along white picket fences or trellises. Picture perfect.

The houses soon led to a small town complete with a grocery store, several restaurants, T-shirt shops, art galleries, and a hotel—painted pink. Her anxiety slipped away as she watched people mill through town, meandering at a snail's pace. No one seemed to be in a hurry to get anywhere. The change of pace might be nice.

Five minutes later, Max turned onto a gravel and sand driveway with a sign indicating they'd reached Sunrise Island School. The view opened up into a panorama of one-story wooden structures, palm trees, and the aqua-blue Gulf of Mexico as its backdrop. Totally opposite from Valen with its stately oaks and century-old stone buildings.

"We're not in Jersey anymore," she said under her breath as she opened the car door.

Drawn from the Jeep by her surroundings, Sophie breathed in the warm, salty air and lifted her face to the sun. Her eyes closed against its brilliance, and her sense of sight was replaced by sound. Palm fronds brushed against each other in the breeze, birds chirped and sang from their perches, and the sea lapped softly against the beach in the distance.

She couldn't remember the last time she'd been to a beach. Vacations had been substituted for teaching, volunteering, and running the Summer Teaching Academy. She had no time for idyllic interludes while working toward her goals.

Max pulled her luggage from the trunk and grabbed one of her suitcases. "Come on. We'll drop these outside of your cabin, then I'll show you to Andy's office." His tone was all business.

She dragged her other suitcase and attempted to keep up without success. Although their initial meeting at the airport didn't rise to the level of warm and friendly, sometime between then and now, he had turned sullen.

Maybe he was just a grump.

He peered over his shoulder and watched her struggling to pull her luggage over the sand and shell walkway but didn't offer more help. "Dan Myers, our program director, will be chomping at the bit to add you to the daily activity roster." His chuckle couldn't be misread as anything other than what it was. Wicked glee at her expense.

An odd tingle crept through her veins. She might have made a huge mistake by reaching out to Andy and then accepting this temporary job to keep her mind off her devastating suspension. Boating and camping were hardly on her radar screen, and now she was expected to be doing these activities, and more, on a daily basis.

She dragged her suitcase along the sandy pathway, and the effort had her huffing and puffing. Clearly, she would have to beat herself into shape while living on this island, if she were to adapt.

Sweat pasted her blouse to her back, and all at once she felt sticky and overheated. And out of place.

Finally arriving at her cabin, they left her luggage beside the step and walked from there to a building designated *Eden Hall*. Max opened the door and stood back for her to enter.

Andy glanced up from his desk. A shy grin inched over his mouth, and a twinkle reached his eyes, magnified by gold-rim glasses. He stood and opened his arms in welcome. "Sophie. You're finally here."

She gave him a warm hug. She'd missed him. "It's so good to see you again."

His once pale, northeastern skin had been tanned by the sun, and his pressed chinos and button-down shirt had been replaced by cargo shorts and a T-shirt.

"You look wonderful," she gushed. "Island life certainly agrees with you."

"As I'm sure it will with you." He turned to Max. "Thanks. I'll take it from here."

Max waved and smirked. "Good luck," he said, although Sophie wasn't sure whether those words were meant for her or Andy.

"Have a seat." Andy's warm welcome set her at ease. "Any word on the culprit behind the video?"

Her stomach plummeted, and that familiar, nauseous feeling returned. Just last week, she'd been summoned to Headmaster Ryan's office for what she thought would be a congratulatory meeting following her nomination to become the next chair of the English department. Instead, he blindsided her with a video posted to social media with her in the starring role. She was standing in front of a group of students from her alma mater, encouraging them to practice their debate skills with the goal of gaining confidence. Someone had edited her words to make it sound like she was coaching them to compete against Valen's debate team—a clear violation of the loyalty clause in her contract—except that she had never said those words. What had started out as her volunteering one day a week after school to help struggling kids with their writing and oral skills had turned into a traumatic nightmare.

"No. Not yet. It was probably posted from a fake account. The name wasn't familiar or connected with anyone at the school. The board is doing its own internal investigation, which worries me. I want this fraud uncovered. Fast. And you know how slowly the board tends to do things."

Andy nodded. "I can't believe someone would do

this to you. You're so well liked at Valen. Whoever it was can't think they'll get away with it."

Sophie sighed. Approximately ten days, twenty hours, and fifteen minutes ago, her world had been turned upside down. And instead of reveling in her nomination for chair of the English department, she'd been forced to wrestle with the possibility of losing her career.

"How's Headmaster Ryan dealing with all this?"

"At first, he was angry. He claimed his phone had been ringing off the hook with irate parents, especially those with kids on Valen's debate team. They'd been up in arms about what they'd seen posted. And of course they shared it with anyone they could think of, which made matters worse. Even after I explained to Ryan that those weren't my words, he was skeptical given the evidence. And he made it clear that perception is everything. He suspended me on the spot." Even now, she felt the painful stab to her soul.

She had been doing something good for students at her alma mater who couldn't afford private school—those in similar circumstances to herself back in the day. Who would surreptitiously take a video of her, edit her words, and post it with the intent to cast her in a very bad light?

"He must have felt cornered by the parents for him to suspend you like that. You've always been one of his favorite teachers, and I know you considered him to be your mentor."

She nodded, a heavy sadness weighing her down. "Eventually he came around and was apologetic over his angry reaction. He suggested I tell everyone I'm taking a sabbatical, despite the board's vote to continue my suspension while the investigation ensues. Neither he nor the board wanted any negative publicity to spread internally or to the outside world."

"Your secret's safe with me. I'm sorry this happened, Sophie. But at least I get the benefit of your little break."

Her sigh echoed around the room. "I'm not sure I made the right decision. From down here, it will be impossible to keep the pressure on the investigation and make things happen quickly. But…I'm here, so there's no point in worrying about that now."

She continued, trying to keep the uncertainty out of her voice. "I just hope that when the investigation is over and I'm reinstated, my reputation will bounce back."

That's what haunted her the most. She'd worked tirelessly for the past seven years to build her status as a premier educator, making a difference in her students' lives as well as that of other educators. Her next goal was soon to be accomplished. At least until this fiasco happened. What would become of her well-planned future? She shuddered at the possibility.

Andy broke into her thoughts. "While they're up in Princeton playing Sherlock Holmes during the cold, snowy winter, you'll be down here kayaking, swimming, and teaching English lit in the balmy, warm breeze of Sunrise Island." The conviction in his voice told her she'd won the prize—at least in his view.

If only she could feel the same.

Chapter Two

"Come on. I'll show you to your living quarters, then give you the two-cent tour." Andy stood and smoothed his wrinkled shorts before heading outside.

Within minutes, they arrived at Sophie's cabin at the end of a row of similar abodes—one-story whitewashed cubes with blue aluminum roofs. Andy pushed open the door and helped deposit her suitcases just inside the threshold.

She took a moment to survey her domain, and an odd sense of calm fell over her. "This is adorable!"

She walked through the tiny living room, sparsely furnished with a couch, coffee table, kitchen table, and two chairs. The bedroom contained a full-sized bed, which took up most of the space. She'd have to squeeze past it in order to get to the three-drawer dresser and small closet on the other side. A diminutive bathroom and kitchenette could be seen from any spot in the cabin. End of tour.

She turned to Andy. "I don't have to share this with anyone, do I?"

That elicited a chuckle. "No. It's all yours." He gave her an evaluative look. "I'll wait outside while you change into something more casual. Then I'll take you around." He paused. "I hope you packed more appropriate clothes in those suitcases."

"I went shopping before I left. I couldn't be sure

you'd have stores down here to match my tastes."

He grunted, then stepped outside and closed the door.

Sophie dragged her suitcases into the bedroom and unsnapped the clasps before digging out one of her new pairs of shorts—khaki—and a white, sleeveless, collared blouse. She quickly changed, then slipped her feet into a pair of sandals while looking at her naked legs. *Ugh.* Ivory, dry skin had been uncovered. Hurriedly, she spread sunscreen on her bare limbs, more to make the dryness go away than with the thought of protecting her pale, winter skin. Taking a fortifying breath, she went to meet Andy.

They ambled along a sandy path as he talked about the school. "The academic classrooms are over there." He pointed toward a long building just before the beach and a breathtaking view of the Gulf of Mexico. "Our teachers incorporate marine studies into their curriculum. For example, if you have your class read *The Old Man and the Sea*, you may decide to take them on a fishing trip where you can discuss the themes of the book as well as the author's connection to the Keys."

She slowed her gait. "Oh. I thought I'd just be teaching in the classroom. And helping out with some field trips." This latter knowledge had only come to light through Max.

"Teaching the subject you were hired for is only a small part of the semester program. Sunrise Island School's philosophy is to teach students academic subjects while applying that knowledge to the environment they're living in and vice versa—in addition to learning about protecting the marine environment."

"But I don't know anything about that."

"I guess we'll be teaching you as well. As for the outdoor activities, anyone can learn."

A laugh escaped Sophie's mouth. Most of her days were spent in her classroom or the library or working with her students. Inside.

"What's so funny?" Andy glanced over at her as they wound around a sidewalk parallel to the sea.

"You seem to have more faith in my abilities than you should. But I appreciate the confidence."

"I know you don't have much experience with water sports, but you should start learning as soon as possible."

He must have seen the dread carved into her face, because he clapped her on the back. "Don't worry, Sophie. It'll be interesting." Unfortunately, he didn't say *fun*. "A totally different experience than you're used to. You may even learn to love it here and beg me to stay on at the end of the semester."

"Andy, I really appreciate you doing this for me. But I assure you my sole goal in coming here is to work my way through my so-called sabbatical so I don't go crazy. I won't be asking you to accommodate me for more than one semester."

"Well, just know that I'd do anything for you. You helped me realize my dream."

Her heart expanded with warmth. He could be so focused when it came to his school, yet he'd really come through for her when she needed his help. He knew she wouldn't fit in with the other teachers—that she didn't meet the school standards. Yet he'd hired her anyway.

She reached out and touched his arm, and an overwhelming bond of loyalty swelled between them.

"I hate to harp on this," he stated tentatively, "but if

I were you, I'd do everything possible to get up to speed on the basic water activities, or you're not going to be able to join in on our adventures."

Almost afraid to ask, she ventured, "Could you be specific, please?"

"First on the agenda should be learning how to snorkel and kayak."

She nodded emphatically, although a sick feeling attacked her gut. "Okay." That didn't sound too ominous.

"You'd better brush up on your swimming too. Start with a quarter mile in the Gulf and build up. And eventually you're going to have to go camping."

Visions of creepy night crawlers covering her body as she lay immobile on the hard ground flashed though her brain. She swallowed her impulse to beg off. Yet the favor he'd granted her was huge. She couldn't repay him by asking for an exemption—at least not yet.

"No problem," she said, her voice wavering.

Thankfully, Andy's to-do list of sporting activities was interrupted when they ran into Ben Knightly, the math teacher. He hailed from Somalia but had found a home here. His dark cropped hair and unshaven jaw did nothing to mask his exotic looks. They also encountered Maddie Cuthbert, the art teacher—a transplant straight from New York City. Although dressed in shorts and a T-shirt—the apparent uniform of the school—her all-white outfit had an air of sophistication, as did her subtle makeup and highlighted golden hair.

To Sophie's chagrin, everyone she'd met so far had toned bodies kissed by the sun and a relaxed, casual personality. Except for Max, of course. By comparison, she was a little more Type A, and her coloring was close to the hue of Maddie's clothing. Although she had a gym membership back home, going once a week provided scant definition to her untaxed muscles.

Circling back past the dining pavilion, they came upon another teacher, and Andy's face brightened. "That's Kristin Sandler, our social studies teacher."

Kristin strode over to Sophie, and her smile glowed. "You must be Sophie Kearns. I've heard great things about you. I also know about your amazing teaching academy. I'm planning to attend next summer if I can get away from here for a few weeks."

Pride rushed through her at Kristin's accolades. "Thank you." She held out her hand, and Kristin shook it with warmth.

"It's nice to have another woman teacher here besides Maddie and me. The men are taking over." She elbowed Andy, who actually blushed at her jibe.

"Now, Kristin. You know we love you and would never discriminate against women."

Sophie noted that Kristin must be the person who brought out the best in everyone. And if she could cause Andy to let down his guard for a few minutes, she must be very special.

"I'll see you at dinner tonight, Sophie, and give you the scoop." Kristin's hazel eyes sparkled with mischief. "I'll teach you all about these characters who work here so you'll know what you're getting into."

"Don't you have a camping trip planned for tonight with some of the students?" Andy arched his eyebrow a bit menacingly.

"Nice try, Andy. But not tonight. I'm totally free to give up all your secrets."

He actually laughed as he steered Sophie back

toward Eden Hall. "We'll see about that," he called over his shoulder.

The sparkle and camaraderie he had so easily displayed while in Kristin's company dissipated. "The rest of the teachers are working with some of the students off site. I know Keith Johnson, our chemistry teacher, is on the beach with his class this afternoon. You'll meet him, as well as the others, at dinner."

They walked in silence for a few moments before parting ways. As she headed back to her cabin to unpack, she thought about Andy's time at Valen. He was a talented teacher, but he'd wanted so much more. His goal had been to start an environmental school. Once he'd gotten the initial grant, his school had become his mistress. And if anyone did anything to jeopardize the vision he had for Sunrise Island School, she was sure he'd have them quartered and skewered.

This adventure she had embarked on was way out of her league. How had she mistakenly thought this was going to be a walk in paradise?

****

Dinner in the dining pavilion occurred at five every evening. Sophie found her way to the teachers' table and sat next to Kristin, who had saved her a seat between her and Ben.

"How'd your day go?" Kristin asked. Her cheery demeanor was at odds with the anxiety inching through Sophie's blood.

"Just great." Sophie forced a smile as well as false happiness into her voice.

Kristin looked at her, her expression softening. "I remember my first few days here. They were daunting. Everything's new, and Andy can be a little intimidating.

But give yourself some time. Things will start to fall into place."

Her optimistic attitude was infectious, and even though Sophie wasn't intimidated in the least by Andy, she certainly was by her surroundings. Yet a little of Kristin's positivity worked itself into her being and settled her nerves.

"You must be the new lit teacher," came a male voice from behind her as a hand landed on her shoulder.

She turned to see a brawny, long-haired thirty-something. His blue eyes danced, and he stuck out his hand to shake Sophie's, introducing himself as Dan Myers, the program director.

"I'm the guy who tortures the teachers into signing up for kayaking, scuba diving, and camping with the kids." His brilliant smile gave testament to the glee he encountered in doing his job.

"I'm afraid I don't know how to kayak or scuba dive. And I've never been camping."

A groan from the other side of the table caught her attention. "Andy hired a prima donna," Max said in a none-too-friendly voice.

Why was he being so surly? "I am not a prima donna." She glared at him for effect.

"If you can't pull your weight around here, then the title fits."

"What makes you think I can't pull my weight? I have a PhD in English literature from Rutgers, and I won the Chasten Award for my thesis on women's emerging roles in twentieth century classics."

"Well, that should help us all out when it's your turn to pitch a tent or fish for food."

The look of disgust on his face and the sarcasm

dripping from his mouth had the effect of slapping her in the face. No one had ever discounted her credentials. Yet, in this atmosphere, they seemed to have little merit. Worse yet, he was making it sound like a Girl Scout would have been a far superior candidate for the job. And why was he talking about her fishing for food anyway? Was he out of his mind?

"Why would I have to go fish—"

Kristin jumped in. "Max, maybe you could be a little less skeptical and give Sophie a chance. She just got here today and is trying to settle in." Kristin gave her a reassuring pat on the arm as she chastised the bully in the playground.

But Sophie needed to protect herself. She didn't want to be perceived as a wimp, so she pulled her strength around her like a cloak. "I realize I'm the new kid on the block, and it may not seem at first blush that I belong here." She glanced around the table and inwardly groaned at that understatement.

Every teacher here was toned, agile, and capable of doing the activities necessary. To make matters worse, they all had that healthy glow from working outdoors and looked comfortable in their skin as well as their casual clothing. On the other hand, she looked like she had drenched herself in white paste and then tried to cover it up with expensive, conservative clothes.

She plowed on. "But I'm an excellent teacher and a fast learner. If I have to pitch in and go kayaking or scuba diving or camping with the students, I'll do my best to get up to speed and help out. I don't intend to be a drain on this community. I just hope you will be kind enough to give me some time to pick up the basics."

"I'll help you, Sophie." Ben playfully elbowed her

while giving her a grin.

"Me too," chimed in Kristin as she shot Max the evil eye.

"That's great," said Max. "Because she's going to need all the help she can get." He scraped his chair against the floor as he pushed back and got up. "See you guys around."

Sophie watched his back as he headed in the direction of the beach. The brooding loner. While he'd been civil when he first picked her up at the airport this afternoon, his attitude toward her had steadily declined during their twenty-minute ride. He was clearly angry that she'd been hired. Yet why it should affect him was a mystery. She wasn't taking over his job.

"What's his problem?" she asked of no one in particular.

"Oh, don't worry about Max," Kristin said kindly. "He didn't mean to be such a cad. He just can't help it sometimes." She glanced past Sophie and exchanged a look with Ben before continuing. "He doesn't always trust other people to do the job they were hired for until they prove themselves to him. He's a bit of a control freak."

"He doesn't have a hard time trusting all people." Maddie's low, sexy drawl was followed up with a sly smile.

*Are Max and Maddie an item? Poor Maddie.* Although she seemed more than capable of handling herself.

Dan stood up and clapped his hands, getting all the students' attention in the dining hall.

"Whoever is on cleanup duty, get to it. The rest of you hit the books. I understand there's a math quiz tomorrow and a social studies quiz on Thursday."

A combined groan moved through the dining pavilion as students brought their trays to the kitchen area and exited the pavilion toward their dorm rooms. A certain few stayed behind to clean up.

"How'd you all like to gather round the campfire and tell scary stories?" Dan directed his question to the teachers while rubbing his hands together.

"I'm fresh out of scary stories." Maddie tossed her long, blonde hair over her shoulder. "But I wouldn't mind listening to Ben play his guitar."

"Me either," Kristin said. "We do this a few nights a week, Sophie. It's fun."

"And a good bonding experience," Ben added.

Kristin rolled her eyes and slapped Ben on the back. "Come on, Garth. We could use some upbeat music tonight. Your friend Max has put a damper on things."

"I'll meet you there in a few minutes. After I grab my guitar." Ben's genuine smile helped lift the negative attitude Max had dumped on Sophie, and she followed Kristin to the beach.

Before long everyone had assembled and took their spots around a blazing campfire. The family-like atmosphere surrounded her, but she couldn't help the penetrating feeling that she didn't belong.

Would she ever?

For at least the dozenth time since her sudden fall from grace, the air leaked from her system and sucked her spirit from her core. She couldn't let it happen now, here. She knew what she had to do. Find a way to fit in. And while it wouldn't be easy, she could do it. She had to. For her own sake.

At nine thirty, the small band of troubadours tossed

sand onto the fire and headed to their respective cabins. Apparently, breakfast was at eight fifteen and the first class at nine. If she wanted to learn how to kayak, scuba dive, snorkel, and swim, she had better be up by six thirty every morning. She pushed from her mind any further thought that taking this job might have been a big mistake.

"Hey, Kearns!" A familiar male voice came up behind her.

*Max*.

"Yes?" she questioned suspiciously.

"Sorry about before." He gave her a sideways glance and an engaging smile. "I was upset about an earlier discussion with Andy and let it get the better of me."

Sophie raised her eyebrow but kept her silence. She wasn't ready to dive in to the politics of Sunrise Island School just yet. Nor did she want to get taken in by a gorgeous face.

"Where'd you get those frumpy clothes?" he asked.

The abrupt change of subject threw her off balance. She looked down at her Bermuda shorts and button-down blouse, scouring her brain for the source of her attire. "A small boutique at home."

"No wonder."

Was he insulting her? "What's wrong with them?"

"Nothing if you're taking a jaunt through New York City with some straitlaced bankers or lawyers on a hot summer day. Is that who you're used to hanging around with?"

His smile showed perfectly straight, white teeth, and she thought she saw a dimple.

"No, of course not. I'm not from the city. I'm from Princeton."

"Well, that clears it up. Many of those stuffy lawyers and bankers who work in the city live in those mini-mansions in the suburbs. And of course, they dress in their conservative long shorts and button-down shirts on their days off."

Despite his criticism of her apparel, a grin escaped. "That's a huge generalization. And besides, how would you know how Princetonians dress?"

"Their moniker sounds even stodgier than I picture them to be." His brown eyes danced, and his laugh did funny things to her stomach.

Sophie crossed her arms over her chest and tilted her head, watching him. "Since I work at a Princeton prep school, I dress to fit in there. But…I guess I'll have to reassess my clothing choices."

Not only did her clothes stand out, but so would her lack of athletic ability and life experiences. If she let her anxiety over her ill-conceived agreement to teach here take over, she'd be on the next plane home. But she was not a quitter.

Instead, she glanced down at her outfit, and a bubble of laughter started deep within. It worked its way up and joined with Max's rumbling chuckle before it took over her entire being.

And it felt so good to be standing in the warm sea breeze at the end of the Florida Keys, laughing with a manic-depressive stranger.

Chapter Three

The sun rose at seven, but Sophie had already been up for a half hour, anxiously contemplating her kayak lesson with Kristin. As she shuffled toward the water, she tried to take her mind off the potential dangers she was about to encounter by focusing on the orange ball of fire inching its way above the horizon.

Carrying her sneakers, she relished the cool granules of sand sifting between her toes—an odd and almost unfamiliar feeling.

Kristin stood casually on the dock, paddles beside her, as she tented her hand over her eyes and scanned the Gulf. From Sophie's point of view, the water looked as calm as a lake, thankfully, and it had better stay like that when they took the boat out. She had never learned to swim, although she could doggie paddle with the best of them. But she'd keep that bit of information to herself.

"Ahoy, sailor. Welcome to heaven on earth." Kristin gave Sophie a broad smile before jumping off the dock onto the wet sand. "Are you ready for your lesson?"

"As ready as I'll ever be." She hoped she didn't sound as scared as she felt.

"Where's your bathing suit?" Kristin frowned, assessing Sophie's shorts and blouse.

"I thought we were going boating, not swimming." Her defensiveness came through, and she breathed a sigh of relief when Kristin just shrugged.

"We usually wear a bathing suit on the water. You never know." Kristin's grin unsettled her even more.

"Never know what?" She had no intention of getting out of that boat.

Kristin ignored her question. "You're going to love kayaking." She handed Sophie an oar with a paddle on each end, then held the boat still in the shallow water for her to get in. "You take the front seat. I'll steer from the back."

The kayak rocked when Sophie got in, and her heart hammered as she quickly dropped down and grabbed onto the side of the craft in an effort to stabilize herself. Kristin pushed the boat out a little farther before jumping in, and a screech escaped when the boat rolled precariously back and forth.

Kristin chortled. "It's only water, Sophie. What's the worst that can happen?"

Apparently, Kristin had no fear of stingrays or jellyfish or barracudas or whatever else lurked beneath the surface. Besides, if Kristin did fall in, she'd be able to swim away from the frightening sea monsters. Little did she know that Sophie would end up as fish food.

With great effort, she ignored the dangers below and instead concentrated on Kristin's instructions on paddling. Only a stray thought here or there—like the fact she might truly anger a shark if she bonked it on the head with her paddle—intruded. But Sophie soon learned Kristin's rhythm and was able to follow her lead. They glided through the turquoise expanse of the Gulf of Mexico between Sunrise Island and small, uninhabited islands of mangrove trees, without seeing another soul. Kristin pointed out different vegetation as well as birds, and before long, she started to relax.

"It's so peaceful out here," she whispered, not wishing to interrupt the quiet solitude of their surroundings.

"I know. Isn't it great? This is my favorite time of day. It's not too hot yet, and there's no one else to share the water with. You can talk to yourself or think or sing or just be."

Sophie pictured herself alone in her boat as she rowed and sang into the breeze. So carefree. Without thought, she sighed.

"Is everything okay?" The concern in Kristin's voice, along with the peaceful aura surrounding her, converged and encouraged her to share a piece of herself.

"I still can't believe I'm here." The turmoil of her last days at Valen was the polar opposite of life on Sunrise Island.

"What brought you here?"

Kristin's question was so innocent, yet Sophie's blood pulsed through her veins at the fate that had changed her life. Her pat, evasive response to the million-dollar question was nowhere to be found, and instead the truth slipped out.

"An edited social media post portraying me as a traitor to my school."

A gasp escaped Kristin's mouth. "What happened?"

Sophie stopped paddling and gingerly turned in the boat to face Kristin. Then she poured out her story, and it flowed like waves rushing to the shore. Nothing could stop her once she'd started.

"Oh, Sophie. I'm so sorry. But I'm sure it will all work out in the end. You're such a nice person. It's hard to believe someone would do that to you."

"Thanks." Kristin's kind words wended their way

into her soul, and it felt good to have another ally. "I didn't think I had any enemies."

She gazed out over the calm sea, hoping its sereneness would wash over her and sweep away the sick feeling living in the pit of her stomach. The underlying truth of the matter was, if the slug wasn't caught soon, her reputation might not survive the scandal.

"I gave every moment I had to that school, to the kids, to other teachers. I wanted to become headmaster there."

This last statement was spoken so softly, so reverently, as if she were afraid to say it out loud. As if Kristin might think her aspiration too grand, too unattainable.

"That's a wonderful goal. And I'm sure you'll reach it. Andy says you're very determined once you set your mind to something."

Sophie inhaled deeply and straightened her shoulders. "I'm sorry. I'm dragging you down on this beautiful morning. I guess it was all too near the surface, and when you asked if everything was okay, the floodgates opened. But please don't tell the others. Only Andy knows."

Kristin gave her a supportive smile. "I'm glad you told me. And even though you'd rather be back at Valen, this is the perfect place to wait out the investigation."

She reached over and patted Sophie's hand. Such a simple gesture, but it warmed Sophie's soul.

"I hope that whoever did this to me gets what they deserve."

"Well, of course they will." Kristin's defiance couldn't be missed. "You'll be able to sue him or her, right?"

She had thought that too, at first. "I spoke to an attorney who advised me that even if we do find out who did this, a civil suit could take years, and if I land back on my feet, there may not be any damages. It seems like the only way I could win a judgment is if I become a basket case and can't function."

"Great." Kristin's sarcasm mirrored Sophie's own. "Where's the justice in that?"

With so many scams, fake reports, and edited posts on the internet these days, a criminal prosecution seemed unlikely as well. Her only hope was that the investigation would clear her, she'd be reinstated to her rightful position at Valen, and her reputation would be restored.

"We better start heading back. I don't want to be late for my first class. Andy has been so wonderful. I can't disappoint him."

"Sure." Kristin started paddling. "Andy's a different kind of guy, isn't he?"

Sophie smiled. "Yes. He is."

The ultimate science geek at Valen, Andy, with his short-cropped hair, tall wiry body, and shy quietness, had existed squarely in the nerd category. But once he broke out of that mold and found his calling here on Sunrise Island, he'd morphed into an attractive, if not quite handsome, benevolent leader with a noble mission.

They moved through the water in silence for a while before Kristin picked up the conversation thread. "This school of his is really something. I don't think there's anything else like it in the country."

"How did you end up here?" Sophie's goal was to learn as much as she could about all the teachers. It would help in her quest to fit in.

"Through a long, winding road which doesn't

necessarily make sense, since I have a degree in archaeology. After I spent a year in Egypt on an artifacts dig, I decided I wanted to teach, so I got a master's in education."

"Where'd you go to school?"

"Columbia for my bachelor's, then Yale."

"You came here after Yale?" She tried to keep the surprise from her voice.

"No. Not quite. Just before I committed to a teaching position at a private school in Boston, my then-fiancé decided he wanted to work at his family's vineyard. In California. Not being the family dynasty type of woman, I broke off the engagement."

She looked over her shoulder and saw the wistfulness on Kristin's face that she'd heard in her voice. "He went without you?" How sad for her.

"Yup. It was probably for the best, though. He wanted me to give up the career I hadn't even started yet, and work side by side with him and his family growing grapes. That was not a career switch I wanted to make."

"How did you manage to move on?" Perhaps she could take a page out of Kristin's book and learn how to handle a change in life plan, if need be.

"I drowned my sorrows by taking a vacation mountain climbing in Nepal. That's where I met Dan, the program director here."

"That was your idea of a vacation?" Now she understood how Kristin's incomprehensible quest for adventure had landed her here. Even her vacations were feats in athleticism.

"Dan told me about the school where he worked, and I couldn't believe there was something like this in existence. What could be better than teaching at an environmental school where you get to go snorkeling and scuba diving and camping as part of the curriculum?"

She could think of at least a hundred things that would qualify as better, but kept her mouth shut.

Kristin continued her enthusiastic praise. "And soon, we'll be doing research on preserving the marine environment if Max gets his way. I've been here for a year and a half, and I think I've found a home."

"What about the others? Do they like it here as much as you?"

Kristin grinned. "Max is a loner. He loves spending time working on his research projects. He's been in Andy's ear, trying to convince him to let him start an environmental research institute. I think Andy's almost ready to give him the go-ahead. If he does, Max'll be here for the long haul."

An egret flew low, just skimming the water near their boat, and Sophie screamed and ducked, causing their kayak to teeter back and forth. Kristin balanced it from the back, thankfully keeping her mirth in check. She continued, as if nothing had happened.

"The rest of them are free spirits. They go with the wind."

"What about Maddie?"

"This is Maddie's second semester. She's from New York. A real city girl and an NYU grad with a master's in art and a second master's in ocean science. But even though she loves high heels and designer clothes, I have to give her a lot of credit. She's our number one snorkel and scuba instructor and leads the way on our coral reef dives. And she's so charismatic that even the least likely of artists spends free time in her art studio. The kids love her."

Sophie closed her open mouth. Here she'd been spouting off about her degrees and awards, and these people not only had excellent credentials from some of the most prestigious schools in their fields, but they had science and research experience as well as athletic ability. If she hadn't known it before, she now knew it would take more than a few kayaking lessons to assimilate with this crowd.

"This is going to be harder than I thought," she admitted.

"Why do you say that?"

"Because I'm a disaster when it comes to this outdoors stuff."

"You're doing fantastic kayaking. Isn't it fun?"

"I am beginning to enjoy it out here. And this is a great way to get around. But my arms are going to fall off before we get back." She would not only have to take daily lessons on outdoor skills, but she'd have to add an exercise regimen to her day if she had any hope of keeping up with the others.

"You'll get used to it." With that, Kristin's paddle came up and out of the water, soaking Sophie's shirt with a well-placed splash.

"Oh, now you're in trouble." Sophie back paddled and gave Kristin a taste of her own medicine.

Then the water fight began in earnest.

Paddles flew, water cascaded, and shrieks of laughter filled the early morning air.

Maybe, just maybe, being one with nature wasn't going to be so bad after all.

Chapter Four

Max rowed toward the horizon as the muscles in his upper back and shoulders stretched and burned with the effort. Boating during the early morning hours off Sunrise Island always energized and invigorated him. With nothing to interfere with his thoughts but the sound of his oars cutting through the Gulf and the birds calling to each other as they dove for food, it was his favorite time of day.

And the perfect time to think.

Yesterday, after his chat with Andy and his foreboding hunch that Ms. Sophie Kearns' presence was about to sabotage his efforts to start a research institute, he'd had every intention of finding out her plan, directly from the horse's mouth. He'd offered to go pick Sophie up at the airport, shamelessly counting on Andy's insane work ethic to toss aside any compulsion he had to greet his old friend the minute she arrived. Once he had Ms. Kearns in the Jeep, it didn't take long to learn that Andy had asked her to come down and teach, instead of the other way around, as Andy had insinuated.

Unfortunately, his plot to corner Andy last night at dinner and demand an explanation was foiled. Andy hadn't shown up.

Of course, he could have been a little nicer to Sophie at the dinner table. He hadn't meant to verbally attack her in front of everyone. Andy was the one who deserved his ire. As a result, he'd decided on a different strategy. As the saying went, it's easier to catch bees with honey. So he'd turned on the charm in the dark of night and even gotten her to lighten up—a feat given their previous exchanges. Unexpectedly, her ability to laugh at herself drew him in, along with her captivating smile and sparkling eyes.

A piercing sound disrupted his thoughts.

He turned his craft toward the clamor and saw the miscreants—Kristin and Sophie battling it out with their paddles, soaking each other with salt water when they weren't laughing so hard they couldn't even raise their oars.

His temporary annoyance with the invasion of his peaceful haven improved with Sophie's shrieks as she begged Kristin not to rock the boat. Like that was going to happen when they were having a water fight. He chuckled to himself.

"Stop. Stop." Sophie sputtered on a mouthful of water that Kristin had just sent her way.

Kristin doubled over with laughter, causing the kayak to teeter. Sophie dropped her paddle as she clung to the side of the boat, but it was too late to get it back into balance. The kayak rolled over and dumped its passengers unceremoniously into the sea.

Max chuckled in amusement.

Kristin's head bobbed to the surface first. "Sophie…Sophie…are you all right?"

Sophie's head bobbed up next, on the opposite side of their kayak. She grabbed for the overturned boat but missed, splashing furiously as her arms worked to keep her afloat. Her head went under, then came back up, her mouth sputtering in her attempt to respond. *Uh-oh.* She was panicked.

Max put his arms into overdrive as he hastened to her rescue. He leaned over his boat and grabbed Sophie under her arms, hauling her up and over the side of the boat as she continued to flail.

"Stop fighting me." He gritted his teeth as he used all his strength to deposit her onto the floor of his rowboat.

She landed on her butt with a thud, splaying limbs in every direction. Long, gorgeous legs emerged from her ridiculously long shorts, which were now bunched up to the length they should have been. Her wet sleeveless blouse clung to delicious curves—a narrow waist and full breasts, which heaved up and down in her effort to breathe.

She pushed a heavy mass of chestnut hair from her face, uncovering the aqua-blue eyes that had captured his attention the night before. Her mouth moved, but nothing came out.

"Sophie, are you all right?" Kristin had just reached the rowboat and hung on to its side.

Sophie transferred her gaze from him to Kristin. "Y-yes, I'm fine."

Although she truly didn't look it. Her usual pale face looked even paler, and she coughed as her lungs worked to rid themselves of the salt water she must have ingested. Jeez, she could have drowned.

"You don't look fine." Concern etched Kristin's face. "Don't you know how to swim?"

Sophie lowered her eyes as bright splotches of red colored her cheeks. "I can doggie paddle. But I guess I panicked."

"I'd say." Max immediately regretted his response.

Kristin gave him the same evil eye as yesterday before slipping away from his boat to retrieve the kayak.

"Thanks for saving me." Sophie's voice was barely audible, and she refused to look at him.

He shrugged as if it were no big deal. "Just trying to help a lady in need."

Despite his outward nonchalance, his heart kicked at his ribs. Her panicked face slipping into the water brought back the recurring nightmare he had of his brother wrestling with his scuba diving equipment as he fought for breath. In his dream he couldn't reach Dean, and his own screams always woke him. He exhaled the angst building in his chest.

"It's not smart to go boating if you don't know how to swim."

"Great advice." She hoisted herself upright with her arms and pulled her limbs closer to the rest of her body, a shiver working its way through her. Her taut nipples pushed against her soaked bra and shirt as the breeze picked up, and Max felt a slow, erotic stirring in his groin. He shifted his body, along with his eyes.

She then inched cautiously toward the seat, but the rowboat rocked unsteadily.

"I wouldn't do that if I were you unless, of course, you want me to rescue you again."

A rosy blush crept into her face, and she remained where she was, threading her arms around her knees as her teeth chattered.

He threw her a towel, hoping to toss with it his unreasonable anxiety. Kristin had been right there. She wouldn't have drowned.

"So you can't swim. And you already said you can't snorkel or scuba dive. Just what was Andy thinking when he hired you?"

Maybe now was the time to get his answer. He had her trapped. Would she admit that Andy had invited her here to see if she would come down permanently and transfer her already successful teaching academy to Sunrise Island? It would give Andy's school even more credibility and bring dozens, if not hundreds, of new people here during the summer to see firsthand what he had going the rest of the year. Free publicity. And prestige. All through one acquisition. Sophie Kearns.

Her silence just fueled his theory, and steam built in his head. He refused to look at her, instead keeping his eyes on the horizon as he rowed toward shore. How could Andy do this to him? After all the discussions they'd had about his environmental institute. All the preliminary work he'd done, just waiting for Andy to give him the go-ahead to start applying for grants.

Down the drain.

Of course that's why he'd hired Sophie—the fish out of water. There could be no other reason.

"People usually wear bathing suits when they go out on the water," he growled, knowing the only purpose of his statement was to attack her. "Although, maybe you don't own one. Swimming may be too outdoorsy for you."

Even that didn't give rise to a comment from her. She just pulled her knees closer to her chest and stared ahead. But he needed a fight. And even though Andy should have been his target, he had Sophie sitting in his boat.

"You must have really snowed Andy for him to give you a job here. Unless there's another motive." *Come on. Tell me.*

"You make it sound so sinister. I am not here for any disingenuous reason, as you seem to think." Her words steamed through gritted teeth.

She wasn't going to admit it. He'd just have to hit her over the head with it, then. "Has Andy talked to you about bringing your teaching academy down here? Is that why you came?"

"What?" Her eyes flew open wide, along with her mouth. "What are you talking about?" Genuine shock emerged at his accusation.

He was either totally off base or witnessing a superb actress at work.

She sat up straighter. "I'm here because I wanted to take a break. Andy was nice enough to give me a job for the semester. Why would he want me to bring my teaching academy down here?"

Irritation put more color in her cheeks, and she seemed to be breathing easier. He guessed mouth-to-mouth resuscitation was uncalled for. Too bad.

She continued. "Andy has done a great job in creating this school exactly as he envisioned it, and he's hired very impressive teachers to carry out his concept. He doesn't need my academy to make it better."

"The teachers here meet your standards?" He added just the right amount of sarcasm to irk her even more.

"I never said they didn't." Blazing blue eyes zeroed in on his, and her exasperation flashed and burned clear through to his core. "I'm not sure what I did to make you treat me like I'm some sort of snobby intellectual, but I assure you I'm not."

"Maybe it's because you pointed out your credentials within minutes of meeting everyone at dinner." He dragged his gaze away from hers and continued rowing toward shore, putting all his muscle into it. The sooner he could get away from this bewitching woman, and this toxic conversation, the better. Although, he had started it.

"I only recall talking about my credentials because you attacked my worth. It was in response to your rude comment that I couldn't pull my weight around here. As a matter of fact, you called me a prima donna." She inched her chin up a little higher, clearly attempting to mask the biting sting of his ridicule.

"You have to admit that you don't fit the mold of any of the teachers here."

She ignored his opinion and started pulling at her shirt to unstick it from her body, no doubt her attempt to keep his eyes off her chest and on their destination. Moving farther down, she tugged on the hem of her shorts which had ridden up her thighs, and he couldn't help chuckling at her out-of-place modesty. She'd learn soon enough that the teaching crew here were like brothers and sisters to each other. Discretion often went right out the door, especially if they shared a tent or ended up on an overnight fishing trip.

He surreptitiously glanced her way again, hoping she wouldn't notice. Other than the fact that she could use a tan, from what he could see, she had very sexy curves. And her face wasn't too shabby either. Those blue eyes looked luminescent in the sunlight. Really quite beautiful.

Approaching the dock, he slowed down and brought the boat to rest on the beach. Kristin stood there, towel drying her hair, obviously waiting to rescue Sophie from him.

"I hope you minded your manners." Kristin's

reprimand hit its mark as she helped Sophie from the boat.

"I was a perfect gentleman."

A scowl furrowed Sophie's forehead, but she remained silent. Too bad. He liked when she gave it back.

"See you around campus, ladies." He placed the oars in the boat and headed toward the dining pavilion for breakfast.

He needed some space.

Only eight fifteen and he'd already rescued a non-swimmer, argued with her about her motives for being here, and felt his libido kick into high gear over that arguing non-swimmer. He had come here to get away from it all, to turn his energy into something more constructive than living with the constant regret that he'd never achieve his lifelong dream of working side by side with his brother. And to continue his promise to himself and his brother that he'd never allow a woman to turn his head again.

So why was Sophie getting under his skin?

A smile tugged at his lips as he replayed her laughter when she and Kristin were splashing each other. It had been infectious. And he'd found himself rooting for her when she gave Kristin a run for her money with a mouthful of water.

But what really had him going were those eyes—crystal clear in the sunlight—but revealing a host of emotions.

She was an enigma. That must be the reason for his intrigue. The snobby professor from the Valen School. Who had shown up here to teach a semester for reasons unknown. Who had spirit and spunk despite her shortcomings. Who had an easy and engaging smile when talking to Kristin, but whose smile disappeared when talking to him. His fault, of course.

He shook his head.

*Stay away from her.*

\*\*\*\*

"I don't understand why he's so rotten to me." Sophie pulled at her wet blouse as she and Kristin walked back toward their cabins to change.

"I don't know why either. Although Max is a moody fellow. You never know what's going to bring it on."

"He makes me feel so inadequate, and I can't remember feeling like that since high school. I know I have a lot to learn in order to adapt to life on this island. I guess I better be quick about it before I end up doing something stupid while I'm in charge of the kids. Do you think you could teach me how to swim?"

Kristin's warm smile accompanied her nod. "Of course. We'll start this afternoon after classes. Meet me on the beach at three thirty. And we'll continue to go out in the morning for boating lessons."

"I can't thank you enough, Kristin. I know you have your hands full with your own classes. And now you're taking me on too."

"I'm happy to do it. We'll have fun."

Maybe Kristin would have fun. She didn't hold such lofty aspirations. But with a plan in place to learn the ropes, she felt infinitely better than she had yesterday.

Sophie returned to their conversation about Max. "You said last night that Max doesn't always trust others. Do you think it's because of some failed relationship?"

Kristin laughed. "Max doesn't do relationships. He meets someone, dates her for a short time, then before long, it's over. I don't know whether it's because his version of the ideal woman is an impossible standard to attain, or whether his need to control everything sends every woman running." She shrugged. "But once you get to know him, you'll see that he truly cares about everyone here, especially the students. And he will do anything he can to make his classes and field trips fun and exciting."

"I haven't seen that side of him yet."

"He has been surly lately. Something's bothering him. I don't know what. Something out of his control, though."

Sophie rewound back to her conversation with Max on the boat. He'd accused Andy of hiring her so she'd relocate her teaching academy to Sunrise Island. Which he clearly believed would affect his dream to establish an environmental research institute here. With Kristin's assessment of his need to control, along with his accusation of her motive for being here, she now understood him a little better. And his antagonism toward her made more sense.

She sighed over the monster she'd unwittingly created just by showing up.

Kristin broke into her thoughts. "Maddie tries her best to snap Max out of his funk when it takes over, but in the past two days, it hasn't worked."

"They're dating, right?"

"What?" Kristin sputtered her astonishment. "Where did you get that idea?"

Sophie recalled Maddie's insinuation the previous night. "Something Maddie said."

"Whatever she said, she was teasing. Maddie and Max are definitely not a couple. They're good friends.

Andy's not big on teachers or staff forming romantic relationships. Although there's no written rule against it."

"Have you ever dated anyone here?"

"No." Her wistful tone gave Sophie pause. "My last boyfriend was the owner of a restaurant from Marathon Key. But now I'm dateless. There are so many other important things that take up my time. Sometimes it's better that way."

Sophie nodded. Somewhere along the way, she had come to the same conclusion.

Chapter Five

The shades were drawn tight, not only keeping the mid-afternoon sun at bay but sending the room into near-total darkness. Max viewed the heart monitor doing a dance in neon colors as his eyes adjusted to the dim surroundings.

"You finally made it here," Andy rasped from his hospital bed.

"I heard you didn't want visitors." Max inched closer to his friend.

Both of Andy's legs were casted and connected to overhead metal bars with wires and pulleys. His torso was bandaged to his armpits, and an IV line ran from a plastic bag to the needle in his forearm. His swollen face was black and blue, with cuts and contusions sprinkled over almost every uncovered skin surface.

"You look horrible." Max's true statement did nothing to break the ice.

"Thanks. I feel worse."

The gloom of the room was in sharp contrast to the glorious day beyond the walls of the hospital, and Max's chest tightened with a familiar dread.

"The doctor says you'll live." Max meant his words to be light and funny, but in view of what had happened to Andy, they fell flat between them.

"Yeah," grunted Andy. "But I'll be out of commission for the next four to six months. Not bad for a near fatal boating accident but impossible to fathom for this workaholic."

Max swallowed to hold his tongue. Telling Andy he was crazy to race speedboats wouldn't help. It was way too late for that. Besides, Andy hadn't listened to any of them before. For as long as Max had been at Sunrise Island School, he could recall comments, discussions, warnings, and even pleas from his colleagues that Andy give up his crazy infatuation, or death wish, as he'd heard Kristin call it.

But Andy persisted. He knew what he was doing. Besides, he drove state-of-the-art boats, and the races were strictly regulated.

He hadn't counted on someone else's stupidity.

The crash had thrown him clear up in the air, and he'd landed dozens of feet away, hitting the water at a rate of speed that must have felt like slamming into concrete pavement.

Luck kept him from breaking his neck. That and the swiftness of the rescue team that pulled him from the water before he'd had the opportunity to drown.

"You're one fortunate dude." Max tried to swallow his anxiety in an effort to calm his racing heart.

Every time he thought about what could have happened, an involuntary shiver coursed through his body. It was the same feeling he'd had when he rushed to his local hospital after his brother had been brought in. Ten years earlier.

Andy's eyes watered, as if to acknowledge his luck. "Amazing how your life can change in a second. But we all know that."

"What's your prognosis?" Max needed to move away from the depressing accident to his hopeful recovery.

"At least a month here, maybe more, depending on how quickly my bones heal. My femur's broken in my left leg. My other leg is fractured, and my ankle's broken. A few broken ribs. Broken wrist. Sprained fingers. I don't know what else. I nodded off when the doctor went through the list."

Max chuckled. At least Andy was trying for a little humor.

"How long in rehab?"

Andy sighed. "They don't know. At least two months before I can become an outpatient. I'm going to lose this whole semester."

"That's the least of your worries. And you shouldn't give it another thought. You have that school set up so well it can run itself. We'll all make sure there are no problems. You just have to concentrate on getting better."

"It's not in my nature not to worry. You know that. Besides, if the school could run itself, then why am I there?" He attempted a scowl.

"You're our guiding light," Max teased, although it was true. "But I assure you we'll make it work." He cleared his throat. "I can take over for you while you're gone. I realize I don't have much administrative experience, but I know that school inside out. I'm sure I could handle any problem that comes along. And I'll meet with you as often as you like. Just to let you know that everything's running smoothly."

Andy's eyes shifted away from him. "Could you hold up that cup of water with the straw? I'm thirsty."

Max did as requested, then waited for Andy to respond to his offer. The silence was deafening.

"Did you hear what I said?"

"Yes." Andy paused. "I appreciate your offer, Max. Really. But I don't think you're the right person for the job. I want Sophie to step in for me."

His heart stopped for at least five seconds. "Sophie? Why her? She just got here. She doesn't know the first thing about the school." The drugs must be affecting Andy's thinking. He couldn't be serious.

"She knows more than you think. Having written those grant proposals with me a few years ago, she understands my philosophy for the school, as well as how all the parts make up the whole. Besides, she also has administrative experience from running her Summer Teaching Academy."

Max's gut sank. He desperately wanted this opportunity to run the school. To prove to Andy he had what it took to be an effective administrator. And if he did a good job, Andy would have no further doubts about allowing him to start the research institute. Maybe he could even figure out a way to get it jump-started while Andy recuperated. But not with Sophie in charge. What was Andy thinking? He was wrong. Plain wrong. Sophie didn't know anything about the soul of the school. Maybe she knew about its mechanical workings on paper, but she had none of the passion for the environment that Andy did. That he did.

"Andy—" He paused, trying to choose the right words that would convince his friend to change his mind. "Sophie couldn't possibly feel what you feel about this school. She's an English teacher who spends her time in classrooms and libraries. She doesn't even know how to swim! Why would you choose someone to take your place who isn't a natural in this environment?"

He thought back to her near drowning while learning to kayak. She was a ridiculous choice.

He was just getting ready to tick off other reasons when Andy stopped him with a body blow.

"I already gave her the job." As if that wasn't lethal enough, he added, "and I want you to help her out if she needs it."

\*\*\*\*

It was six thirty, and Sophie had missed dinner for the third evening in a row. Funny how she didn't mind at all. She sat at Andy's desk, poring through the last of his binders on the organization of the school. If Andy was anything, he was a stickler for systematization. But a brilliant stickler.

"Sophie, you've been here since eight this morning. Don't you think you should take a break?" Sue, Andy's administrative assistant, closed a file drawer, stood, and pushed her chair under her desk. "I know I've had enough today."

Sue took care of all organizational matters for the teachers as well as the students and smoothed over problems with competence and charm. She laughed easily, and her light, cheery manner made a visit to the office a favorite pastime for the teachers if they had a break—as long as Andy was off doing something else.

Sophie took an energizing breath. "I probably should take five. All this information is starting to blur. I was hoping to get through the last of Andy's operational guides today. I can't get to the day-to-day administration until I see how things are set up." She held up the binder. "This is like a treatise on private school management. He should publish it."

A huge dose of pride in her friend's

accomplishments streamed through her, and having been involved with this school from its inception, she couldn't help the satisfaction she felt from having had a hand in it.

Sue chuckled. "Yeah, Andy's organized. He has to be going crazy that he can't rule this place from his hospital bed."

Sophie stood up and stretched. "I feel so bad for him. This is his baby. When I went to visit him yesterday, he seemed really depressed that he'd be away for so long."

"He should be thanking his lucky stars he'll be able to come back after a few months." A shadow crossed Sue's face.

Sophie knew the inherent censure in her statement wasn't meant as a criticism but concern for her boss and friend.

Sue shook her head. "He could have been paralyzed. Or died."

That thought had crossed everyone's lips over the past week since the accident. Something of this magnitude, hitting so close to home, had Sophie and the others talking about mortality. Something she didn't often think of.

"I guess I better give it up for today. I have to prepare for my class tomorrow." Sophie closed the binder and set it back on the bookshelf in chronological order. "The kids here are really great—so excited about literature. We're reading *The Old Man and the Sea*, and they've shown a true appreciation for Santiago."

"They're all lucky to be here. Jeez, I didn't have the opportunity to live in an island paradise for a semester when I was in high school, did you?" Sue pressed the button to turn off her computer and pulled her purse from her desk drawer.

Sophie grabbed her briefcase. "Hardly." Although her wish back then had been to attend Valen, not an island environmental school. And while she'd had the grades, with no scholarship, her dream was destroyed.

She bit her lip and stared at the desk.

"Are you okay?" Sue brought her back to the present.

Not wanting to discuss her huge disappointment from so many years ago, she came up with an adequate reason for her preoccupation. "Tomorrow, I have to review the budget. I need to understand what's going on there."

"No problem. I can help. Accounting is my forte." She smiled and clicked off her desk lamp. "Now, let's blow this joint. The morning will be here before we know it."

Sophie stowed the day's mail in her briefcase, hoping to get to it later tonight. "I never realized how time consuming this job could be. Just dealing with all the requests for funding from the different teachers could take up most of the day."

"Don't let it overwhelm you. It's all so new. Once you're more familiar with the different aspects of the job, it'll be easier."

Sue's perky, upbeat attitude was an incredible help to Sophie, and her positive spin on things calmed her anxiety over her temporary position.

She flipped through a few piles of paper on the desk while considering whether to bring something more home.

But Sue came over, grabbed her by the arm, and

pulled her to the door.

"Enough," she said, attempting a stern voice. "You're going to burn yourself out before the week is up. Then who is Andy going to rely on?"

She capitulated. "Okay, okay. I'm outta here too. See you tomorrow." She paused outside, then called after Sue who was heading toward the dining pavilion to scrounge up some leftovers. "Sue? Thanks."

Sue held up her hand in acknowledgment and continued on her journey, a bounce in her step.

Walking down the pathway toward her cabin, Sophie relished the warm breeze wrapping around her body like a light, soft blanket—so comforting. It riffled her hair and blew it in tendrils around her face, tickling her cheeks. The salt air awakened her senses, and she inhaled its tangy aroma. She would have liked nothing better than to drop off her briefcase, discard her sandals, and head for the beach. A walk would do her wonders.

Maybe the brooding loner would be there and say something to make her laugh—like he had that first night. Or, more likely than not, he'd say something mean. Weighing the odds, she decided against taking the risk. Besides, she didn't have time anyway.

Andy had bestowed upon her a huge responsibility. And she wouldn't disappoint him. Or herself. This was going to be an invaluable experience, which would hasten her climb to the top of the ladder. Headmaster Ryan planned to retire in a few years. And even though she anticipated applying for his job, she knew her young age would hinder her chances. But now, with this coup, it just might change things. Assuming she'd be back at Valen with her reputation intact.

Her slow, meandering walk home abruptly changed

to a stride. She had a job to do, and although it would take every waking moment, she was not only up to the challenge but looking forward to it.

Chapter Six

The weekend finally arrived. No classes, no environmental trips, and no mentoring duties. Even though Sophie could spend the next forty-eight hours dedicated to her new undertaking, a well-needed break would assuredly re-energize her.

Besides, this particular Saturday was a free day for the ladies. As a result, Maddie, the ultimate material girl, had organized a day of shopping and pampering in Key West. While Sophie could have done away with the shopping and pampering part, she had been dying to see Key West while down here. This seemed the perfect opportunity.

"Hey, Sophie, we've decided to help you buy a new wardrobe," called Maddie over the noise of the engine as they cruised through the ocean in the school's powerboat.

Sophie cringed but wasn't surprised. She had been deflecting negative comments about her choice of dress since she arrived. And not just from Max. Apparently, no one appreciated the fine quality walking shorts she had purchased, and they liked her cotton, short-sleeved, button-down blouses even less.

"You're going to get a golfer's tan," Ben had commented—one of the nicer remarks she'd had to endure.

Max had resorted to shaking his head at the first

sight of her each morning, and Maddie had offered to lend her some clothes so she wouldn't be embarrassed in front of her students. *Very touching.*

"Kristin, are you in on this too?" Sophie feigned hurt feelings.

"No, of course not." But Kristin's telltale grin told Sophie otherwise.

They docked in the marina, then walked toward Mallory Square, the historic pier that boasted time shares, condos, shops, and restaurants—and a nightly party of sorts that brought everyone from the island to applaud the setting sun. Immersing themselves in the throngs of cruise ship visitors who had disembarked just minutes earlier, they maneuvered toward Duval Street, the one-mile strip of stores, galleries, and bars that stretched from the Gulf of Mexico to the Atlantic Ocean.

"Follow me." Maddie took the lead as they outpaced the cruisers. "I know just the store."

They ended up in a boutique that favored Italian designers but also catered to the bohemian taste of so many inhabitants of the Keys. The polar opposite of Sophie's tailored clothing.

Maddie headed straight for the rack of shorts and began pulling out what she deemed an acceptable length—although too short in Sophie's book. Next, shirts. But not cotton button-downs. Clingy, sleeveless numbers made from Lycra that looked more like tank tops.

Sophie swallowed in her effort to tamp down her apprehension. She hadn't worn such revealing clothing in years. It wasn't how teachers dressed. At least in private schools in the northeast. But now she was in a totally different environment. And, she supposed, these clothes were more practical for life on an island—more movement, less restrictive, less wrinkly. She grudgingly acknowledged she should give it a try. It would help her fit in, at least physically. But should that still be her goal? As the acting director, maybe she needed to distance herself from the others. Just as Andy had. Make sure she didn't blur the lines of authority.

While the debate continued in her head, Maddie pushed her into the dressing room with an assortment of clothing. Encouraging statements from Kristin and Sue diminished her hesitation. They were really sweet and waited patiently for her to emerge a changed woman.

Kristin slid the dressing room curtain aside to view Sophie's potential new style. "You look perfect."

Leave it to Maddie to pull Sophie out into the middle of the store so she could see herself reflected in the three-way mirror.

"Why so shy?" Maddie failed to use her indoor voice, causing other customers to glance her way.

"Shhh. People are looking at me."

"Well, if I were you," said Maddie, hands on hips, "I'd sure want them to. You look great. Why in the world would you walk around in those dreary clothes when you look like that?"

"It's just not who I am." Her face burned to prove it. Or at least not who she had become.

Over the past fourteen years, she had worked meticulously toward reshaping herself from the teen who couldn't afford to attend Valen, to the woman who would take over the school. And then with one altered video, her world, as she knew it, had splintered into a million pieces.

"You look terrific, Sophie," Kristin interjected,

taking her out of her painful musings.

Kristin's playful tone also worked to diffuse the tension instigated by Maddie. "You're even starting to get a nice tan. See the stripes on your legs and arms?"

Sophie had already noticed the clear lines of demarcation on her thighs and upper arms where the lower part of those limbs were bronzing nicely.

The vibrant colors Maddie had chosen for her were so unlike anything she had in her drawers that her eyes blinked from their brilliance. But, she had to admit, they worked wonders in brightening her disposition. As did the women's comments. Within the hour, she had shorts and shirts in every color of the rainbow, including the yellow outfit she had on.

Surely, this new wardrobe would stop Max's derogatory remarks about the length of her shorts and the design of her blouses. Maybe he'd even compliment her. Although why she cared what he thought was beyond comprehension.

The other women made some purchases as well, and then they were on their way, all talking and laughing at the same time. Ahh, the power of shopping.

"Next stop, the salon." Maddie ushered them down the street.

"Are you getting your hair done?" Sophie asked. There was nothing wrong with Maddie's hair.

"We all are."

"Why?" Sophie furrowed her brow as she looked from one woman to the other. Sure, she hadn't had her hair cut in months, but it was easy—all one length. Besides, she generally wore it pulled back—perfect for island living.

"Because it's time to get pampered. Manicures,

pedicures, haircuts, highlights, the works."

"That seems like a waste. The polish will just come off in the ocean, and no one needs their hair cut." She realized her lack of self-indulgence sounded judgmental about how the others should spend their money, which was not her intent. "Everyone looks perfect." In fact, they looked like cover girls with their shiny hair and bronzed skin.

"Haven't you ever had a pedicure because it feels good?" Kristin wiggled her toes in her flip-flops.

"No. I guess I haven't." In college, she hadn't even had enough money to pay her tuition, much less go to the salon. By the time she did earn a living, she had decided on a conservative course, both financially and physically. The preppy business style allowed her to be judged for her talents, not her looks. And the money she could have spent on pampering instead went into her retirement account to secure her future.

"Then you're in for a real treat." Sue grabbed Sophie's arm and led her into the Coral Salon and Day Spa.

Three hours later, they emerged, and Sophie felt and looked like a new woman. Her long tresses had been trimmed, layered, and highlighted. A facial had removed dead skin cells, and moisturizers and emollients had given her a fantastic glow. A makeup specialist had talked her into a sun-kissed blush for her cheeks, a touch of velvet mascara to enhance her eyes, and a neutral lip gloss to protect her lips from the burning sun. Just enough to make her feel pretty without overdoing it.

"Wow, Sophie," Kristin gushed, "I'm not sure we should have brought you here. Now none of us will have a chance with any of the single men around town."

"Nice try, Kristin." Sophie gave her a friendly elbow to the side, knowing Kristin could stop a bar full of men from watching football in the last minute of overtime with her sculpted body, hundred-watt smile, and hazel, doe eyes.

"I agree," Sue chimed in. "I think we all look fabulous." She patted her short blonde hair, which had been lightened and cut to look adorably messy.

"Sophie's our modern-day Eliza Doolittle." Maddie's teasing sarcasm was evident in her voice. "A little makeup and a haircut can do wonders not only for the body but the soul." She flipped her long, freshly highlighted hair over her shoulder and strutted as she walked down Duval Street.

And it worked. Men's heads turned, even those walking next to their girlfriends. Tall, statuesque, and dressed in white—a knock-out contrast against her tan—Maddie lived to be noticed. The complete opposite of Sophie, who had never wanted the attention. But in seeing Maddie enjoy the interest of others, she started to think it might be nice to get just a little of it. Whether this recognition came with her new friends or her new environment, she loved that she felt a little more comfortable in her skin.

A left turn off Duval and a short block to the corner led them to The Pilot House, an outdoor bar and restaurant secluded behind lush, flowering bushes. The others seemed to know everyone in the joint, including the owner, who seated them at a long table in the center of the backyard garden. Margaritas appeared without order, and fresh shrimp and cocktail sauce arrived shortly thereafter.

As a guitarist sang about island life, a warm buzz

spread through Sophie's veins, washing away any lingering doubts about emerging from her shell. Wearing colorful clothes and a little makeup felt good. And she couldn't help giving her hair a little toss every once in a while, as she brushed her fingers through newly highlighted layers. She felt attractive, and the men coming over to their table to say hello to the other three, were also flirting with her!

"So, Sophie," asked Maddie, when their host of admirers had died down, "what brings you to Sunrise Island School?"

Sophie's heartbeat kicked up a notch with the question. "I needed a break." Hoping her standard but vague answer was sufficient, she glanced over at Kristin, who kept her eyes downcast while picking at her shrimp.

Maddie's stare penetrated Sophie's eyes, telling her she needed to come up with a better reason than that.

Sophie shifted in her seat and took a fortifying sip of her margarita. "I'm up for the position of chair of the English department, and I decided to take a sabbatical before jumping in with both feet. I figure that if I get the position, I won't have the opportunity for a break in a long time."

There. She had come up with a plausible explanation. Even under Maddie's scrutiny. And it was now out there. Was it good enough? She looked at Maddie for validation.

Maddie's clear blue eyes didn't move from Sophie's face. She wasn't buying it. Her skin tingled with the realization she'd have to invent something more.

Maddie finally spoke. "This is a great place to take a break. Except that you ended up as acting director. Hardly a walk in the park. I think I would have just taken a vacation." She shrugged. "To each his own."

Sophie breathed a little easier. In her new position of authority, now more than ever, she didn't want her suspension exposed.

Kristin jumped in. "Maybe you'll love it so much here you'll decide to stay."

A chuckle escaped Sophie's mouth. "I don't think so. We all know I'm not quite what this school is looking for." A momentary flash of disappointment zapped her. "In case you haven't noticed, I'm not an outdoors, camping, boating, hiking kind of gal." She laughed despite the sad truth.

"Kristin's been teaching you how to swim and kayak," Sue said. "Some of the other stuff you just have to do. After a few times, it'll seem like second nature. Like camping. It's no big deal. You pitch your tent and commune with nature. Anybody can do it."

Sophie ventured a glance at Maddie who still seemed to be puzzling over her answer. She needed to turn the conversation away from her.

"What brought you here, Maddie?"

"A bad relationship. If I hadn't gotten away when I did, I might have ended up in a mental institution."

"Don't get her started," Sue warned, shaking her head for effect. "We'll be here for the next two hours listening to her tale of woe."

Maddie threw a shrimp tail at Sue, laughing. "You have a lot of nerve. Your story's not much better."

"Yeah, but at least I'm over him. There's no use giving the bum another moment's thought. I like to live in the present and make sure I'm having fun doing it." Sue nodded to affirm her statement, and her short blonde waves bounced in unison. "Besides, I'm too young to be tied down. I want to experience life."

"Here, here." Kristin raised her glass for a group toast.

They all followed her lead and clinked their glasses, causing a few spills in the middle of the table. But not to worry. The shrimp tasted even better with a little margarita drizzled over them.

Sophie smiled as warm fingers of affection slid around her and pulled her into their group. At least Kristin and Sue's group. And while she had been a little worried about spending an entire day in Key West with the women, it had proven to be a wonderful connecting experience. Maybe she'd even feel closer to Maddie in time.

And maybe…in enough time…she'd fit in.

\*\*\*\*

Her alarm buzzed incessantly, and Sophie rolled away from the sunlight streaming through a broken slat in the blinds. She hit the off button and, with one eye open, peeked at the time. Seven thirty.

She bolted upright before flopping back against her pillows, her eyes gritty and her body aching with overuse and insufficient sleep.

Snippets of yesterday's shenanigans, which had extended well into the night, made her smile.

Laughter, conversation, singing…oh my, had they actually been singing? Arms around each other's shoulders, swaying. Dancing. More and more people…men…women…chairs squeezing in around the table…more people squeezing into the chairs.

What time had they finally arrived back on Sunrise Island? Her smile turned to a groan over the hours spent having fun with no thought of what Sunday would bring.

She was on food duty today—whatever that was—and she had to be at the dining pavilion at eight. She grudgingly rose.

As acting director, she could remove herself from such activities, but she didn't want to. That would just isolate her more, and her goal was to assimilate.

She hastened through her morning routine, catching a glimpse in the mirror of the new Sophie—complete with highlighted hair and a contemporary outfit. But after slathering on sunscreen, she reverted to her old ways by pulling her hair into a ponytail and donning a baseball cap. She pushed her sunglasses onto her nose and headed to the dining pavilion with no time to spare.

The teacher's table was half full, and she slid into her unofficial seat between Kristin and Ben, placing her sunglasses on the table. "Morning." Her voice was hoarse from overuse the night before.

"The second musketeer has arrived." Dan grinned before digging into his bowl of oatmeal.

"Are you as exhausted as I am?" Kristin held on to her mug for dear life.

"Ugh." It was all she could say, until she smelled the aroma of fresh brewed coffee. "I need some of that." She surveyed the distance she would have to travel to get a cup. "I don't know if I can make it."

"I'd suggest you get your coffee and whatever else is going to open those eyes and move that body 'cause it's our turn to go fishin', darlin'."

Sophie knew that voice. Slowly, she looked over at Max, whose huge, smug smile immediately grated on her tired nerves. "Fishing?" She must have heard him wrong, but it sure sounded like he said fishing.

"That's what I said. We need to catch dinner for

tonight."

"Stop joking. I'm not in the mood this morning. As you can see, I'm a little tired." And now a headache was working its way from the base of her skull to her temples—insufficient rest and one too many margaritas the culprits.

Just then, Maddie plopped into a chair and growled. "A little tired doesn't begin to describe how I feel." She laid her head on her arms. "If I conk out here, just move me to my bed."

"What were you women up to last night?" Dan asked, a chuckle in his voice. "I hope nothing that would get back to Andy."

Maddie lifted her head marginally. "Oh, Dan, puleeze!" Then she closed her eyes again.

Dan turned to Kristin. "Well?"

"We went into Key West for the day and did some shopping. Then we stopped by The Pilot House for a margarita or two and ended up dancing the night away." Kristin lifted her coffee to her lips and inhaled a mouthful.

"Sue, were you there too?" Dan directed his gaze to the other side of the table.

"Of course. It was girls' night out, and I'm one of the girls—women I mean."

"Touchy, this morning, aren't we?" he teased. Then he pivoted back to Sophie. "I guess the women are breaking you in, director or no director."

Sophie's stomach did a little flip. Had she overstepped her bounds by taking the day off with the other women? Should she have stayed here and worked, giving the best impression she could? Honestly, she hoped she hadn't made a colossal mistake. But how could it have been? She'd had a great time and had gotten to know the women a little better. That would only help her in the long run. She needed allies here.

"Dan, cut it out." Maddie lifted her head, and her tone proved she hadn't caught on to his lighthearted banter. "We are responsible adults who put in hours and hours of hard work and effort in making this school what it is. If we want to go out dancing the one night we have off every so often, I really don't think you should give us a hard time about it. Maybe we got a little carried away and stayed out longer than we should have. But don't worry, we'll suck it up and get to our jobs." She looked directly at Dan. "What is it that I'm supposed to be doing today?"

"You're going hiking with me and ten of the students." His mischievous grin was unmistakable as he nodded toward the buffet table. "You'd better get something to eat before we leave."

Although the throbbing in Sophie's head cautioned her otherwise, she spoke up, feeling the need to take on her authoritative role. "Even though we all had a great day in Key West, I guess we stayed out a little too late last night, given our responsibilities today. We'll have to consider that next time."

She inwardly cringed at her prudish tone, but thankfully no one commented.

Then she whispered to Kristin. "Fishing?"

Chapter Seven

It wasn't long enough before Max and Ben ushered Sophie to the fishing boat. She inhaled huge breaths of salt air, hoping the oxygen would perform some magic on the dull throb in her head.

"I know you're going to find this hard to believe," she started hesitantly, "but I don't know how to fish."

"What a surprise." Max didn't even bother to moderate his sarcasm.

Sophie's scowl fell on his back as he and Ben gathered up rods and reels, a tackle box, and cartons of what she could only assume contained live bait. He had been sniping at her for days. Ever since Andy had asked her to cover for him as director. It was as if she had caused Andy's accident intentionally, just to take over his job and keep it from Max.

She followed them onto the dock and into the boat, wishing she had brought her bottle of aspirin to dull the pain of this ill-conceived trip.

She sat on the bench, quiet as a church mouse, as Max steered the boat out toward the ocean. Her eyes betrayed her as they were drawn to the muscles in his back and shoulders, stretching and straining with each movement. His tawny, bronze skin glistened with a layer of sunscreen and ocean mist. A work of art. His jaw was square and tight, his cheekbones chiseled. Soft, wavy brown hair blew straight back from his forehead, giving her a bird's-eye view of one very gorgeous man. Oh, so easy on the eyes. Too bad he wasn't as easy on the nerves.

As the boat gained speed, the cool spray from its wake misted her face while the whipping wind infused her lungs with oxygen. There was something to be said for natural remedies.

She dragged her gaze away from Max and looked over at Ben.

"Don't worry, Sophie, I'll help you." His warm smile accompanied by a pat on the shoulder acknowledged his support.

"Thanks. I appreciate that." Maybe he would even bait her hook.

Before long, Max cut the engine. He grabbed a rod and opened one of the Chinese food boxes. Disgusting squirmy things crawled inside.

"Stop crinkling your nose and bait your hook," Max demanded without apology.

She looked to Ben who mouthed that he would do it.

She relaxed a tad.

"You shouldn't be helping her." Max directed his uncalled-for animosity toward Ben. "She'll never learn."

*Keep your comments to yourself, Max*, she bristled from within.

"You're right," Ben agreed.

*Uh-oh.*

"Come here, Sophie." Ben held a rod in his hand and a sympathetic expression on his face. "I'll show you how to do it so you can bait your own next time."

She stood slowly, getting her sea legs, and inched her way over to Ben. He took a squiggly thing from the box and speared it with the hook. *Ugh!*

"See, it's easy." He gave her a friendly wink and a smile. "Now, here's how you cast." He moved the rod around to his side and snapped it toward the ocean. The line whirred as it flew through the air and then sank into the sea. It looked fairly easy. For him.

"Hold it until you feel a tug. When you do, reel it in by turning this lever. If you have a fish on your hook, take it off and put it in the bucket." He paused, taking in her reaction. "Why are you looking at me like that?"

Sophie tried to wipe the trace of disgust off her face but knew she was doing a horrendous job of it. "Sorry."

She turned toward the ocean and pretty much decided that even if she did feel a tug, she was just going to leave the line where it was. Who would know if there was a fish on it or not?

Unfortunately, the ocean was packed with grouper, snapper, hogfish, and cobia. Both Ben and Max hooted and hollered every time they had a bite, then gleefully reeled in their lines and displayed their catch before tossing it into the bucket.

"Hey, Sophie," called Max, "maybe you should reel in. There must be a fish on your line. They're biting like crazy. Unless they can tell you're scared of them and are staying away." He chuckled, annoying her even more, if that were possible.

She rolled her eyes. His knack for pushing her buttons was more prevalent than usual this morning, but she vowed to ignore him. Especially since he was right. There was something pulling on her line, but she wasn't about to pull it up.

Ben must not have received her mental memo since he came over and took the rod from her hands. He wound the line in, and there it was. A medium-sized fish hanging from her hook, flopping in the wind.

"Nice." Ben nodded. "Why didn't you reel her in?"

She answered with her eyes, a pitiful plea to leave her alone so she wouldn't have to say it out loud, in front of Mad Max.

"It seems that Ms. Kearns thinks she's too good to have to work for her food." Max's sarcasm kicked in at full force. "The job of director must have gone to her head. Perhaps we should tell Andy she's not pulling her weight around here. It might get her off this island sooner and back to her precious Valen."

Wouldn't he like that. The perfect excuse to knock her out and take over as acting director. What he had wanted. What he hadn't gotten. Heat spread across her face, and steam was about to explode from her head. She'd had just about enough of Max and his superior attitude.

"I do not think I'm too good to work for my food. I just can't bring myself to touch those disgusting wormy things or take a slimy fish off a hook." Her stomach jolted with the thought of it, although she couldn't be sure that it wasn't Max's effort to control her, making this whole event much worse than it had to be.

"Well, you'd better get over it, because if you don't start contributing, I can guarantee you that Andy will have something to say about it."

"Andy is not in charge." She barely held her temper in check. "I am, in case you've forgotten." She stared at him through slitted eyes, hoping the venom she sent his way found its mark and entered his soul. What a cad! A gorgeous cad, but a cad just the same.

"Come on, Sophie," Ben said appealingly. "Just try.

You don't want to be known around here as a diva. That reputation will get you kicked out of this school the day the semester is over."

Why did everyone seem to think she would want to stay on? That she could stay on? Sophie glanced at Ben. He was so sweet, compared to the evil Max.

She swallowed hard and licked her dry lips. After reaching for the fish dangling from her rod, she grabbed it around its middle and lifted it up slightly, trying to disengage the hook. It didn't work.

"Like this." Ben put his hand over hers and did the same thing, just more forcefully. It slid off the hook, and Sophie tossed it into the bucket as fast as she could.

Now for the bait. She leaned over and saw the squirming mass, which caused a violent reaction in her stomach. She stood up and breathed in through her mouth, closing her eyes for a moment.

*You can do this. You have to do this.*

Closing one eye, she held her breath and tried again. She got one!

"Good, Sophie," coached Ben. "Now put it on your hook."

Since she couldn't wait to get the squirmy, slimy thing out of her hand, she quickly jammed it on the hook and looked around for some disinfectant to pour over her fingers. There was none.

Ben gave her a lopsided smile. "Here." He handed her a towel.

"You've got to be kidding me."

Max's annoyance grated on her last nerve, but she ignored him. "Thanks, Ben." What a nice guy.

Now, to cast. She tried doing what Ben had shown her, but the line didn't release very far, and the hook plopped in the water just a few feet in front of her.

"That's okay, Sophie. There are so many fish out here you'll probably catch one even though it's too close to the boat."

She glanced over at Max who had mumbled something under his breath, then shook his head.

"What?" she asked.

"You'll never fit in here. You don't have it in you."

His words cut through her like a knife, and tears stung the backs of her eyes. But she wouldn't cry. It would just prove his point. She blinked to bat the tears away and inhaled as a backup.

Then she counted to ten.

"You are a despicable person, Max. You know I'm not exactly the outdoorsy kind of person, but you also know I'm trying. Yet you take every opportunity to disparage me." She slammed her rod against the side of the boat and focused all her attention on her intended target. "I've met Kristin every morning at seven to go kayaking in an effort to improve my skills and learn about the wildlife in the area. When I'm not doing that, I'm out there practicing to be a stronger swimmer so when I have to go on a field trip with the kids, I'll be prepared. At night I've been reading study guides on marine life, just so I'll have some idea of the basics when I'm called upon to 'pull my weight' as you've so aptly put it." She didn't add that in addition, she'd been studying Andy's manuals so she'd be better at running this place in his absence. That would only add fuel to his ire.

"Good for you. You're learning all the things you should have known when you signed on for this job. You're only about four years behind. Which just goes back to my question. What was Andy thinking when he hired you?"

The two of them squared off against each other as if readying for a boxing match. Not a bad idea. Except Sophie didn't know how to do that either.

She stared straight into his eyes, the color of melted chocolate with golden flecks sparked by the sun. Or by anger. Although what he had to be angry about, or at least the degree of it, baffled her.

"Let me ask you a question, Max." She placed her hands on her hips and spread her feet apart for better balance. "Why is it that you care so much about why I'm here? Am I a threat to you in some way? Don't you trust me to run this place? Or do you find it impossible to deal with having a woman in control? Just because you have issues shouldn't mean you can't trust anyone but yourself." The second the words were out of her mouth, she knew she'd gone too far. But he had started it. And frankly, she didn't care if she had struck a nerve.

His jaw clenched, an almost imperceptible movement. After a few seconds he bowed his head and sighed. Then he turned his back to her, picked up his rod, and cast the line into the ocean. No comeback. No smart remark. A minor victory. Had she really gotten in the last word this time?

Unfortunately, she couldn't let it go.

"Is that how you deal with conflict? You turn around and ignore it?"

She was definitely pushing the envelope now, but he deserved it. One didn't just end an argument by turning away. He needed to stick with it. Fight it out. Until the bitter end.

She watched him in profile, the brooding, detached

fisherman whose lips rarely inched into a smile, whose eyes rarely sparkled, and whose cutting words were meant to slice—and hurt. Which they did.

Sophie looked over at Ben, who had remained quiet during their little altercation. He held his finger to his lips as if to say *enough*.

She itched to continue but followed his unspoken suggestion. He knew Max a lot better than she did. And sometimes, she just had to let things settle down. At least for the time being. She'd have plenty of time to show him she was capable of fitting in.

For the next hour, other than some small talk between her and Ben, the boat was silent. She got the hang of baiting her hook and casting her line. And she began catching a boatload of fish, along with the other two.

She couldn't be accused of failing to do her job now.

Inhaling, she ventured a smile. Whether the fresh breeze carrying sea air, the salty aroma of the cerulean ocean, or the liberating argument with Max, she couldn't be sure which had eliminated her headache.

But she began to feel infinitely better.

****

By one, they had docked, and the three of them hauled their buckets of fish from the boat to the beach. While she and Ben unloaded their equipment with care and precision, Max threw things, slammed things, and generally clattered about. Obviously, the calmness and serenity that had finally overtaken her had missed Max.

"Hey, Max, careful there." Ben jumped as a tackle box crashed next to him on the dock.

The only response was a grunt.

A smile crossed Ben's face, although Sophie was in

the dark as to its reason. And given Max's mood, she was not about to ask.

Even though she felt extremely proud of herself for overcoming her initial aversion and getting right in there and fishing, she was glad it was over. She'd had enough of fish for one day. After carrying their buckets with the fruits of their labors into the kitchen, Sophie turned to Ben.

"Thanks for your help today. I'm going to get going. I need to douse myself in shower gel to get rid of this smell."

Max finally broke his silence. "Not so fast. These fish have to be gutted and cleaned."

She glanced over at him. He must be joking. But no hint of a smile crossed his lips. Only that infuriating, serious set of his jaw and unnerving determination on his face.

"Come on, Max. I really think I've done my share today. Don't you?"

When she received no response, she persisted. "Isn't one major conquest per day a limit around here? I learned how to bait a hook and toss my line out. I even started taking the fish off the hook. Can't you give me some credit for coming around?"

"Credit's given. Now help Ben clean the fish." He dropped his buckets on the floor by the kitchen sink and walked out the door.

Sophie stood there with her mouth open and her hands on her hips. "How does he get out of it?" She turned to Ben.

"The only reason he's not helping is because he's too angry with you." He moved one of the buckets of fish closer to the counter. "It's probably better that he left.

Lord knows what would've happened once the two of you had knives in your hands."

He grabbed a rubber apron from a storage closet and threw one to her. "Let's get started. We have to clean these babies up, package them, and freeze the ones that won't be cooked tonight." He walked over to a drawer and removed assorted knives. Then he got two cutting boards and placed them on the counter, side by side. "We caught enough for the week." He surveyed the five buckets of dead fish.

"Great." She sighed, resigning herself to the fact that she would be knee deep in fish guts for the next few hours. "Where are the rubber gloves?"

She started opening and closing drawers and cabinets in search of yellow latex, the only thing that would keep her hands from touching the disgusting slimy entrails of the disgusting slimy fish. She finally found a pair in the cleaning supply closet. "Aha!"

Ben just ignored her and got to the business at hand. And sooner than she would have liked, Sophie got to it too.

Chapter Eight

"Hey, Max, pass the tartar sauce." Dan's request came from the other end of the table, and he obliged, keeping his culinary opinion to himself.

"This snapper is so good you don't need condiments." Sue moaned over the morsel she'd just placed in her mouth. At least she knew not to ruin fresh fish with mayo and relish.

"You guys must have had a great day out on the ocean." Kristin, the ever-present optimist, turned to Max, smiling. "I hear the fish practically jumped onto your hooks." She then directed her question to Sophie. "So how was it?"

Sophie shrugged. "It was a little hairy at first, but Ben was nice enough to show me what to do. After I got over my initial revulsion, I think I did pretty well. Don't you, Max?"

Her gaze targeted him for a few seconds, and the electricity of a lightning bolt ran through his body. Unable to look away, he studied her as some unknown emotion clouded her beautiful eyes. Then she lowered her lids as the corners of her lips turned down.

He was such a dolt.

Max had predicted disaster as soon as he learned Sophie was slated to join him and Ben on their fishing trip. She hadn't gotten enough sleep, she had a headache, and fishing was not an activity high on her list of must-dos. Further, their rapport was fraught with friction. Even more so after Andy had named her as acting director of the school.

He should have been patient with her, but this outing proved Andy's mistake in spades.

When he and Ben got to the dock, Sophie was still yards behind them, lagging as if that would prolong their departure. When she finally followed them onto the boat, she sat on a bench, as far away from him as possible. Which didn't stop his gaze from wandering to the woman who unnerved him.

Gone were her boxy, conservative clothes, and in their place were flattering navy-blue shorts and a white tank top that fit her to perfection. Her long limbs had started to tan, and those swimming lessons had created definition in her upper arms and gorgeous long legs. But those eyes were the biggest draw—sometimes crystal, sometimes aqua—their depths were impossible to ignore, especially when fixated upon him. Beautiful.

At one point she had removed her hat, along with the elastic from her ponytail. The wind blew through her chestnut strands threaded with gold, and his fingers had itched to lace through them. Just as they did now.

Why he'd felt it necessary to cut through her like a knife, he didn't know. Maybe it was because he didn't want to feel the stirrings she elicited in him. Pushing her buttons would assuredly keep her at arm's length.

Unfortunately, she'd struck back with fiery words and blazing irises—a dangerous mixture of turquoise and sass. And her sting was poisonous. Of course, it was precipitated by his biting remark that she'd never fit in, an arrow he knew would hit its target. He really needed to get ahold of his emotions when he was around her, or the next few months would be intolerable.

He had been an overbearing ogre this morning. Things had gotten out of hand, too hot. They needed to let things settle down. At least for the time being.

He raised his fork and ate without tasting while trying to concentrate on the conversation around him. Yet his eyes were drawn back to her. She had showered and dressed in white shorts and a pink top. Chestnut hair, lush and sun-streaked, fell around her shoulders in cascading layers. Full lips outlined a wide mouth uncovering a perfect smile—when directed at someone other than him. His gaze stayed on her mouth as she ran her tongue over her lower lip, drawing his attention even more to his desire to kiss those lips. He mentally thumped his head. What was he thinking? Sophie would never kiss him. She didn't even like him, thanks to his animosity toward her.

She caught his stare, and a rosy blush seeped into her cheeks before she jerked her head to the right—cutting off their connection, cutting off his fantasy.

In his quest to detach himself from her hold over him, he entered into a conversation on the next few weeks' activities. A field trip to Big Pine Key for a night of camping was on his agenda, as well as a kayaking trip through the backwater mangroves. Perfect outings to keep his mind where it should be and not on the delectable Sophie.

He felt rather than saw her get up from the table, and her absence brought his thoughts right back to her.

He was in big trouble.

\*\*\*\*

The beach at dusk emitted a solitary aura as Sophie walked barefoot—the cool sand soft and inviting. Gone were the students who had populated the area this afternoon, playing volleyball or relaxing on blankets in groups. The day of rest was coming to a close, and obligations slated for the week ahead, whether studying for academic tests, planning for environmental experiments, or preparing for field trips, had everyone in their living quarters, teachers included.

She raised her face to the sea breeze as it blew against her cheeks. The sky's colors streaked a low path across the horizon—a myriad of pinks, purples, and blues painted by the setting sun. Although she too had to prepare her lecture for tomorrow, this environment was too new for her to take it for granted. If she were back in New Jersey, no doubt, she would be holed up in her apartment poring over her notes for *The Odyssey*. But here she could see, feel, and grasp these incredible surroundings with all of her senses.

She strolled for a while, then sat before pulling her knees up and resting her chin on them, contemplating nothing more than the ebb and flow of the tide.

"What brings you down here?" Max's deep voice broke through her trance and sent shivers through her pores. Surprisingly, not bad shivers, which perplexed her. His tone was friendly. As if their morning altercation and awkward moments at dinner had never occurred.

Without waiting for an invitation, he sat down beside her, cross-legged.

She mimicked his breeziness. "This place is just so beautiful. I know that sounds like a cliché, but it's paradise. All so different from what I'm used to." She glanced over at him. "What about you?"

"Even though it's not new to me, I'll never get bored with this view. This is the golden hour."

His mood was mellow, almost melancholy, a nice change from his combative persona this morning.

"I'm sorry about earlier." He started cautiously. "I was a bear—not at all helpful. And what I said about you never fitting in was cruel. I know my words were cutting." He grimaced. "I've been upset about something else. You didn't deserve being the target of my disappointment."

She let his words sink in and curl around her.

"Am I forgiven?" Vulnerability pierced through his question.

"I suppose." She tried to keep her grin in check, but it emerged.

"Thank you." A smile flashed across his face, and Sophie's heart stopped, just for a second.

He continued. "You came around today…after a while. And Ben told me you were a real trooper gutting and cleaning the fish."

"So glad to hear I'm moving up a notch in your estimation. We would have finished a lot faster if you had done your part and helped out." With just the two of them, it had taken nearly three hours.

"Sorry. But I figured you'd have your nose wrinkled and your head turned while you stabbed at a dead fish. You didn't need any more negative comments from me. You'd already put up with your share for one day."

"The reason you didn't help was to save me from your scorn? That's a sad excuse for not *pulling your weight around here*." She deliberately threw his words back at him, knowing it would either make him laugh— the hoped-for outcome—or force him to get up and leave.

He chose the former. "Touché." His chuckle

jumbled her insides.

Silence enveloped them, but it wasn't uncomfortable. Max had, at least temporarily, put the gloves down, allowing her to enjoy not only her surroundings but the pleasure of sharing them with a very handsome maverick. He had seemingly opened a door to a possible friendship, and Sophie didn't want to give him the opportunity to close it.

But in order to get to know him better, she needed to ask the tough question. "Since you brought it up, what was the real reason for your foul mood?"

He didn't answer right away, and she wondered whether he intended to at all.

"I've had a chip on my shoulder ever since Andy made you the acting director here. My misguided anger has been unfair to you."

His confession was unexpected, even though she knew of his views on the subject. "Word travels fast around here. I know you don't think I'm qualified."

"Sorry. I should have kept my mouth shut." His jaw clenched, then relaxed. "You were right about what you said on the boat. I do have trust issues. And control issues."

Mocha-brown eyes stared at the sea, and he seemed miles away. "My brother, Dean, died in a scuba diving accident. It was ten years ago. We always went on dives together, but that day, I had bailed on him." His words rasped. "That decision cost me my brother."

His words punched her in the gut. She hadn't been expecting such a devastating confession in response to her question. She didn't know what to say, so she remained silent.

He closed his eyes and tilted his head back. The pain

etched on his face was palpable. "When we dove together, we always used the buddy system. It's when you dive in pairs so that you can help or rescue each other in case of an emergency. That day there were others on the trip, and from the police report, it appears that they dove as a group with no two in particular pairing up. Dean's oxygen line got caught up in some ocean trash and cut off his air supply. No one noticed. At least not in time. He was unconscious when they pulled him out of the water. He died a day later at the hospital." He exhaled. "If I had been there, I would have seen that he was in trouble and been able to cut him free. But I wasn't. I had something better to do that day—or so I thought."

Max's voice was raw with emotion, and the guilt he carried rose to the surface.

Tears flooded Sophie's eyes, and her throat clogged with pain. "I'm...I'm so sorry." Her words were totally inadequate, but she was at a loss.

A heavy sadness tugged at his lips. "I will always carry the burden of his death."

"It wasn't your fault." She rustled around her brain for other appropriate, comforting things to say. "You had every right to do what you wanted to do that day. Your brother chose to go diving without you just as you chose to do something without him. It wasn't only your choice that triggered the outcome." Would that rationale lessen his guilt? Probably not. "I can understand why you feel responsible. I'm not trying to dismiss those emotions. We all carry around *what ifs*, and sometimes we convince ourselves that if we had only done something differently or not done something at all, we could have prevented a misfortune. But we are not clairvoyants. We can't let those *what ifs* strangle and suffocate us. We can only embrace the fact that fate had a hand in our destiny and move on—to a new beginning."

"Is that what you're doing?"

His eyes found hers and held them, looking for the answer. She lowered her lids and turned her face to the Gulf. She hadn't expected her words of wisdom to come back around to frame her. She wasn't ready to bare her soul to him. She was only trying to help.

"She doesn't answer," he said quietly. "Very telling."

Her cheeks burned, and she hugged her legs in closer, knowing the gesture would give him more food for thought.

More silence. More introspection.

"This isn't a new beginning for me," Sophie ventured. "It's a pause—a breath of air before I go back to Valen." At least she hoped so. She'd heard nothing about the investigation. If the board couldn't determine if the posted video had been edited, they might fire her.

"Thanks for trying to ease my guilt, but nothing works. I've been to therapy over the years. I know intellectually I had a right to do whatever I wanted that day. I had no obligation to Dean to go scuba diving. He was with experienced divers. All the facts that should help me appease my guilt have been hammered into my head." He eased his body back, leaning on his elbows. "So yes, I know it wasn't my fault. But it happened because of a choice I made. Since then, I've had this overriding need to control what I can. If I make the rules, if I'm in charge, I'll make sure that nothing bad happens. I can't seem to put my trust in others. Dean did, and look what happened." He angled his head as if waiting for her to endorse his theory. "It's not a man versus woman thing, as you assumed this morning. My trust issues aren't gender specific. They're universal. In my current view of the world, everyone who participates in any activity or venture should know what they're doing so nothing bad happens."

"I understand where you're coming from. But one has to learn before they can become proficient." How had they shifted from Max's guilt over Dean's death to her shortcomings?

"In my opinion, which as I just pointed out is very skewed, any teacher here should be well-versed in all school-related activities before they sign on. It makes no sense to me that someone who doesn't have that background would even come here. That's the missing piece where you're concerned."

"You shared your theory that Andy brought me here so I'd transfer my teaching academy to the school. But I already told you you're way off base. Andy and I are friends from Valen. I helped him obtain the grants he needed to get this school off the ground. He's always wanted me to see the end result, to experience it." She refused to share the real reason that brought her here, even though Max had just bared his soul. Trust was a two-way street, and their relationship was so tenuous and ever-changing that she couldn't rely on one seemingly open conversation. "Since I was taking a semester sabbatical, it seemed like the perfect time to visit. It just so happened that Andy needed an English teacher for the semester. End of story. No hidden agenda."

Of course, there was more to his cynicism—her quick rise to acting director. So she addressed it. "Maybe Andy should have chosen you to run the school while he's out. But from what I see, you're all about teaching and doing. Why would you want to be holed up in an office, poring over requests for funds from every teacher here, or dealing with parents' issues with their kids, or kids' issues with their teachers or fellow students?"

He sat up and tossed a shell into the sea. "When you put it that way, you're right. I was looking at it more as an opportunity to get the school more recognition. To get a marketing plan in place. Andy's been reticent about my ideas, but if I were in charge, he'd see how well my plan would work."

So that's why he wanted the position of acting director. Now it made more sense. "Instead of antagonizing me at every turn, why don't you bring your ideas to me and we can discuss them?"

His lips quirked up in a grin. "I never thought about that."

"Of course not. You'd rather point out my flaws and make my life miserable than work alongside of me." She smiled to lessen the barb. "If you want to accomplish something—anywhere, not just here—you need allies. The more, the better. Trying to wrangle control and stuff your ideas down everyone's throat doesn't usually work out so well."

"Are you saying you'd be my ally?"

"You have to convince me your ideas have merit. Your current goal is to get Andy's or my approval for your marketing ideas. But your ultimate goal is to establish an environmental research institute."

Surprise lifted his brow. "How do you know?"

"Nothing is a secret around here. I'm sure you're aware of that."

He nodded, and a smirk took over. "Since Andy won't consider my institute until the school becomes more prominent, I've suggested that he market the school. With that would come name recognition."

Sophie considered his words, not wanting to crush his ideas out of hand, but they needed more work. "What is your marketing plan?"

He jumped right in. "Send information about the school to as many high schools as possible, starting on the East Coast. And market through social media and an updated website."

"Is there a brochure already in existence that could be sent out? Do you have the names of all the schools you want to send it to? What social media platforms do you want to use? What does the website need?" She could have gone on and on, but those questions should start to make him see that a lot of effort went into a marketing campaign.

"There is a brochure. I don't know what schools are already on our contact lists, so I don't know what others should be added. With regard to social media, we should have a presence on Facebook and Instagram at the very least. Maybe others. The website is bare bones. So much more content should be added."

"Is your proposal in writing?"

"No. It's just something I've been batting around with Andy."

"You can't just drop it in Andy's lap and assume he'll figure it out. If you have a good idea for marketing and you want it done, you need a structured plan. In writing. And you need to be involved."

"Is that how you got your teaching academy off the ground?"

She shook her head. "Valen already had a great reputation—not only in New Jersey but on the entire east coast and beyond. But I did have to create a plan to market the academy since any potential grant maker would want to know about that plan before investing in it."

"How did you go about doing that?"

"I reviewed grant applications to see what information they'd want. I met with the school's communications officer to discuss marketing ideas specific to the academy, and I came up with something solid. I spoke to dozens of teachers to find out what type of continuing education they preferred and how any new program should be communicated to them. I also analyzed other programs out there to see what they did well and what they lacked. I didn't go to our headmaster until I had answers to any and every question he could possibly throw at me."

"How long did all that take?"

"About a year."

He sighed. "I've done the research you've talked about as it pertains to the institute. But I didn't do any marketing research. I figured that if Andy hired an outside consultant to improve the school's website and increase the school's social media presence, more people would become aware of the school. And once the school's reputation expanded, adding the institute would give the school more credibility."

She nodded. "All of that makes sense. Except that you've hit a roadblock. Andy isn't doing anything to market the school other than what he's done in the past. Probably because of the money it would cost. If you want to convince him to increase his marketing efforts, then come up with a concrete plan, including how to fund it. Make it easy for him to agree with you."

"I guess I have my work cut out for me." A wry grin took over his mouth. "I appreciate you sharing your thoughts. It's very helpful."

"So you see there is a benefit to working with others as opposed to taking total control?"

His chuckle tickled her heart. "Now I do. My head hurts from thinking about the tasks you just suggested if I want to see my project come to fruition." He lay back on his elbows. "Let's talk about something else. My brain needs a break."

At least he still wanted to spend time with her. "What would you like to talk about?"

"It appears to me that you love teaching. Why do you want to rise up the ranks at Valen? As you said before, it's an administrative headache."

Kristin must have shared her goal of becoming headmaster with him. "That's a complicated issue." One that could be broken down into parts and parceled out, depending on how much she wanted to share. "You're right. I do love teaching. Kids are like sponges. So inquisitive. So open to learning. They make me see things in a different light all the time. It's amazing. But I could help those students even more as chair of the English department—which is a stepping stone to my ultimate goal. I'd be the one in charge of implementing the curriculum and instructional practices. I would also assist the teachers in their professional development—all with an eye toward helping students engage more and therefore achieve more."

"That sounds like a lot of work. Would you still have time to teach?"

"I'd make the time, although I might have to cut back on a few classes."

He seemed to ponder her explanation. "There's something I'm missing." His steady gaze had the effect of placing her under a microscope.

She sighed, contemplating whether to reveal another piece of herself. "You are very suspicious about my motives—not only for being here at Sunrise Island School but for reaching for the top job at Valen."

"I've seen what a great teacher you are. The kids here really flock to you even though you're new."

"You mean even though I don't fit in?" She elbowed him, hoping to lighten his mood.

And it worked. He laughed out loud this time.

She shrugged. "I try to make it fun. Literature can be a little difficult to get through sometimes, so I figure out ways to make it relate to their world." She paused, thinking back to her high school lit teacher, Miss McCarthy, and a warm cocoon wrapped itself around her, making her smile.

"Why the smile?"

"I had a teacher in ninth grade who set me on my path. Ever since then, I wanted to be like her—to reach out to students, especially those who feel like they don't belong, and lasso them in. Whether it's dressing up in character, participating in some playacting, going to Renaissance fairs, watching movies, debating issues raised in a particular book... Turning literature into something you can get lost in." Sophie smiled over some of her more outlandish ideas.

"Did you feel like you didn't belong in high school?" His voice was caring, caressing.

She stretched her legs before her and brushed at some sand. "I went to a large public high school, but that's not where I wanted to be. I had applied for a scholarship to Valen—my dream school. I got in but didn't receive a scholarship. So I couldn't go. My parents didn't have the money to pay the tuition. I was angry." Embarrassment warmed her cheeks as she remembered the skipped classes, the detentions, the below average grades. And the disappointment in her mother's eyes. "I had been an A student but was quickly turning my grades to D's. I rarely brought assignments in on time, and I never studied for tests. I was rebelling for not being accepted on scholarship into the school I was dying to go to. Miss McCarthy, my English lit teacher, was my saving grace. She lassoed me in and wouldn't let go."

Sophie smiled at the wonderful memories. "She would bring in costumes from the local theater she was involved in, and let me try them on after class. She would too, and we'd pretend to be Romeo and Mercutio or Desdemona and Emilia."

Max threw his head back and let out an infectious laugh. "And that was fun?"

She stared at him, biting her inside lip to keep from showing any mirth, waiting for him to stop.

"I'm sorry," he sputtered. "I could just picture you speaking in your Shakespearean voice, dressed in some dusty old gown." He looked at her, the sparkle of amusement not dying in his eyes. "Come on. That's funny."

He pushed at her arm to encourage her to share in his enjoyment, and a momentary jolt flashed through her system at his touch. Electric. Dangerous.

She needed to focus on something else. "Anyway, Miss McCarthy got me back on track academically, and I was able to get it together from there." She paused, contemplating whether to open herself up even more—

to fill in the missing piece he surmised about her career choice. She shrugged and threw caution to the wind. "This might sound vindictive or vengeful, or at the very least immature, but once I decided I wanted to teach, my sole goal was to teach at the school that wouldn't accept me. To show them I made it despite their choice to keep me out. Once I got my foot in the door, I wasn't going to stop. I would get to the highest position possible. And that's headmaster." She lifted her chin, taking on her leadership mantle. "With that job, I'll be able to steer the entire ship. I'd task the director of development with obtaining more scholarship funds for those who have the ability but can't afford a private school education."

"Aaahhh. The Sophie Kearns Scholarship Fund."

Her face flamed at his suggestion. "No. I would never put my name on it."

He placed his hand over hers, and the heat from her face traveled to her limbs.

"I didn't mean to insinuate that. I just meant that it would help students like you. It sounds like you would make an excellent headmaster."

His words showered her with validation, something that had not been forthcoming from him since the day they met.

He continued. "That's a great reason to choose a career path. I can't say I had any similar experience in high school, especially when it came to English class." He grimaced.

"Don't you like literature?" Disapproving judgment peppered her voice.

"I'm not much of a word guy. I like science. Experiments. I want to see things, smell things, touch things. It's so much better than reading impossible-to-understand prose." He glanced at her, his grin still in place.

She swayed at the thought of him touching her—his fingers caressing her cheek, his arm sliding around her waist and pulling her close. She had to refocus.

"If that's what you think about literature, then you should take one of my classes. I'll show you how much better it is."

He raised his hands in surrender. "No, that's okay. I believe you."

Their difficult conversation had given way to easy banter, which spun warm fuzzies within. She couldn't remove the smile from her face. She and Max were finally having a nice talk—not sniping at each other. The enchanting feeling settled around her as they sat in the dark.

After a few minutes, he pushed himself up, unfolding his legs and brushing the sand from the back of his shorts. He held out his hand, and she took it, rising with his force. His heat radiated through her blood, and when she stood, she came up against his hard, broad chest. His pine soap and beachy scent enveloped her senses, and she raised her eyes to meet his. Desire flamed through them—the same desire that flowed through her core.

Then reality struck. *What are you doing?* She was the current director of the school. The person in authority. She had an image to uphold. She couldn't act like a lovesick schoolgirl. Especially with Max. He was trouble—had been since day one.

She pulled away and lowered her eyes, refusing to let him see the passion he had ignited. "I better get back to my cabin. I have to prepare for tomorrow's class." Her voice rasped, the result of electrified blood.

"I'll walk you back." His tone was nonchalant, as if nothing had just happened between them.

She had ruined it.

He had ruined it.

They walked side by side, but she kept her distance, not daring to touch, not daring to acknowledge their near lapse. Her steps synced with his, but her walls crept back up between them.

And now she had nothing more to say.

Chapter Nine

Max sat on the brick wall near the classroom building, watching Sophie through his aviator shades, careful to angle his head in such a way that she wouldn't know he was observing her. A current of electricity sizzled through his veins, and he couldn't turn it off.

His usual mode of indifference, leaning toward detachment, had drastically changed over the last few weeks. Starting with the arrival of Ms. Sophie Kearns. His preferred aloofness had turned to paranoia when he'd thought she was here to move her teaching academy. Paranoia became resentment when Andy named her as the acting director.

But then he'd stood toe to toe with her on a fishing boat, and although her words were fighting, she'd zeroed in on his real problem. Very perceptive. And aware.

When he ran into her on the beach the other night, all his built-up negativity came crashing down. In one soul-baring conversation—in one bewitching touch—in one almost kiss—she had zapped him with an enchanting potion so strong he was still drugged by its powerful effects.

His gaze followed her as she walked beside the building with a stack of books. Her outward transformation was impressive. But he'd also seen a glimpse of her inward beauty, and that beauty dazzled.

"Hey, Ms. Kearns," Mike, one of her tenth-grade

students, called from across the patio. "Do you have a few minutes?" He ambled toward her with his best friend, Ken, in tow.

"Sure." Sophie moved toward one of the outside tables, half covered by the fronds of a palm tree and half baked by the intense sun. She chose the shade. "Have a seat."

Max was close enough to hear their conversation but far enough away to appear unobtrusive. He was just one of the teachers hanging outside between classes for a shot of sunshine.

"Ken and I wanted to ask you about Jay Gatsby. What does he really do for a living?"

A smile played around her lips. "We're not quite sure yet, are we? He's certainly managed to accumulate a lot of wealth. He's a self-made, self-invented man. How do you think he's done it?"

Their conversation continued in that vein as the students sat down with Sophie and actually discussed the American classic. If he hadn't seen it with his own eyes, he wouldn't have believed it. According to Sara, none of the kids ever wanted to discuss literature outside of the classroom. She'd constantly complained about their lack of interest and how unfair it was that she had to compete with the classes that took the students kayaking and camping. And it wasn't just Mike and Ken asking Sophie questions. He had seen others with her before. She obviously had that certain something that drew them in.

Him included.

It had taken her a few weeks, but she seemed to be adjusting to life in the Keys. She was no longer that repressed, uptight, northeastern prep school teacher who shunned the outdoors. Her new confidence appealed to him.

So did her feistiness.

He thought back to their argument on the boat. With eyes flashing and face burning, she had given him an earful and then some. The electricity she generated could power the entire island. But then he'd seen a different side of her on the beach. One that forgave him his sins and accepted his reasoning for his many flaws. And despite those flaws, she shared her wealth of knowledge on how to accomplish his goal. She had so many facets that he had trouble keeping track. She'd miraculously flipped the switch inside him and shrouded his negativity in darkness while casting a bright light on his future dream.

But the absolute best moment—the one he couldn't let go of—was the moment he pulled her up from the sand and into his space. Her lips had been kissing close. All he had to do was close the gap and freefall. But he'd gotten lost in her eyes, their blue depths hypnotizing him with their intensity.

Until she shut him out.

He shouldn't have let her go so easily. He thought about that almost-kiss far too often—the close encounter that sizzled through his veins.

His gaze slid down to her long, shapely legs, crossed, with one dangling over the other. She had slipped off her sandal, and her foot was bare, except for the pink polish on her toes. She spoke with her hands as well as her entire being—so expressive and engaging.

He inhaled, trying to tamp down the fog she created in his brain. He didn't want to fall under the spell of any woman. He'd made a non-negotiable promise to himself that kept any stray feelings of ardor under wraps. It didn't matter that she was a caring, generous, thoughtful woman who, in one night, taught him to garner allies and give up his demand for sovereign control.

Unfortunately, he still harbored a niggling feeling that he couldn't trust her a hundred percent.

Because he still wasn't sure why she was here. She had dissuaded him somewhat of his theory that Andy wanted her Summer Teaching Academy down here. And Andy couldn't have known he'd need her to act as temporary director. Although she'd come up with a plausible reason for her sabbatical from Valen, she was clearly hiding something.

He watched as her leg bounced back and forth, her audience captivated by her discussion of *The Great Gatsby*. She laughed at something Ken said, a sparkling, open laugh that set the teens at ease with their mentor. If she had been his teacher at that age, he would have been stuttering and sputtering. Kids these days had a lot more going for them.

"Looking at anything in particular?" Kristin stopped to follow his gaze.

"No. I just find it hard to believe that high school kids here like literature." He tried his best to scowl.

"For some reason, I don't think that's what has you so fascinated." Her brow arched with skepticism.

He ignored her comment and jumped off the wall. "Take a walk with me." He moved away from Sophie and her entourage.

"Sure. What's up?"

"What's her story?" He knew he didn't have to identify "her."

A grin washed over Kristin's face. "So Max likes Sophie." She singsonged like a teenager. Very annoying.

"No, I don't. I just want to know why she's here. It's not because of her undying love of the environment. She didn't even know how to swim when she arrived."

"You've been after the reason since the day she got here. Why don't you ask her yourself if it's that important to you?" She slid her sunglasses from her head to her eyes, a sign his questioning made her uncomfortable.

"I have. But every time I ask, she maneuvers around it or gives that bit about needing a break before becoming chair of the English department. It doesn't make sense to me. Maddie agrees." Her opinion validated his own.

"Just leave it alone. Not everyone wants their secrets known." While Kristin's words responded to his complaint about Sophie, they contained a double-edged sword, and he felt the blade purposely cut into him. But instead of accusing him of keeping his own backstory a mystery, she turned and started heading back toward the building. "I have to go. My next class is starting soon."

Max caught hold of her arm. He'd been right. Sophie did have a secret. "Come on, Kristin. I won't let on that I know. I won't do anything with the information."

She removed her sunglasses and looked at him with her huge hazel eyes, as if to gauge his sincerity. He let her see into him. She hesitated, and in that instant, he thought he had her.

Then she hammered him. "You have some nerve, relying on our friendship to find out some morsel of gossip about Sophie. I expected better of you."

He hung his head, duly chastised. "I guess I am a little infatuated with her. I just don't want to get burned."

"Yeah, right." She chuckled. "I know your type." An edge of sarcasm floated through her words.

His forehead furrowed. "What type is that?"

"The brooding, detached type who waits patiently for his prey, then swoops in for the kill. Only to toss her aside a few weeks later."

His uncomfortable chuckle came from deep within. "Are you kidding?"

"No, I'm not. Over the past year and a half, I've seen you in action at our hangouts. You sit apart from everyone, watching, listening. Scoping out the place for that one woman who snags your interest. Then you reel her in, working your magic. You date for a few weeks—maybe even a month or two. Then poof. Onto the next."

"Is that what you think? That I'm a serial dater who's just in it for the catch?" She was wrong. Although he did enjoy the chase, he had other reasons for never sticking around long enough to form an attachment.

A smile played on her lips. "Yes. That is what I believe." Then her playfulness evaporated. "She's going back to Valen, you know."

"I know." Was she trying to protect him or Sophie?

"Don't hurt my friend." She stood with her hands on her hips, her expressive face taking on a stern set. There was his answer.

"What makes you think I'll get close enough to do that?"

Kristin didn't respond. But it didn't matter. Despite his irrational attraction, he had no intention of getting close to Sophie. Just as he hadn't with any other woman. He had a different plan formulating in his mind.

"Hey, Sophie," he called, as he and Kristin approached her table. "How'd you like to come on a kayaking trip with my environmental class later this afternoon?"

Kristin jabbed him in his side with her elbow, as she whispered to him out of the corner of her mouth. "What are you doing?"

He ignored her. "You could put your new skills to good use. We're heading out toward the back country to identify different types of fish and birds."

Sophie looked up, a smile playing across her face. "I'd love to."

If they hadn't been in the middle of the patio, where not only Sophie and her students but several others milled about, Max was sure Kristin would have demanded an explanation. Instead, she bored into him with her eyes, eyes meant to pierce and maim.

"I'm coming with you," she hissed.

"Now, Kristin." He used his silky, charming voice. "I'm sure Sophie doesn't need your protection."

Kristin was about to respond when Sophie broke in. "What are you two talking about?"

"Kristin was just telling me she's too busy to come on our field trip, and I told her the only way I would let her off the hook is if you came."

Kristin's glare was lethal.

"I haven't been to the back country yet," Sophie admitted. "I've been dying to go."

"Sophie, you don't have to—" started Kristin.

"Great," broke in Max. "Then it's all set. Meet me down by the dock at three. See, Kristin? Sophie's there for you too, when you need her. Now you can grade those papers."

If looks could kill, he would have been down for the count. "I have to go," he said breezily. "I hear Maddie's been looking for me." He left Kristin standing there with her mouth open and Sophie glancing back and forth between them, looking adorably befuddled.

A ripple of amusement washed through him.

Perfect.

**\*\*\*\***

Max looked up as Sophie ran toward the dock one minute before three, a towel and sneakers in one hand, shorts and T-shirt bunched in the other. Her red one-piece bathing suit was cut high on her thighs, and his breath caught in his throat. Could his *Baywatch* fantasy have come to life?

The mousy private school professor turned cover girl. His heart beat double-time, and heat coursed through his veins. Damn. Not the reaction he wanted; certainly not the one he needed. This was strictly business.

"Sorry, I'm late," she said, a bit out of breath. "I just got out of class and had to run back to my cabin and change."

With some effort, Max closed his mouth and glanced at a few of the teenaged boys standing next to him. She apparently had the same effect on them.

"Let's get going," he shouted. "Two to a boat. Sophie, you come with me. I'll take the rear."

They set out on their journey, six kayaks in all, prepared for a lesson on the wildlife making this environment their home. The group paddled around the shallow waters of uninhabited keys and mangrove islands, which were no more than the root system of the mangrove trees.

Max looked up and saw an osprey making its plunge for food. "Look right," he called to the group as the bird hit the water feet first, with a great splash, before seizing its prey in long, slender claws.

Sophie screamed in surprise.

"You're going to scare all the birds away." He chuckled. "See up there to the left. That's a frigate bird. It has a wingspan of about eight feet." He stopped paddling, as did the rest of the group, while they watched the graceful bird soar through the sky.

"What's that up on top of that tree?" Sophie pointed to one of his favorite species.

"A blue heron. Although it looks like it's sleeping, it's patiently waiting for a fish to come by."

He turned his lesson from birds to fish and pointed out eagle rays, southern stingrays, bonefish, tarpon, and permit as the fish swam beneath them in the emerald-green water.

Sophie's eyes glowed with excitement when she spotted a starfish and made him stop to pick it up so she could study it more closely. Exactly what he wanted. This was his opportunity to teach her firsthand about this magnificent natural paradise. For her to enjoy marine wildlife in the Keys as much as he did.

And his students clearly felt the same way.

Their questions about the environment, their enthusiasm, their sponge-like grasp of the names of different birds and fish, made him proud of his role in teaching them about marine life, which would eventually segue into marine resource management.

They wound through the back country for two and a half hours, and the time had come to head back. Max purposefully allowed the students to blaze the trail, and he and Sophie lagged behind.

"How'd you like it?" He was sure he already knew the answer.

"It was fabulous...educational...really beautiful."

She paused. "You are one incredible teacher. The kids hang on to every word." Her sincerity warmed his heart.

"Thanks. It's what I love. And the marine environment is my passion."

They paddled in silence for a few minutes, and he hoped she was enjoying the scenery and sounds of nature as much as he was. Given the inroads they had made in their relationship, he decided now was a good time to push for more information. "I know I've asked you this before, but you never seem to give me more than a vague and very general response. Why would you take a break at Valen—a sabbatical—just when you were poised to become chair of the English department? It's not like you've slowed down any. You not only teach here, but you've taken over as the acting director." He was quick to add, "Of course, you couldn't have contemplated Andy's accident. That took us all by surprise. But even coming down here to teach is hardly a break."

Her back stiffened, but her tone was even. "I told you why I'm here. I'm sorry if that's not a good enough reason for you."

So today wasn't the day he was going to get the full story. Maybe there was nothing more to the story. Maybe his distrust was misplaced. She'd opened up to him about the reasons why she wanted to ascend at Valen, and it all made sense. If she thought she needed a break, maybe he should accept that at face value and stop harping at her, trying to get her to divulge more. His innate cynicism had the capacity to upset the delicate balance they'd achieved in their relationship over the past few days.

"I apologize for trying to get at motives which may not be there. As you know, I have an issue with trusting people. You've been open and honest about your goals and the motives driving you."

He hoped his apology would wipe away the tension in her body, but his words didn't have the intended effect, and she continued paddling with stiff shoulders.

Curious over her reaction, but not wanting to get off track from the discussion he did want to have, he let it go. For now. They were alone, or at least as alone as two adults could be at this school. Private discussion time was at a premium where the kids were underfoot morning, noon, and night. Not that he didn't love being with them. But now that he had Sophie's undivided attention, it was time to dive in.

All afternoon, he had been building up to this moment. He knew he had to be careful with his presentation. He didn't want her to take it the wrong way.

"After our talk the other night, I now understand that I've been going about attaining my goal in the wrong way. Since you have not only the background and knowledge concerning this school but also your teaching academy, I wanted to run an idea by you." He slowed his strokes to give him more time to talk. "In the past, I was trying to convince Andy to market the school to get more kids in attendance since he thought more recognition was instrumental before starting a research institute. But maybe we should do both at the same time. Kill two birds with one stone. Since we'll have to market the research institute before it can take off, all of our efforts can go toward both goals—getting more students because of the great school it is already and also because it's going to have this incredible research component." He watched Sophie as she kept paddling, long, smooth strokes that matched his, waiting for her reaction. "What do you think?" He held his breath.

"Why do I think you're not telling me the whole story? Why doesn't Andy want to dive headfirst into this research institute?"

"He believes we'd have more interest from grant makers and other funders if the school is better known. That's why I suggested he market the school more. His response has usually been that it will cost too much money and manpower. But I'm working on a marketing plan, as you suggested, that won't cost a lot."

"Are you trying to get me to sign on to your plan as acting director, hoping to bypass Andy's approval?" Thankfully, her voice held no hint of sarcasm.

He chuckled, hoping to deflate his bold ask. "Well...yes. But giving me the go-ahead is just the beginning. I'm asking for the green light to work on content for the website and other social media platforms, which would include information about a future research institute."

"So you're suggesting that the website and other marketing efforts include information about an environmental research institute in the future, without any specifics."

He couldn't tell if she liked or hated the idea. Having this conversation in a kayak with her back to him was not the best design.

"I do have specifics. I know how it will function. I've done the research."

"Is it wise to dangle a carrot in front of potential students who will never see the institute because it's only a germ of an idea?"

"If we work both prongs together—marketing and getting the institute off the ground—it will become a reality. Once we agree on the overall concept, I can present the details to you, work on the marketing aspect, and start applying for grants. I know in my gut it will work. Once we get the information out there, corporations will be clamoring to help fund research that's important to them. It would attract the best and brightest environmental scientists. Marine biology teachers would jump at the chance to spend their summer months participating in hands-on projects to take back to their classrooms. It would be amazing."

The adrenaline rush he experienced every time he talked about the research institute fizzed through his blood. To start something like this from scratch, to be instrumental at every level, and then to see his dream come to fruition—he just couldn't wait. And if he could get Sophie to buy into his dream, maybe, just maybe, it could all occur much sooner than Andy would have allowed.

"Making your proposal shine and getting grants based on that proposal is a long, hard process, which Andy knows all about." She laid her paddle across the kayak and swiveled in her seat to face him. "So do I. It's tedious. And frustrating. But so worth it in the end—if you get the funding."

He thought he saw promise lighting up her eyes. Then she faced forward again, so he was no longer able to read her expression.

Max paddled in silence for a while, optimistically hoping his idea was working its way onto her agenda.

"Why is this research institute so important to you? Not that I don't think it's a fabulous idea, but what makes you so passionate about it?"

"My brother's death."

His words stilled her paddle, and she turned toward

him again. "Oh. I didn't realize they were tied together." She looked into his eyes.

He swallowed. "He died because of ocean trash. Other divers have too. But so are the fish and other wildlife. We need to do more to save our environment. Dean loved marine biology. He loved the ocean. He was always questioning why more wasn't being done to stop pollution. We had often talked about how we'd work together after college—at Woods Hole Oceanographic Institution in Massachusetts. We were going to become famous marine biologists who would be known for our efforts to save the ocean." He laughed at their childish dreams. So big. So unattainable. But so real.

"You did work at Woods Hole, right?" Sophie started back with her paddle.

"For five years. But without my brother there to share it with, it didn't mean the same. When I heard about this place, I was on the next plane. Along with my dream to honor my brother."

"Now that I know why the institute means so much to you, it's even better. Passion is important. If it's not there, you're never going to get your project off the ground."

"Are you agreeing to my proposal?"

"No. There's a lot more to discuss. When would you have time to do all the work involved? We're only six weeks into the semester. You have your classes to teach and your field trips to guide."

The balance tipped in his favor one minute and teetered in the other direction the next. He needed to put more weight on the favor side.

"I'll share with you the proposal I've been working on. I also have a preliminary list of possible funders. My next step is to work on a budget."

"Have you asked Sue for help with that?" She looked over her shoulder with eyebrow raised and a smirk on her lips. "Of course you haven't, because you want to be in control of the entire project."

He chuckled, a welcome feeling after giving such a serious pitch. "I'll ask Sue for help."

"While you're at it, ask her for help in putting together a marketing budget to revamp the website."

Unable to hold his tongue or his enthusiasm, he plunged in further. "My plan is to photograph some of the teachers and kids doing various sporting activities and write up the content so the cost of a web designer would be less. I'd also like to add some video to the website. Maybe you'd like to participate. You could be teaching your lit class, discussing *The Great Gatsby* with your students. That would show potential students and their parents that the academic subjects taught here are just as important as the environmental courses." Sophie's connection with her students would jump right out of the video and wrangle any vacillators right in.

"Absolutely not."

Her definitive statement and icy tone chilled his blood. "I just thought that…you have such a great rapport with…the kids are so engaged with you." He stuttered like a fool.

"Stop, just stop." Her voice pierced the peacefulness of the day's end.

"What's the matter, Sophie?" He was at a loss.

She turned in her seat. Bright red slashes colored her cheeks. "I will not be in any video or on any social media platforms. I'm an English teacher. A well-respected member of the faculty at the Valen School. I will not participate through videos or otherwise in helping this school compete against Valen."

"What? There's no competition between Sunrise Island School and Valen." Had he heard her correctly?

"Never mind. It doesn't matter. The answer is no." Her words were clipped, bitter.

And in that instant, he knew he'd lost her.

Chapter Ten

Sophie couldn't get off the boat fast enough. She threw her paddle on the dock, grabbed her towel, and started across the beach in a near run. Her cheeks burned, and her blood boiled, the replay of Max's words adding fuel to the fire.

After their encounter the other night on the beach, her path hadn't crossed Max's until today when he asked her to go kayaking with his students. She had been thrilled with the invitation. Not only did it confirm that their relationship was on steadier ground, but it also gave her hope that he was more confident in her outdoor abilities.

But now she saw the truth. The butterflies. The tingly feelings she experienced when her eyes met his. She'd been naïve. He was just trying to get on her good side so he would have an ally.

He didn't care about her. He didn't feel what she felt every time his arm brushed hers.

To add insult to injury, he was trying to rope her in by having her participate in a video with her students. That was the bucket of cold water that had opened her eyes. The reason for her suspension flashed before her like a neon warning sign.

She was transported back to Headmaster Ryan's office where he'd blindsided her with a video posted on social media of her purportedly offering to coach teens from another school to compete against Valen's debate team. His words crashed into her brain.

"The evidence is right here." He tapped the face of his cell phone. "Perception is everything these days. When I have dozens of parents calling to complain about a teacher aiding the competition, I have to step in and take control of the situation."

At the time, his accusation had circled her head but refused to sink in. She explained in detail that she had been doing something good for students who couldn't afford private school—those in similar circumstances to herself back in the day. She volunteered once a week at her alma mater to help struggling kids with their writing and oral skills. Occasionally, she had them debate each other because it made the whole learning process more fun. They loved it, and it helped them with their confidence. But she never said she would coach them to compete against Valen or any other school. Her encouraging words must have been edited to frame her.

His response—"You're suspended until further notice."

As if she hadn't understood his very plain English, she argued that she couldn't be suspended. She'd been nominated to become chair of the English department.

At least Ryan didn't laugh in her face at her refusal to acknowledge her horrific predicament. But his next statement was even worse. He planned to pull her nomination and nominate Gregg Nelson in her stead. Gregg Nelson, the arrogant, self-absorbed English lit teacher who didn't have a compassionate bone in his body, was going to slide into her position—the very position she had worked so hard to achieve.

Of course, Max didn't know any of this. But he

didn't need to. She would never purposefully put herself in that position again. Even though Sunrise Island School wasn't competing against Valen, one never knew who their enemies were. She would from now on always be more aware, more vigilant of what could possibly be posted online and do whatever she could to prevent such a thing from happening again.

Although her guard had lowered from her initial run-ins with Max, she didn't know him. Would he edit his proposed video in some nefarious way to get her fired from this school so he could be in charge?

Her feet pounded the sand as she distanced herself from the man she had begun to have feelings for. A big mistake. She gulped in oxygen as her heart pumped in her chest, threatening to explode.

She counted to ten in an effort to calm herself.

She had almost given in to his charms. He had been so nice to her the other night and today. A complete reversal from his treatment when she'd first arrived. Or when he'd learned she was to take Andy's place as director.

Because of his change in attitude, she had doused her reactive hostility and encouraged him to find allies, to come up with a concrete plan to pursue his dream. She shouldn't have gotten involved. And she certainly shouldn't have given him a blueprint to follow. What was she thinking? This was Andy's school, not hers. She'd be leaving in a few months and wouldn't be here long enough to help Max or Andy see this plan through.

Heat rushed to her face, and her skin was on fire. The fire of embarrassment.

Her feet moved, but her pace had slowed to that of a snail. A heavy heart weighed down every other organ, every limb. She pushed herself to get to her cabin before anyone could see her total humiliation.

Before Max could see it.

\*\*\*\*

"I'm sorry to have to tell you this, Sophie," Headmaster Ryan began, his voice tinged with just the right amount of sympathy to send her anxiety into orbit, "but the board has voted to terminate your contract."

He didn't even look at her as he said it. As he ended her career at Valen.

Her blood pulsed through her veins as if readying for a fight. She opened her mouth to plead her case, but the headmaster held up his hand, motioning for her to keep quiet. Hot tears streamed down her face, and her throat tightened and burned.

She gasped for breath as her eyes flew open and she sprang up in bed. Her heart raced out of control, and she placed her hand over her chest to quiet its thundering rumble.

The nightmare had returned.

Just when she'd thought she had gotten control of her emotions and could now think straight, the haunting issues raised by the video had, again, insinuated themselves into her dreams.

All because of Max's absurd proposal.

If he hadn't asked her to be filmed, her fears would have stayed in the compartment she had locked them in. But it seemed that every time something reminded her of what had happened at Valen, they escaped.

She had to get past this trauma and obliterate it from her life. She needed closure, but the investigation was moving at a snail's pace. Could she actually lose her job over this fiasco?

Unfortunately, ruin came in all shapes and sizes, from an outside physical force over which one had no control, like a scuba-diving accident, or from events someone else set in motion, like an edited video. Sophie sighed. Yet both could cause unalterable changes in one's existence, all in the blink of an eye.

Exhausted from her disturbed night's sleep, Sophie dragged herself from bed at seven and stumbled into the shower. She needed a clear head before taking over her administrative duties today. She had to keep her emotions in check, not like yesterday when she had stormed off the kayak in a haze of fury.

Max had looked so bewildered—stunned actually—at her reaction to his suggestion. He hadn't realized that more was at play than his mere request that she participate in a video. Her suspension, her feelings for him, her dashed hope that he had feelings for her—they were all tied up in her crazed reaction. And while his ideas were valid, she hadn't been able to separate her issues. Self-control had been startlingly missing. Not a great quality to lack when in the position of temporary director.

Respect came from acting in a calm, persuasive manner, not unreasonable anger.

She stood under the stream of hot water pelting her neck and shoulders as she inhaled the tropical, floral scent of her shampoo. Then she exhaled, hoping to blow away her mortification.

Finally turning off the water, she toweled herself dry and formed a new resolve to deal with Max more effectively. She'd bury her unwanted attraction to him and interact with him as she would any other staff member requesting the green light for a project—with impartiality and common sense.

After dressing quickly, she headed toward Eden Hall. Sue would be there and have the perspective she needed.

Sophie put on her happy face and mentally injected herself with an upbeat attitude—quite a stretch from the way she was feeling.

"Good morning," she sang upon entering the office. "How are things going?"

Sue looked up from her computer and smiled. "Hi, Sophie. I didn't see you last night at dinner or this morning at breakfast. Are you okay?"

"Sure. Fine." She plopped into a chair in front of Sue's desk. "I went kayaking with Max and his class yesterday. He might be seeking your help to put together two budgets. One for a marketing plan that would include a website redesign, and one for his proposed institute. I told him you might be able to help him. But if you're too busy with everything else, you can put it off."

"He already called to schedule an appointment." Sue handed Sophie a few phone messages. "He's very…determined."

"I'm sorry. I shouldn't have even suggested he speak to you. I'll talk to him later and tell him myself that you don't have time."

"I don't know if you know this, but Andy's not big on spending money on marketing. He thinks the school will gain a bigger reputation through word of mouth. That it's better to grow slowly so he can handle greater numbers of students over time."

"I've heard. I was having a weak moment when Max made his pitch to me. With Andy out of the picture for a while, he had a new ear to bend." And if he hadn't blown it with his suggestion that she be in one of the videos, it might have worked.

Disappointment washed over her. In herself for falling for his passion project, and in Max for charming her into supporting it.

Sue got up and walked over to the coffee machine. Petite and sculpted, she exuded energy and athleticism. She would have been a better choice for Max's video. Even though she wasn't a teacher here, she participated in the water sports and camping activities. Her bouncy, short blonde hair and perky attitude would have leapt off the video and hit its mark.

"Would you like a cup?" Sue held up the carafe.

"I'd love some." Sophie's stomach grumbled at her refusal to feed it. But that grumble was nothing compared to the noise in her head. Charming Max. How dare he try to manipulate her like that.

Sue handed her a mug of coffee and sat at her desk with hers. "What's wrong? You seem preoccupied."

"I am." Sophie hesitated, then admitted that Max had almost won her over with his plan.

Sue shrugged. "That's Max for you. He's so focused on getting his institute off the ground that he'll try anything. He's been relentless with Andy, so it doesn't surprise me that he'd do the same with you."

Sue's nonchalance made Sophie sit back and consider. "Do you think Max thinks I'm an easier target than Andy?"

Sue laughed. "Anyone would be an easier target than Andy. No matter who was in the position of acting director, Max would have used his best efforts at persuasion. Getting a lukewarm response from Andy has done nothing to slow his enthusiasm. He just keeps at it.

I say good for him."

Sophie considered Sue's assessment as she sipped her coffee. "Max thought it would be a great idea if I appeared in a video on the website interacting with my students. I blew a gasket. My reaction was totally out of character." She didn't confess to the reason for her meltdown, though. "But it made me stop and take pause. That's when I realized I was being played." The annoyance in her voice was a mere trace of the anger that had rolled through her last night.

"That conclusion is too sinister." Sue's statement advised Sophie that she might be off base. "Max wants his institute. Period. He doesn't care what he has to do or how he has to go about getting it. He's not hiding anything. He was upfront with you. Even asking you to participate. But I guess you told him no."

"You might say that." Embarrassment at her outburst reared its ugly head for the tenth time this morning.

Sue made Max's pitch to her sound so matter-of-fact. An opinion Sophie might have concurred with if she hadn't been so sensitive about the video. But given her irate state after his suggestion, she'd absurdly thought he might use his proposed video to get her fired. By this morning, with a clearer head and saner thinking, she didn't believe he'd do any such thing. He loved this school and only wanted to see it succeed—along with his institute.

If she looked at this reasonably, she'd see that Max was merely trying to convince her of the merits of his idea. Especially since she'd told him to find allies. He was just following her advice. And in doing so, he was so persuasive she could see herself potentially aligning with him. Although she hadn't given him the go-ahead he sought, she did suggest certain actions that needed to be taken before the project could gain legs.

What was wrong with her? She'd made mountains out of molehills and simple requests into manipulative plans. All because those requests came from Max, the man who pushed all her buttons. And who heated her blood.

Now she had to face him—act normally—and somehow explain her irrational behavior.

This day could only get worse.

Chapter Eleven

Sophie avoided the dining pavilion—and Max—asking Sue to bring her a sandwich back for lunch while she worked at her desk. To busy her mind, she dealt with the budget and other daily problems that presented themselves. But by five o'clock, her stomach was again grumbling, and she couldn't avoid seeing Max forever. The time had come.

"Where've you been, Sophie?" Dan nudged her before she sat down at the staff table with a salad.

"I had administrative duties to take care of today. Sue helped me get them straightened out." She pushed the lettuce around with her fork, her stomach tied in knots at the prospect of facing Max.

She breathed easily for a moment. Max's chair was empty.

"I missed you this morning," added Kristin. "Why didn't you tell me you couldn't meet? I would have slept in."

Sophie's hand shot up to cover her mouth. "Oh no. I'm so sorry, Kristin. I completely forgot. I was preoccupied this morning and..." And what? She couldn't admit that her total misreading of a situation with Max had her in such a tizzy she'd forgotten to meet her at the dock as she had every morning since the day after she started.

"No problem. Just let me know next time." Kristin

smiled, letting her off the hook for her lack of consideration.

Conversation swirled around the table, no different than any other night. Although, tonight Sophie failed to participate unless spoken to directly.

Then the air changed. An almost imperceptible crackle, a warmth cocooning her from the outside, then penetrating her skin and moving inward. She didn't have to look up. She knew Max had arrived.

He sat down across from her. She tried to avoid looking at him, but her eyes betrayed her, and she found herself studying his face. His strong jaw with day-old stubble moved methodically as he ate. His lashes, thick and dark, cast shadows on his cheekbones.

She repositioned her gaze to his hands—long, lean fingers, turned bronze by the sun, were sprinkled ever so lightly with golden hair. She swallowed as she recalled the electric shock they'd sparked within when they entwined with hers. But after her performance yesterday, it seemed clear that would never happen again. Not from his perspective, and certainly not from hers.

The cool chill of disappointment washed through her.

Max appeared to be in a melancholy mood, not so odd for the sulky, complex loner she knew him to be. Or could it have something to do with her bizarre reaction to his idea?

Maybe he was just avoiding conversation with her because he thought her to be insane. Once Sue had put things in perspective, she wasn't so sure she disagreed.

She had to get out of here. She wasn't contributing a thing to the conversation around her, and the more she stared at Max, the more uncomfortable she became. She wiped her mouth with her napkin and started to rise.

Then his eyes locked on hers.

Gravity pushed her back into her seat. Her heart leapt in her chest, threatening to cut off all oxygen. He made an ever-so-slight gesture with his head toward the beach.

What could he possibly want to talk to her about? Yesterday afternoon, at least the end of it, had been a nightmare. And now that she knew he wasn't interested in her romantically, the thought of being alone with him had no appeal.

Max pushed his chair back, took his plate to the kitchen, and with steady purpose, crossed the room and headed toward the water.

Her fingers grasped the table before her, rooting her to her place, giving her time to watch, to think, to decide. Her gaze followed him.

Slowly, she stood, her legs like rubber beneath her. She excused herself from the rest of the group, urging herself to turn right and head for her cabin.

But within seconds, she too was heading for the beach.

\*\*\*\*

Max focused on the orange sun hanging low in the sky, the wispy clouds just above turning pink and red. Within minutes the huge fireball would disappear into the Gulf of Mexico and the sky's colors would turn to purple and gray.

The golden hour. He loved dusk even more than dawn and made a point of coming out to the beach every night to celebrate the end of the day. Usually alone with his thoughts, surrounded by nature, he relished the contented peacefulness that would wash over him, making him one with the universe.

But tonight, Sophie's aberrant behavior weighed heavily on his soul. Why would his suggestion that she participate in a school video turn her inside out? Yet as soon as his suggestion had spilled from his mouth, he'd known he'd made a mistake. She'd looked so tortured. It had become evident it was worse than he'd initially thought when she jumped out of the kayak and practically sprinted to get away from him.

And now he'd let a full twenty-four hours elapse without saying anything to her.

Had he allowed the excitement over his project get in the way of his judgment? Of course she wouldn't want to be one of the images of Sunrise Island School when her loyalties and attachments were to Valen.

He moved behind the trunk of a palm tree so they wouldn't be observed from the dining pavilion. They didn't need an audience.

She walked toward him on the beach. Her long strides, usually made with purpose, were slow tonight. She bit her lip, looking tentative, vulnerable. The usual blaze in her eyes was disappointingly missing.

He switched his stare to the water ebbing and flowing on the shoreline.

"You wanted to see me?" Her voice was husky.

"I...I just wanted to apologize... For yesterday." The words stuck in his throat, but he pushed them out. "I wasn't thinking. Sometimes a problem of mine." He chuckled without humor to cover his embarrassment.

He glanced over at her. She didn't look at him, just gazed out toward the horizon.

"You're going back to Valen," he continued. "I guess you wouldn't want to be seen as a representative of this school."

She shook her head, then sank to her knees—her face holding a mixture of emotions: sadness, pain, anger, disgust? But even if he couldn't identify the correct one, none of them were good.

After too many seconds of silence, he ventured, "What's going on, Sophie? I don't understand." He sat down beside her.

"I know." She sighed. "I'm sorry I overreacted yesterday. You hit a nerve. I should have just told you *no*. That I didn't want to be in a video. That you should find someone else. It was very unprofessional of me."

"Unprofessional? What are you talking about?" Why was she turning this into an administrative discussion? "I thought we were becoming friends. I thought I could bounce ideas off you and see what you thought."

"A few things were going on in my head. One had to do with being in the video itself. But the other had to do with your intentions. Were you manipulating me, as acting director, into giving you the go-ahead for your project?"

The arrow had been shot, and he felt it pierce his skin. His plan had been to convince her to buy into his idea. But there was no scheming. And certainly no manipulation intended.

She folded her legs underneath her and kept her eyes downcast.

"No, absolutely not. I wasn't using our friendship to get what I wanted. I was trying to convince you it was a good idea. Just like I do with Andy."

She didn't respond. Her eyes shimmered, but it could have been the sinking sun reflecting off the water that gave them that glow.

"Say something. Please. You're worrying me."

She picked up a shell and idly pushed sand around with it, making lazy circles in front of her. He knew better than to speak. She'd talk when she was ready.

And she did.

"While your suggestion may have seemed harmless, it opened up a very recent wound." She paused. "One that obviously hasn't healed."

She told him about her passion to help teens at her alma mater who were struggling with their academics. How she was paying it forward, in part, as a tribute to the teacher who had helped her over a rough patch, and in part to give them hope that they could succeed just as she had. At times, she smiled when talking about the students she helped, and at others, she swiped at a tear or two that escaped onto her cheek. Sometimes her voice was matter-of-fact, and sometimes it shook, in anger.

But she finally got out the whole sad, infuriating story about the edited video, about her suspension, and about her frustration.

He wanted to hug her, envelop her in a blanket of support—to show he cared. But he couldn't. He didn't want to care. And he was sure she didn't want him to, either.

So he dwelt on the details. "How could something like this happen in the halls of such a well-respected institution like Valen? Do you have any enemies there?"

"No. Not that I know of." She sighed. "But I must. Why would anyone take a video of me talking to some students at my alma mater, edit it to make me look disloyal, and post it?"

"Somebody wanted you fired."

Sophie had the intelligence and the drive to make it all the way to the top, and clearly, someone intended to stop her. While it infuriated him that any human being would have done something like that to her, it wasn't implausible in this day and age of scams, fake news, and edited photos.

"I guess. The board is investigating."

"Who do you think it was?" She had to have some idea.

She took a while to respond. "I can't be sure, but I have my suspicions." Her voice was flat, unemotional. "It could have been a colleague of mine who wanted to become chair of the English department." Her brow furrowed. "I just can't imagine him going to those lengths to get the position."

"Did you share your suspicion with the board?" He could feel the anger on her behalf well up inside.

"No. What if I'm wrong? I can't ruin his reputation without proof. And I have none. I need the board to come up with the culprit on their own."

He exhaled. He'd finally learned why she was here. His never-ending quest to find the answer had come to an end. Disappointment in himself welled up and threatened to choke him. Even though she'd outright denied his theory that Andy had hired her to bring her Summer Teaching Academy down here, he'd never fully let it go. Always watching, always worrying whether Sophie had a leg up on him. Now, come to find out, she'd been betrayed beyond belief, and she just needed a safe haven while the investigation ensued.

She glanced at him, her crystal-blue eyes holding a multitude of emotions. "I should have been more aware of my surroundings. I never saw anyone videotaping me or my class."

His stomach clenched, and he felt her pain even more acutely than before. Without further thought, he wound his arm around her shoulders and pulled her into him. A totally involuntary move that sent sparks through his blood as she came into contact with him. He closed his eyes and breathed her in. The floral scent of her hair blended with the salty mist covering her skin, creating her own unique fragrance.

"I'm sorry this happened to you."

"Me too." Her attempt at a smile didn't quite make it to her lips. Then she pulled away, and the momentary warmth disappeared. "Up until last month, I had my life planned out. Then, by a twist of fate, I've been derailed, and I'm powerless to get back on track." Sadness clouded her eyes, and her shoulders sank.

She stood up, so he stood too, as their fragile closeness slipped away. She drew in the sand with her foot, moving a little farther away from him. "I know I sound like a pathetic soul. And maybe I am. But just when I think I'm getting it together, a request to participate in a video spins me out of control. Sometimes I think I'm losing my sanity. A very dangerous thing to lose."

She had turned away from him, her body stiff, her eyes fixed on the circle she'd drawn. He couldn't help himself. He reached out and took hold of her hand, pulling her closer, turning her around to face him.

"You need to be proactive in this investigation. You can't rely on others."

That was his mantra. Why he pushed so hard to make things happen—like the research institute. If he didn't do it, no one else would. Sometimes one just had oneself to rely on. A very hard lesson to learn. If he had been there with his brother scuba diving, Dean wouldn't have died. He would have made sure of it.

Sophie broke into his thoughts. "I don't know if pointing a finger is the right thing to do." Her reluctance resounded in her words. As well as her vulnerability. She needed to get herself back on stronger footing.

Guilt washed through his being. He'd set her adrift with his video suggestion. Now, if he could only help her find her center again.

"First of all, stop blaming yourself. You were engaged with your students. Teaching them. If someone was secretly videoing you, he or she wouldn't want to get caught. They'd be hiding somewhere. And if that person was out to get you, they would have found a way to do it. If not through the edited video, then with some ugly rumor. You can't let this person ruin your career."

A spark flashed in her eyes. A good sign.

"You're right. For the past seven years, I've been working nonstop to get where I am and continue my rise. I can't let some evil actor interfere with my career that easily." Although she'd said it with conviction, caution showed in her eyes. "I just don't feel right about naming names. It might sound like I'm on a witch hunt."

"You'll figure out the best way to present it."

Her blue eyes searched his, as if looking for strength, and his heart stopped beating for those few moments.

"I feel like I'm down here hiding," she confessed. "Being suspended was so embarrassing, even though it was couched as a sabbatical. Since the headmaster didn't want to bring in the authorities to report the crime, I had little faith that it would be solved quickly. So I called

Andy to see if I could visit for a week or two. A vacation of sorts to get my mind off my troubles. When he offered me the job because Sara was out for the semester, I jumped at the chance. It was the perfect solution to keep me out of town."

The pain etched on her face made him want to caress her cheeks with his hands and crush his lips to hers. But fevered kisses weren't what she needed right now. She needed motivation.

"You should stop hiding and face the problem head-on. Someone betrayed you. Someone maliciously interfered with your career." He put his hands on her upper arms, as if to give her strength, but the mere feel of her satin skin sent tremors to the pit of his stomach. He swallowed. "Fight back, Sophie. Don't let your embarrassment keep you from putting on the pressure. Have you spoken to the headmaster to find out where the investigation stands?"

"No." She bowed her head.

"You can't let this criminal get away with it."

His words hung between them on the still air, and he knew he had at the very least lit a match within her. He watched her struggle for a response.

When she said nothing, he jumped in with both feet.

"Let go of your wounded pride. If you sweep this travesty under the rug, you're letting someone else win." He paused, allowing his plea to sink in. "Get angry."

Shadows played over her face as the sun dipped into the ocean, casting its last light. She moved from anguish to resentment. And finally, defiance. He could see it in the glow of her eyes, in the set of her jaw.

Eventually, she found her voice. "You're right. What that person did was criminal. If it's who I think it is, I can't let the kids at Valen or the board think he's a pillar of the community. I can't let him benefit from ill-gotten respect and recognition. He's probably already been voted in as chair of the English department while I'm gone." She straightened her spine. Then her voice gained strength, and the wheels of anger finally gained some speed. "How dare he do this to me. To the students. The school has to be made aware that he's the number one suspect."

"That's more like it. There's the spirit you so often show me." He grinned at his tease, then continued. "It's hard to hide something. Worse yet to run away."

What a hypocrite. Here he stood, telling Sophie that it was good to get everything out in the open. Not to run away. Yet that's exactly what he had been doing.

"What's going on in that head of yours?" Sophie asked, her brow creased. "You morphed from being my cheerleader to being benched."

"I've also been sweeping something under the rug."

Now that the words were out there, he would have to follow through. Sophie's gaze zeroed in on his eyes, waiting for his revelation. She reached up and laid her hand on his arm—a gesture of comfort, maybe even friendship.

"I told you the reason I wasn't with my brother the day he died was because I had a commitment. I made it sound like it was a job interview or an important doctor's appointment. It wasn't. I didn't go with Dean that day because I had a date with a woman I'd been trying to go out with for months. While that excuse probably doesn't make any difference now, ten years later, it is something I'll regret to the day I die. Because I put a college crush before my brother." The weight of his confession pulled at his shoulders. "I vowed to his spirit and to myself that I would never do that again. And throughout all these years, I haven't. Any relationship that started getting too serious, I sabotaged." A frustrated sound emanated from his throat. "You've probably heard about my reputation around here. I'm apparently some sort of serial dater who's just in it for the chase. Then when I've made the catch, I'm no longer interested. But that's not true. I just can't commit to anyone."

His voice sounded thick, foreign. As if the words were coming from someone else. They swarmed around him, exposing him. He hadn't told anyone here about the guilt he carried or how it affected his relationships—or lack thereof.

Afraid to look at her, afraid to see pity for a man who couldn't move on from a devastating event, he stared out at the water instead.

"That's a big sacrifice to make," she said softly. Her words curled around him.

He glanced at her, and her face held no pity, just true sorrow for his plight.

She continued. "I'm guessing you feel that you should atone for your perceived sin. By denying yourself an intimate relationship. Perhaps you punished yourself enough. Ten years is a long time to be a loner."

"It is."

He'd recently started thinking that he wanted a good, solid relationship with someone who understood him and cared about him despite his flaws. If he were being honest with himself, he would love to start something with Sophie. But he knew how it would end. Hurt, anger, disappointment. The way most of his relationships ended. He couldn't risk it—not with her.

She was too good of a person. Besides, even if he wanted to change, wanted to go back on his promise to Dean, he'd have to rid himself of the guilt first. And he didn't see that happening anytime soon.

He sat on the beach and picked up a handful of sand, watching it flow between his fingers.

Sophie sat beside him. "Maybe you can substitute one promise for another. Instead of punishing yourself, you could put all of your effort into your research institute. You already said you wanted to create it to honor your brother. What an honor that would be."

He closed his eyes and inhaled the positive aura she spun around him.

Sophie reached for his hand, and her comforting touch began to warm his damaged heart.

"You told me a few minutes ago that I should face my demons head-on. That I shouldn't let embarrassment cloud my thinking. That I have to confront the situation." She paused, softening her voice. "I think maybe you should listen to your own advice. Not forming any type of relationship with a woman isn't a positive step. It's a penance you laid upon yourself. But establishing a research institute to protect the marine environment is a constructive undertaking that will yield benefits for years to come."

He swallowed and nodded. "True."

"You came here to escape. Just like I did. But we both know that our pasts follow us wherever we go. Look at us." She chuckled. "Two poor souls sitting on the beach on Sunrise Island commiserating about our bad luck. We should be thanking our lucky stars we've found such an incredible place to land while we figure out our lives and move forward."

Her words began to lift his spirits. And the fact that he'd finally admitted to another person what made him who he was today lessened his grip on his guilt.

It was a good start.

He turned to Sophie, her cerulean-blue eyes clear and open to him. A nice change from flashing in anger or challenging his every move. He turned his palm over and held her hand, squeezing it in thanks. At least that was his intent. But that one little move sent sparks shooting through him. He wanted to hide his reaction from her. But he couldn't tear his gaze away. She drew him in and locked him there, without so much as a movement in his direction.

He inched toward her, toward those soft, full lips.

She leaned closer, her mouth lifted to his, so inviting, so sexy.

Perhaps a spontaneous gesture on her part—one she might regret at some time in the future. But he wasn't going to give her a chance to back away. Not this time.

He closed the distance and brushed his mouth over hers, that mere touch shooting flames through his being. Her lips parted, and he ran his tongue over her sultry mouth, tasting, wanting more, taking more. He gave in to the passion she ignited, mating his tongue with hers. His heart beat wildly against his ribs as he crushed her to him, threading his fingers through her thick, shiny tresses, holding her close as he devoured her mouth.

Her body melted against his as her arms encircled his neck. Did she too feel the rapture of a passion so strong that it couldn't be contained—one that had been building just below the surface for the past few weeks, desperate to explode?

His hands roamed over her body, the feel of her

curves and angles feeding his craving for her. He breathed her in like his life depended on her sweet scent. He was addicted. Floating. And on fire.

And his need to feel this connection, this electricity, this passion, took over all reason.

Chapter Twelve

The noon-hour clatter and buzz in the dining pavilion barely entered Sophie's consciousness. She bit her lip as she stood by the buffet table, ignoring the choice of food, while daydreaming about the night before—recalling the magic Max had sprinkled over her. The image wreaked havoc in the pit of her stomach, as butterflies flew and collided, spinning dizzily—making her dizzy.

A swirl of emotion tore through her as she replayed her and Max's erotic interlude on the beach last night. One minute they were talking, and the next they were kissing. He'd moved his mouth over hers, hungrily capturing her lips, her tongue, spreading fingers of fire while awakening a libido that had been hibernating for far too long.

His strong hands had caressed her shoulders, her arms, as he held her close while assaulting her mouth with an uncontained passion. She was breathless while falling into the abyss that was Max. When he brushed his hands over her breasts, her nipples strained against her thin top, aching for more contact. She moaned with desire—her tacit invitation to touch her again, to drive her crazy with want.

Her skin tingled as her shirt slipped away and Max's mouth covered the tip of her breast, sucking until it was taut and hard, nipping at her with his teeth, then teasing her with his tongue.

Before long, the two of them were lying in the sand, naked from the waist up, stroking and kissing and straining against each other like teenagers in lust. And while they were far from teenagers, the lust part definitely applied.

Sophie spread her fingers over his hard chest, feeling the ripple of muscles beneath them as the water of the Gulf lapped quietly against the beach and the crescent moon rose slowly upward in the night sky. But the beauty of their surroundings was lost to her, who only wanted to feel the heat, the passion, the shivers that Max inspired.

Somewhere in the back of her mind, her conscience had whispered, "This is not a good idea." But whether it was or wasn't, there was no way she could listen.

Not then.

Not when she was floating in paradise.

"Hi, Sophie. What's taking you so long?"

Ben's voice cut into her reverie, and she tried to wipe the dreamy look off her face.

"I can't decide what I want." Although she knew perfectly well what she wanted. And it wasn't on the buffet table. She mentally pinched herself and told herself to snap out of it.

"Yeah, it's the same thing every day. Sometimes, I have a hard time too. But there's no use staring at it. It won't change." He chuckled and moved around her to grab a sandwich. "You better get to the table fast before you get signed up for some activity. Our esteemed program director is on a rampage. Have your excuses ready."

"Oh, great." She laughed.

Ever since her indoctrination into fishing a few weeks earlier, Dan had given her some time to get her bearings. And although she had a full workload as acting director and lit teacher, she'd specifically asked to be put back in the rotation for the various activities with the students. Her hiatus was at an end.

"Try to protect me until I get there." Sophie quickly picked up a bowl and filled it with macaroni and cheese—maybe not an island staple, but comfort food and a teen requirement.

As she sat down, she stole a glance at Max. He was engaged in lighthearted bantering with Maddie and Dan, but his laughter reached her ears, and his sparkle reached into her heart.

Momentarily, he looked over at her, but he barely acknowledged her presence. Was he just being careful so no one would suspect anything between them, or was he actually ignoring her?

Maddie was in overdrive flirting mode. Her hand caressed Max's arm as she coyly whispered something in his ear, eliciting his not-often-seen brilliant smile. Jealously tightened her stomach. She tried to relax. This was ridiculous. She had no hold over him.

"Hey, Max," Dan called, his yellow pad in hand, "you're onboard to go fishing today. Do I have any other volunteers to help out?"

Sophie spun through her schedule as her blood rushed through her veins. She could go with Max. Even though fishing wasn't high on her list, spending the next few hours with him on the open sea was. And this time, they could just hang out and have fun, without the tension and stress of their last outing when the gloves were off and the anxiety at a premium. The mere thought of having Max to herself for the next several hours jumpstarted her heart, as if it needed reignition.

"I have a class this afternoon," broke in Kristin.

"I have classes this afternoon too," Ben added.

Sophie opened her mouth to respond.

"I'll go with Max." Maddie used her silky, sensual voice. "It will be fun." She practically purred at him as she glanced at Sophie, then took possession of his arm again.

Another bolt of jealousy struck. She closed her mouth as disappointment washed over her. If she volunteered now, she would have to spend the day watching Maddie fawn over Max. It would be unbearable. And yet, if she wasn't there… What if Max's new outlook on life opened his eyes to what he could have with Maddie? No, she couldn't bring herself to play watchdog.

Max stood, and Sophie watched the scene play out.

"You better be careful, Max." Dan tried without success to temper a smile. "It looks like Maddie intends to reel in more than some fish."

"Lucky dog." Ben slapped Max on the back.

Maddie did nothing to dispel the undertone of their conversation. "Don't worry, boys. I'll take good care of your friend here."

She snaked her arm around Max's waist and led him away from the table. Max looked back over his shoulder and shrugged for his audience's benefit, but he didn't look unhappy.

And there it was. The blow to her heart.

Did last night mean nothing? She'd thought their bond had become stronger than ever. That he was going to try to change his attitude from entering into meaningless relationships to putting his heart into the next one. Surely, he couldn't have his sights set on Maddie. Talk about different species.

She stared at their backs as they headed toward the dock, Maddie's long blonde hair swinging with her movements, her even tan set off by white shorts and a tank top, her toned body lean and perfect. They were obviously kidding with each other, because every once in a while, one of them would push the other playfully.

Her stomach sank.

"Didn't eat much of your mac and cheese," Kristin commented as Sophie pushed her plate away. The others slowly made their way toward the kitchen with their trays.

"I'm not hungry." She sounded like a forlorn soul but couldn't muster up much enthusiasm.

"He's not interested in Maddie, you know."

Sophie swung her head around. "What?"

"Maddie teases all the guys. It's part of her personality. And they all play it up. It's fun. I can assure you they're just friends."

"It doesn't matter to me, one way or the other." Sophie tried for nonchalance.

"Good try, Sophie, but I don't believe you. Your eyes—and that turned-down mouth—gave you away."

Sophie flashed a quick look at Kristin, then twisted her head toward the kitchen in an effort to shield herself from further study. But Kristin's gaze bored into her.

"I thought we…" *We what?* Made a connection? Fell in like? "Oh…I don't know."

She shook her head. An enchanting interlude on the beach couldn't adequately be explained in words. But it was much more than that. Their emotional discussion had peeled away thick layers of protection, leaving them both bare and vulnerable. For weeks, they had taunted and challenged each other. But Sunday night and continuing into last night, they had removed their armor and shared huge pieces of themselves. It had been much more than a physical connection.

The bliss of their new friendship had her humming all morning. At least until Max had practically ignored her at lunch and flirted unmercifully with Maddie right in front of her. She swallowed and balled her fist in her lap. Maybe Max didn't see anything special in what they had shared last night. That was the real problem.

Sophie continued. "I thought we had called a truce. That we were friends. We've had several talks and made a real breakthrough. But he didn't even acknowledge me today." She sounded like a high-schooler. "His flirting with Maddie was like a bucket of cold water being dumped over my head. As if he were showing me that our discussion last night meant nothing."

"Max has always had a hard time opening up. The fact that he did with you has probably spooked him. Maybe he's embarrassed about the things he said."

Sophie grimaced. "Maybe."

"Hey, you two." Dan came toward them with his ever-present clipboard. "Since you don't seem to be otherwise occupied, the kayaks need to be cleaned. Why don't you grab a few students and get to work?"

Kristin rolled her eyes, then grabbed her baseball cap. "I knew we should've escaped while the going was good. I have a class later this afternoon, but we can get the boats done by then. Come on, Sophie. If we do it ourselves, we can continue our little talk."

Sophie didn't mind the distraction. An hour of

sunshine and some physical activity might just be the prescription she needed to drag her out of her funk. And it would help to get Kristin's perspective on things.

"What's really going on between you and Max?"

The pointed question caught Sophie off guard. "What are you talking about?" While she still played it close to the vest, she knew it was only a matter of seconds before she'd spill her guts.

"Come on now. All this angst over Maddie and Max can't be about the two of you getting along better. I definitely see something more than a friendship blooming."

"Maybe you see tension." She flashed Kristin a quick smile as she shrugged her shoulders. "Any peace talks between us could be shattered in a second if Max perceives that I'm not pulling my weight around here."

"Sexual tension is what I see." Kristin smirked, and Sophie couldn't help but laugh.

Then she sobered. "I don't understand him. Just when I think we've made some strides in the right direction and we're becoming friends..." She let her sentence die out.

Kristin furrowed her brow. "Friends? Is that a euphemism?"

Her comedic sarcasm made Sophie laugh. "Okay. Maybe we're heading into the more-than-friends territory. Maybe not." She sighed. "He's impossible to read."

Kristin nodded. "Max. What can I say about Max? He's gorgeous, smart, sulky, complex. He doesn't trust people in general. I haven't figured out his problem with women." She paused. "I feel sorry for him. He seems lonely, and he doesn't have to be." They headed toward the boat hut where eight kayaks were cradled in a rack. "We're a great group here. And we do a lot of things together. Of course there's no one else to hang out with." She chuckled. "But Max stays to himself for the most part. Although he and Ben are good friends." She pushed her hair behind her ear and squinted at the sun's reflection off the water. "He volunteers a lot to do things with the kids. It's like he's afraid of getting close to any of the adults here."

Sophie considered this new information about Max while Kristin sprayed water in two buckets.

"And just for the record, Max isn't Maddie's type either."

Sophie's head snapped up.

Kristin continued. "They couldn't be a less likely couple. Max is a listener, an observer—he sees things beneath the surface. Maddie's impulsive. She sizes up a situation in seconds. She's not one to sit around and contemplate the environment. She's more likely to jump in and experience it firsthand." Kristin handed Sophie the hose and directed her to spray the boats. "Neither of them would have the patience to deal with the other." Kristin chuckled. "They're probably driving each other crazy on the boat as we speak."

"We both know that opposites attract." Sophie quoted the saying while shooting the kayaks with a steady stream of water.

"Not that opposite," Kristin argued.

"They looked awfully friendly when they went off fishing."

"That's just Maddie playing and Max going along with it. Which he doesn't often do. Something must have put him in a good mood today."

Sophie pondered this bit of data as she moved around the kayaks with her hose. Could Max have been in a good mood because of last night? If so, why didn't he share it with her?

Kristin's optimism on the subject was definitely misplaced, but she couldn't let her odd relationship with Max take up any more time. With a million things to do as acting director, she should simply forget about starting anything with him. A romantic relationship with him spelled trouble. And she had enough of that on her plate already. A heavy sigh escaped.

A flashback to the night before interrupted her resolve. Max's soulful eyes had penetrated her being as his exquisite lips brushed over her eyes, her cheeks, her neck, her mouth, flipping her inside out and upside down. Her breath caught in her throat as prickles taunted her skin at the hot, erotic memory.

*Stop being such a spineless wimp,* she told herself. *You made a decision; now stick with it. Max is off-limits.* It was time to change the subject.

"Have you seen Andy this week?" asked Sophie.

A shadow crossed Kristin's face, and a slight tremor shifted over her lower lip. "Yes. I went yesterday."

"How is he?" She had seen him a week ago, but her hectic schedule kept her from going more often.

"He's coming along. He must be getting better because he's really cranky about having to lie in bed." Kristin attempted a smile. "The doctor says he'll probably be transferred to a rehab facility in a few weeks."

For the first time since she'd met Kristin, she noticed a crack in her surface. "You really care about him, don't you?"

Kristin squinted as she looked out toward the horizon. Then she turned back and nodded. "Of course. We all care about him." Her defensive answer was just the thing to open the door for Sophie to go on.

"If I didn't know better, I'd think you have a little crush on our director." Sophie removed her sunglasses and peered at Kristin, attempting to see the truth in her eyes.

But Kristin got back to work scrubbing a boat. Yet Sophie didn't miss the grin pulling at her lips.

"Well, that confirms it." Sophie nodded in approval. "Does he feel the same way about you?"

"I think so. We're in the flirting stage." Kristin's smile widened. "At least we were before the accident. Anytime he walked into my classroom or took me aside to have a conversation, his aura zapped and crackled all around me, and I felt myself lighting up like a Christmas tree. He must have felt it too."

"My, my," Sophie crooned. "Come to think of it, I noticed something between you two the first day I arrived. He actually kidded with you. And smiled. Not an easy thing to get from Andy." How wonderful that two people she adored, cared about each other.

Kristin's smile disappeared. "Unfortunately, it's Andy's belief that he shouldn't get romantically involved with any of the staff."

"Why not? Where else is he going to meet someone?" Just like Andy to make unnecessary rules.

"He's concerned that if the romantic involvement goes south, the ugliness that could accompany a breakup will affect everyone. Including the students. And he doesn't want that sort of bitterness to ruin the atmosphere he's created here. Besides, as the director, he feels he has to distance himself from everyone else, at least to a certain degree, in order to show his authority. In certain respects, I understand his view. But emotionally, I can't stop the sparks from flying."

Kristin's happiness from just moments before converted to gloom. Even her shoulders slumped. Poor Kristin. She was so sweet. She deserved to be happy.

"Maybe you can change Andy's mind," offered Sophie. "He's here for the duration. He can't live like a monk forever. Sooner or later, he's going to have to find someone to share his life with."

"I suppose. But he thinks we should be looking outside the school for relationships. He even introduced me to a friend of his up the Keys. As if he's pushing me away."

"How long ago was that?"

"About six months ago."

"It appears that he's past that now, and since he's searching out your sparks to generate his electricity, you're in a great position to change his policy. With subtleness of course."

"Now that could be fun." Kristin's eyes took on a sly look. "I may just try that."

They both sponged the kayaks with soapy water in silence for a few minutes before Kristin turned the conversation back to Sophie.

"How's the job as director going?"

"It's overwhelming." Sophie hadn't admitted that to anyone. "But it gets a little easier as each day goes by." She paused, wondering if Kristin might be of some help. "I'd like to ask your opinion on something."

"Sure. What is it?" Curiosity tinged her voice.

Sophie picked up the hose and washed the soap from

the boats. "What do you think Andy wants me to accomplish as director?" A very broad, open question that she'd asked herself countless times in the past weeks.

"I'd say he wants you to keep things running smoothly in his absence. To keep the status quo until he returns."

"Which means he wouldn't be happy if I made decisions he might not have made. Even if there're good for the school." Her statements had questions within.

"That depends. Like what?" Kristin picked up her bucket and sponge and headed to the hut to stow them away. Sophie followed.

"Like putting some money into marketing." Sophie almost choked on the words as she said them. A short half hour ago she'd instructed herself to push Max to the sidelines, and now here she was considering his plan again. Was she out of her mind?

"I see Max has gotten to you with his idea." A tiny smile curled Kristin's lips as she sat on the bench near the hut, inviting Sophie to join her.

Sophie was quick to respond. "It sounds like a good one. This school needs to be promoted to continue on. How do people even know it's here?"

"Andy meets with the heads of different schools during the summer months when things are quieter. He thinks it's important to meet face-to-face and pass on his philosophy as well as his enthusiasm for the school. That way all questions are answered, and he's recruiting a select group of salespeople to spread the word."

"But how many people can he talk to during the summer? And what if those headmasters or principals don't spread the word?" Sophie knew enough about marketing to know that mere discussions with headmasters could often be a waste of time. "He should have a communications or development person who could go from school to school while they're in session to meet with the students directly."

This idea had been percolating in her mind ever since Max had started talking about marketing, and it was getting her creative juices flowing. It could really work if some research went into the best schools to attack first.

"That's an awfully ambitious plan for a temporary director."

Sophie had to laugh at her own enthusiasm. "I know I'm getting way ahead of myself. But Max's ideas to energize the website and reach out to as many schools as possible, coupled with Andy's word of mouth philosophy, have tapped into my marketing gene. My wheels started spinning."

"Max is very persuasive. And his proposals may be smart. But Andy hasn't bought into them yet. Andy's the kind of guy who needs time to mull things over—to weigh the pros and cons. He doesn't jump into things quickly. But once he comes to the conclusion that it's the right thing to do, he'll dedicate a hundred percent to seeing it through."

"You know Andy pretty well." Sophie acknowledged that Kristin had tapped into the mind and soul of their beloved director.

"So do you." Kristin paused. "I know how hard it must be to jump into Andy's shoes, without warning, and take over his job. With all the teachers requesting money for their special projects...trying to persuade you that the funds are better spent on their ideas. Not having enough money to go around." She tugged on the brim of her baseball cap. "Just try to keep things balanced by reminding yourself that this school is made up of equal parts—that no one area should take precedence over another. That's the way Andy set it up." She looked into Sophie's eyes. "If you remember that, you'll make the right decisions. Whatever they are."

She nodded, understanding full well what Kristin was telling her. Although marketing covered the entire school, she had one teacher pulling on her to accomplish it for his eventual goal. Even if she thought it was the right way to go, she had to follow Andy's blueprint. This was his school, his baby. She was here at his request.

Kristin glanced at her watch. "Oh. I have to get to class." She turned to Sophie, concern in her eyes. "Sorry I have to run off on you like this."

Sophie nodded. "That's okay. Thanks for your input. About the school—and Max. I really appreciate it." She could feel the warmth of Kristin's friendship settle around her. "See you tomorrow morning at seven?"

"Absolutely." With that, Kristin jogged off to her destination.

Sophie stayed on the bench, taking in the white sandy beach and the turquoise waters of the Gulf. The emotions of the past few days had drained her mentally, and she needed time to regroup. This was as good a place as any to think things through.

Max was beginning to affect every conversation, every decision, and this had to stop. She had to annihilate the feelings he stirred and disseminated to every cell in her body. She was not a teenager crushing on a boy, hoping to catch a glance or have a conversation.

Her best bet would be to forget about the connection they had made. She had a job to do here, and getting involved with the biology teacher was not part of it. If she could just put her nose to the grindstone, concentrate on her duties, and get through the next few months without destroying Andy's school, just maybe she could turn this whole sabbatical into a positive experience. Without the complication of a romance.

She was just about to head back to the office when she heard voices. She looked over toward the dock, and there were Maddie and Max, talking and laughing as they removed a bucket of fish from their boat.

Her heart jumped into her throat and beat wildly as she watched him carry the bucket effortlessly toward the dining pavilion. She held her breath, attempting to quiet the thumping, but it was useless.

The wonderful plan she had just formed had fallen by the wayside with one sighting. The great goal she'd had, to protect her heart, had disintegrated in seconds.

She had failed miserably.

Chapter Thirteen

"What's going on between you and Sophie?" Maddie gave Max a sideways glare as they walked along the beach with their catch.

Discomfort burned the nape of his neck, but he controlled the telltale signs in his voice. "What do you mean?"

"I saw the way she looked at you today at lunch. As well as your stolen glances toward her, even though you tried to be inconspicuous." Without giving him a chance to come up with an explanation, she jumped right in with her next accusation. "There's something you should know about her before you get too involved. I just found out last night. It seems that little Miss Conservative isn't on sabbatical, as she claimed. She was suspended and might even get fired."

Max's heart raced. How had Maddie found out about that?

"Can you believe it?" She chuckled with a certain amount of mirth.

Anger rushed through his system, and he spun on his heel, dropping his bucket of fish on the sand. "What are you talking about?" How had she heard the story that Sophie had just shared with him a mere nineteen hours before? Surely not from Sophie.

"I guess she didn't tell you that little piece of information."

He massaged his jaw to hide the tightness that gripped it. "Who told you that?" He tempered his tone with a hint of indifference, hoping Maddie wouldn't have a sudden attack of guilt by protecting her confidante. Maybe if he could find out the source, Sophie could do something to stop further gossip.

"A teacher I know at Valen. Cassie Steele. She's in the art department. We went to college together." She shrugged. "It's not like I know her well, but when I was rooting around Valen's website to see what it said about Sophie, I saw my old classmate's name. I called her to get the scoop, since Sophie's story didn't add up. Cassie not only told me about the suspension and why—although she said the information was not to go any further—but said some guy by the name of Greg Nelson is the chair of Valen's English department. The job Sophie claimed was hers."

Max's ears burned with rage. He must be the one Sophie suspected of taking the video and editing it.

"Go on," he said through clenched teeth.

"Unbelievably, Sophie was coaching another school's debate team—a team that competes against Valen—and somebody caught her on video and posted it. The headmaster at Valen suspended her on the spot. Can you believe it? Sophie lied to Andy and all the rest of us about her little sabbatical."

Maddie's evil grin was reminiscent of the cat eating the mouse, and Max's insides churned at the thought she was getting such glee from Sophie's misfortune. While Maddie had never appealed to him as girlfriend material, he'd always thought she was fun in that aggressive, New York City woman kind of way. But he'd never believed her to be callous.

Disbelief must have morphed his expression, since Maddie continued to share her information. "Cassie said she'll probably get fired." Her whispered words held a conspiratorial tone.

Fury spread through Max's blood. Not only toward this Nelson guy who had now usurped Sophie's position as chair after presumably altering a video and getting her suspended, but at Maddie for digging around in Sophie's background trying to find any detail that would ruin her reputation here. What Maddie failed to uncover was that Nelson was the snake who had taken and edited the video.

Maddie continued, seemingly oblivious to Max's fury. "Sophie always talked so highly of Valen. I can't imagine why she would help another school's debate team compete against her precious school. Cassie was shocked. But apparently the chair of the English department wasn't. He knows Sophie pretty well."

A jealous jolt zapped through his system, and he inhaled to tamp it down.

Maddie just kept going. "Cassie said Sophie tried to deny her involvement, coming up with the story that someone must have edited her words. But the board didn't believe her." She chuckled. "Neither did Greg Nelson. He'd dated her for a while and obviously knows more about her character than Andy does."

His blood pressure escalated while Maddie chattered on. "Just wait until we tell Andy. She'll be out of here in no time flat. Then you can take over as acting director." She gave him a sweet smile, as if she were handing him a gift.

But he didn't want it. Not like this.

Sophie had dated the slug? Why hadn't she told

him? And what else was she hiding?

Maddie finally stopped her run-on commentary and turned to Max. "Aren't you happy about this?"

"It's hard to believe," he managed.

While he wanted to defend Sophie and reveal what she had told him, he couldn't divulge her confidence. Even though she hadn't conveyed the whole story, it was still hers to share. Or not. Either way, he wanted to strangle Nelson for sabotaging his colleague, and former girlfriend, for his own benefit.

Maddie's exuberance over the whole sordid mess was more than grating. But he couldn't let on that he knew anything.

He turned his sneer from her, picked up the bucket of fish, and started walking.

Maddie ran to catch up. "What's the matter? Which brings me back to my first question. Is there something going on between you and Sophie?"

Max's heart practically beat out of his chest. He had to get his anger under control and figure out the best way to deal with this information. He refocused on her question. "Of course not." His attempt at disinterest fell far short, but it was the best he could do. "I'm just surprised at your apparent glee over someone else's misfortune. I'm sure Sophie wouldn't be jumping for joy if she learned your ex-boyfriend is in prison for fraud."

Maddie's eyes flashed, and she practically bared her teeth. "It's not the same, and you know it. Derick was manipulated by his boss into dealing with those securities. He got caught up in the scam because he was lied to."

"You can believe anything you want. My point is I'm surprised that you, of all people, would believe the worst about someone without knowing all the facts. And you'd go to Andy with this story, without finding out if it's true first. I would have thought you'd be more sympathetic, given your own past."

Maddie's ire deflated, and her face paled. Hopefully she was sufficiently chastised so as to be more understanding.

"Why don't you go ahead without me? I'm going for a swim." With that, she walked to the water, discarded her shorts and top, adjusted the straps on her bathing suit, and dove in.

That was one way to burn off the resentment left by their argument.

He continued on his way, still smarting over the nerve of Greg Nelson. That and the thought that Sophie might not have told him the entire truth about her fiasco. Just when he'd begun letting his guard down with her. But no more.

He strode toward the dining pavilion, his jaw working overtime while the vein in his forehead throbbed with every step.

Honesty. Obviously an overrated virtue.

****

"Hey, Dan, what's up for the rest of the week?" Max slipped into a chair in the program director's office.

"Glad you stopped by." Dan drummed a pencil on a yellow pad attached to his clipboard. "I set up a camping trip for tomorrow on Big Pine Key. You're taking a group of ten, and I was going to have Ben go along. But he ran into a conflict. So I've substituted Sophie."

Max grimaced.

"What's wrong? Do you have a conflict too?"

Oh. He had a conflict all right. And her name was

Sophie.

"Not exactly." He chose his next words carefully. "But you may not want to throw Sophie into the woods overnight so soon. Although she's coming along, I don't know about her camping skills."

"She's been here over a month already. She has to learn sometime. Besides, she asked to be included in the school's activities, even though she could've just as easily decided not to participate." He shrugged. "Since she wants to learn, you're the perfect guy to teach her how to bat."

Max rolled his eyes. Dan's clichés always had to do with sports or outdoor activities, although not necessarily the activity to which he referred.

Rubbing his hands over his face, Max stopped to massage his temples. The last thing he needed, when he was determined to avoid Ms. Kearns, was a night in the woods with her. A potentially disastrous situation. One to beware of. Yet his heart catapulted at the thought.

Sophie. And ten kids.

He blew out a breath and stood. "Did you give Sophie the bad news yet?"

"I told her about an hour ago."

"How'd she take it?"

"She was a bit hesitant. Asked a lot of questions about animals and bugs and bathrooms. The usual newbie stuff."

Max could picture her tossing and turning all night, worried about what creatures went with all the terrifying sounds of nature. If he was juvenile and immature, he'd find this fun. But he was too upset with her to even toy with her neuroses.

"I'm relying on you to follow the rules," warned

Dan, obviously picking up on some thread running through Max's head. "But if she really needs help, you're going to have to break a rule or two. If something happens to her out there, Andy will have your head. And mine too."

"Too bad Andy didn't think about that when he hired her."

His sarcasm was back. Funny how self-preservation reared its ugly head.

\*\*\*\*

They arrived at their destination by four the next afternoon, just as Max had planned. Having walked a few miles from where the bus had dropped them off, each hiker carried a fold-up tent, sleeping bag, and a backpack filled with provisions for today, tonight, and tomorrow morning.

"Let's set up camp here." Max dropped his pack to the ground in a cleared-out sandy area surrounded by pine trees.

They all followed suit, spreading out enough to make room for each of them to pitch their own tent. The weather was warm, around eighty, but the cloud cover kept the heat at bay. Unfortunately, the forecast called for rain tonight. *Sometimes you win; sometimes you lose.*

Max opened his backpack and took out a bottle of water. With a sideways glance, he watched Sophie as she sat on a log and drank from her canteen. Her backpack had looked unbalanced and heavy as she trekked through the woods with them, but he hadn't heard a peep out of her, other than the small talk she made with some of the students as they wended their way to the campsite.

His decision had been to ignore her. She hadn't told him the whole truth—and frankly, he was hurt. Although ignoring her in person and ignoring her in his head were two totally and distinct issues. And while he had avoided all but the tritest of conversations with her thus far, he had not been able to tear his gaze from her long, lean body or gorgeous face. At least when she wasn't looking. Now he wished she would go back to her frumpy persona.

The kids had camped a few times already and were getting proficient at putting up their tents. They worked well as a team and helped each other with the chores. Sophie, on the other hand, had apparently never pitched a tent, and clearly no one had given her directions. She squatted near her poles, picking up one, then another and trying to insert them into the canvas, to no avail.

Max had vowed he wouldn't help her, no matter what, but his resistance was running low. He felt sorry for her. So he made a deal with himself. If she asked him for help, he would. If she didn't, so be it.

And she didn't.

After about an hour, and after the students had come back from a swim, a few of them took pity on her and helped her out. But she had refused to let them do it without teaching her how. Smart lady. She knew she would be in this situation again before her time was up.

Max and a few of the students started a fire for anyone who needed it to cook. The students had learned early on that they were each in charge of themselves. There would be no sharing of provisions. They had been told to pack enough food for dinner tonight and breakfast tomorrow as well as snacks to get them through the rest of the time. Some brought prepackaged food that required no heating, and others brought freeze-dried food that needed boiling water. They also stowed whatever utensils or gadgets they needed to deal with their provisions.

"Does anyone have a can opener?" Sophie held up a can of tuna. "I forgot mine."

The students looked to Max, obviously wanting to help her but knowing the rules. They were here to learn valuable life lessons, and forgetting the utensils they would need to survive would teach them very quickly to pack more carefully the next time.

"Sorry, Sophie," said Max. "But the rules here prevent the sharing of food or utensils or clothing or anything else." He refrained from telling her she should have consulted her camping manual for everything she needed.

Sophie's face fell, and red blotches stained her cheeks. Great, even though he'd kept most of his comments to himself, she would accuse him of embarrassing her in front of the students. But rules were rules, and he needed to set an example for the kids.

She rummaged through her backpack again, taking everything out, but the much needed can opener did not surface. Neither did any other food that didn't require an opener. His heart sank. But he wouldn't have given in if a student had mis-packed, and he couldn't give in for her.

"There are berries on some of the bushes around here," he said, trying to be helpful.

"Are any of them poisonous?" Concern etched on her face.

"Yes," was all he could answer.

Damn Dan for putting him together with her for her first camping trip. Why hadn't anyone clued her in? Why hadn't Dan prepared her better? Why hadn't she consulted her camping manual?

They all got through dinner and sat around the campfire talking as dusk turned to dark. But their conversation was cut short by rain. At first, it just sprinkled, but within minutes the light shower turned into a torrent. Everyone scrambled into their tents.

The rain hitting the top of the tent didn't bother Max, but he was sure it would keep Sophie awake. Always thoughts of Sophie.

He had just dozed off when he heard a noise. He listened intently. Then heard it again.

"Max...Max...can I come in?"

Sophie's voice was almost lost in the beat of the rain on canvas. He sprang up and opened the flaps. She was dripping wet, her hair plastered to her head, her shirt plastered to her body.

He pulled her in.

"Why are you out in the rain?"

"The top of my tent caved in, and the water started pouring in. I tried to fix it, but I finally gave up."

She shivered and folded her arms around herself. The temperature had dropped with the dark and the rain, and although not cold, she had to feel uncomfortable.

"Take off your wet clothes, and I'll lend you a dry shirt and sweatpants." Another rule that shouldn't be broken—but this time he had to help her out.

She sat down next to his sleeping bag, with barely enough room for the two of them. "I'm not changing in front of you."

"Well, I'm not going out in the rain so you can have some privacy."

She seemed to think this through for a moment and then said, "Fine, then turn around."

"There's barely enough room for the two of us to sit

in this tent, and you want me to turn around?"

Here he was bending the rules to help her out, and she was playing the modesty game. He thought back to that day when she was sprawled on the deck of his rowboat, tugging on the hem of her ridden-up shorts and pulling at her shirt, which had molded to her breasts. He shook his head. She was one uptight woman. Thankfully, she couldn't read his thoughts.

He sighed for effect. "My eyes are closed."

"Keep them closed."

The rustle of clothing painted a very graphic picture of her peeling off her soaked T-shirt and shorts, exposing very gorgeous curves and toned muscles. His hands itched to slide up her tight abs, silken skin, full breasts, and so much more. He sighed and counted to twenty, refocusing his erotic thoughts on breathing in and breathing out. "Are you done yet?" His question came out huskier than he'd intended.

"I'm done," she said through her teeth.

He opened his eyes to a sullen Sophie encased in a too-large sweatshirt and sweatpants, but at least she was no longer shivering. Her vulnerable state ate at his heart, and he wanted nothing more than to take her in his arms, capture her mouth with his, and let his body do the talking as he took them both to paradise. But that was not going to happen.

And to assure that, he plowed in. "You come on your first camping trip, and you're not prepared at all. You don't have a can opener to open the only food you brought. You don't know how to pitch a tent—"

He would have gone on if she hadn't cut him off.

"Dan sprang this whole thing on me yesterday. I told him I wasn't ready yet. That I would go on the next trip.

But he said, 'Don't worry about it. Max will help you out.' I looked for you after dinner to find out what I needed to bring, but I couldn't find you. I didn't know I'd have to take my own utensils. I didn't know I'd have to put up my own tent. I thought people helped each other and shared the responsibilities. No one told me about your stupid camping rules."

Her voice escalated with each sentence. He was back with the original Sophie. The one who pushed his buttons and egged him on to argue with her. The only problem was that this Sophie attracted him too. If he had any hope of keeping his distance, he'd need to anger her enough to make her want to stay away from him.

"If you want me to go there again, Sophie, I will. If you can't participate in required activities, then you don't belong here. I don't care what reason brought you here." He knew he was treading on dangerous ground. But her lack of trust in him by omitting her relationship with the snake who had hung her out to dry had him steaming again. But why go there? It was too personal, and he had no intention of opening himself up for more disappointment. Just a little more scolding and he'd push her over the edge. "You're one of the teachers. You owe it to the kids to do your job. And I don't mean just teaching literature. I mean doing everything this job requires. Learn the rules. Learn what you're supposed to be doing here."

He didn't have to study her to feel the tension emanating from her body or the fire blazing in her eyes. By the light of the flashlight, he could see her fingers curled tightly in a ball, her jaw clenched, her knees drawn up to her chest. If she had been a spring, a mere touch would have sent her bounding into orbit. He had done it. But she held her grip on her anger with defiance. And maturity.

A characteristic he questioned his possession of.

The silence turned deafening. It pierced his ears and added to his angst with every passing second. Still, she said nothing.

She hated him. As well she should.

Sadness roiled through him at the thought.

Mission accomplished.

Chapter Fourteen

With the towel secured around his waist, Max finger-combed his wet hair off his forehead, then stretched out on the bed. He was drained.

It wasn't from camping the past two days; he'd always loved that. It was the despondency that came with having spent the previous night in a tent with Sophie. Who now hated him. And so she should. He was a despicable man—pushing her to the edge, then waiting for her to fall. And all because he was afraid to trust his own emotions. Because he didn't trust her.

The other night, he thought he and Sophie could possibly become more than friends. But the information shared by Maddie made any relationship with her impossible. While he'd opened up to her about his past, she'd edited hers. Maddie's words reverberated in his head. Why didn't Sophie tell him she'd been involved with Greg Nelson? She had made it sound like they were just colleagues vying for the same position, when in reality it was much, much more.

She'd left out a huge piece of the puzzle—a relationship gone bad, which Greg must have seen as an additional motive to ruin Sophie. Although Max couldn't fathom any reason that would push a person to wreck someone else's career. Nelson had definitely gone too far to settle whatever issues he had with Sophie. But that didn't excuse her lie of omission.

He had to stop dwelling on her, or he'd go insane. His new prescription was to ignore her and move on. His focus would revolve around moving ahead with the research institute—substituting one promise for another—turning a negative into a positive.

Max closed his eyes. But visions of Sophie took over. The azure waters of the Gulf had nothing over the color of her aqua-blue eyes, eyes that penetrated his until he was sure they could read his soul. He wanted to be back on the beach with her, sitting side by side, talking about their deepest secrets. In so many ways, she was the right woman for him. Chiseling through his walls, ever so gently, careful so as not to damage him any more than he already was. Little by little she had uncovered the demons that weighed him down and encouraged him to toss them aside.

With her, he felt lighter, freer, happier.

She had started a slow fire in his gut that spread through every inch of him with her kind, caring ways. But a more lethal blaze burned through him at her lack of honesty.

He moved his fingers and felt her phantom silky tresses flow through them as they had the other night—strands golden from the sun, catching the light of the moon. The muscles of his body tensed as two opposite versions of Sophie pulled at him.

He swung his feet to the floor, got up, and got dressed, needing to jog off his angst.

No peace for the wicked.

\*\*\*\*

Sophie had survived the camping fiasco.

Not only had she made it back to school without having to speak to Max, but she'd had twenty-four hours to appease her hungry stomach, catch up on her sleep, and look forward to a day off spreading before her. Sundays weren't always work-free, but today was one of those miracle days when nothing urgent required her attention. Sunny and warm with a slight breeze blowing off the ocean made for perfect conditions for a catamaran ride, and some of the teachers were taking off from Key West at noon.

Sophie took the powerboat with Kristin, Maddie, and Sue, feeling infinitely better than she had the day before when she returned from camping, exhausted, hungry, bug-bitten, sticky, and indignant.

Now, as the boat sped toward their waiting sea-chariot, she stretched her legs before her and leaned her head back, closing her eyes behind her sunglasses while the warmth washed over her.

"Sophie, I heard you had a tough time camping." Maddie's teasing inflection couldn't be missed.

"You might say that. I guess I should have talked to one of you before going instead of relying on Max." The irksome knot that had lived in her stomach during most of her camping experience returned with the conversation.

"Dan should have given you a crash course before sending you out there. Or at least warned you that Max is a real stickler for the rules." Maddie's statement surprised her. Shouldn't she be taking Max's side on this subject?

The knot eased, and a smirk crossed Sophie's lips. "Dan told me Max would help me out. But I guess he forgot to clue Max in to the plan."

"Dan's like that," acknowledged Kristin. "He's so preoccupied with running his programs, taking care of the big picture. He doesn't always pay attention to the details. Besides, he's a big rules man too. Two peas in a pod."

"That's the truth." Sue nodded. "Dan's problem is he thinks everyone loves the great outdoors as much as he does. He would never think that someone wouldn't know the basics of camping."

"But I told him." Sophie sat up, insecurity creeping back into her system. "I specifically said I wasn't ready, that he had sprung this on me. I asked him to give me another week and I would prepare. That's when he said the ogre would help out." Her accusatory tone punctuated her words.

Maddie chuckled. "Max can be pretty difficult sometimes. He seems particularly hard on you, Sophie. What's the deal?" Her curiosity came through, along with a hint of awareness—but awareness as to what, Sophie didn't have a clue.

She shrugged. Although she knew about half a dozen reasons which made Max difficult, she didn't know which one of the many contributed to his mood on their camping trip. He had always run hot and cold with her—mostly cold. But then, just when she was about ready to give up on him, he apologized for his bad behavior and opened up to her.

Her face burned at the thought of his lips teasing hers, making her light-headed and faint—his hands roaming all over her body with the expertise of a sex god. She inhaled, hoping to get oxygen to her brain.

She had to forget about their night on the beach. She didn't mean anything to him. He had proven that the other day when he ignored her at lunch. And he'd reaffirmed his apathy when he wouldn't help her while camping. His actions had cut her to the core, and she was still nursing her bruised heart. How could he have treated her so appallingly after they'd shared so much of themselves just a few days earlier?

Maddie cut the motor, and the sudden silence jolted Sophie out of her thoughts. She opened her eyes and watched Maddie expertly dock their boat near a huge catamaran. The guys were already aboard, talking to the captain.

Ben, Dan, and Max. Gorgeous Max with his sun-streaked hair blowing in the wind, his muscled shoulders and upper arms hard as a rock, and his six-pack abs tight and defined. As if that weren't enough, he had those incredible eyes, intense and soulful. And she wanted them to look only at her.

Sophie mentally smacked herself. *Didn't I just have a discussion with you? Mr. Heaton is off-limits. He is not your fantasy man, not your anything.*

"Hey, Dan, why aren't you sailing this boat?" Maddie placed her hands on her hips, giving him a piece of her attitude.

"I have off today too. And I plan to take full advantage. I'm going to drink a margarita, lay on the net, take in some sun. And when the time comes, I'm going snorkeling. Do you have a problem with that, Maddie?" His blue eyes crinkled, and his mouth turned up into a smile as he gave her his undivided attention.

And anyone would have. Maddie, with her no-holds-barred New York City attitude and her white bikini showcasing her perfect body, was impossible to ignore. How'd Sophie end up working with women who could have been in the *Sports Illustrated* swimsuit issue?

She glanced down at her own one-piece halter and

smoothed out an imaginary wrinkle. Not ready to venture back to the bikinis of her college days, she'd chosen a lime-green hue that looked great against her tan. And even though her midriff wasn't bare, the high-cut detail on her legs showed plenty of skin. At least she wasn't embarrassed standing next to Maddie. Or the other two.

She'd come a long way from the buttoned-up professor at Valen, thanks to her new friends here. After their shopping spree in Key West, they'd made sure to compliment Sophie on her new look—obviously afraid that if they didn't, she'd go back to her old ways. And it had worked. Along with the exercise she was getting from boating and swimming, she looked and felt like a new woman.

Stealing a glance at Max, she assumed he'd be staring at Maddie. A slow burn crept across her face when his gaze fell on her.

His mocha eyes blazed a scorching trail as they traveled up her legs, her torso, then stopped at her face. She turned and looked out over the ocean, swallowing hard, to banish this erotic discomfort. But try as she might to ignore his scrutiny, she felt it deep down in the pit of her stomach as fingers of heat spread over her skin, doing much more damage than the sun.

"All aboard," called the captain, not a minute too soon. It spurred her into action and away from Max's lethal stare.

With all on deck, the captain set the boat in motion, and the real party started. Giddiness washed over the gang even before Ben handed out icy, green margaritas. A few hours away from responsibility and obligation had the team in great spirits.

A trampoline that looked like a fishing net was

strung between two pontoons, and Sophie joined the others stretched out under the cloudless sky as the blue-green water passed swiftly beneath them, spraying up a cool mist to counter the heat of the midday sun.

Heaven.

As the catamaran sped to its destination, Sophie joined in the upbeat conversation, hoping to get her equilibrium back. Even though she cautioned herself to ignore Max, her gaze drifted to him as he moved around the boat taking pictures with his expensive-looking camera. Mostly of the beautiful environment. But every once in a while, he would catch two or three of his colleagues mugging for attention. Not her, though. She stayed away from cameras.

"Hey, Sophie," broke in Ben, "are you going to snorkel with us?"

Another sport she'd never done. Another activity to embarrass herself with. Her smile slipped a few notches. "I'd love to try it. Maybe you can teach me?" She inhaled and pasted her smile back on.

"It's easy. All you have to do is breathe through this gadget so you can keep your face in the water to see the sights." He held up the snorkel and comically demonstrated.

Dan threw a mask at him. "Let's see you demonstrate with full gear." He chuckled, tossing over flippers as well.

Ben obliged and had the entire gang laughing uncontrollably as he tried to walk over the net—and bodies—with his flippers, mask, and snorkel in place. Max caught it all on film and swore he was going to post it on the school's website.

It wasn't long before the captain anchored the boat

near a reef. Dan was the first to jump in.

"Come on, you lazy bums. Get in here and become one with the fishes."

"I'm coming." Kristin dove gracefully into the water from the side of the boat—her bright yellow bathing suit streaking through the aqua depths before she surfaced. "Maddie, can you throw my equipment overboard?"

Maddie tossed Kristin's gear to her, then slid into the water from the side of the boat with her own. Max clicked away on his camera. Making memories. Or PR shots. Or both.

Sophie stood on the side of the boat, watching as one by one the crew jumped in and prepared for their adventure. A band of trepidation ran through her, and a prickly sensation crept up her neck. She looked over at Max.

There he was, standing on the beam near the deck, focusing his camera on her.

Flashes of fire ripped through her gut, and adrenaline rushed to every extremity. "Stop," she yelled, holding up her hand, feeling the blood drain from her face. "Don't take my picture. Give me the memory card," she demanded. The din in the water below quieted, but all she could see was red. She practically sprinted toward Max, holding out her hand, yelling indecipherable words, grabbing the camera from his hands.

Then it slipped through her fingers—as if in slow motion—heading for the water.

Max reached out and snatched it just in time, saving it from a salty death. At the same time, Sophie tilted precariously forward—off balance—her arms flailing in an attempt to steady herself.

In one fluid motion, Max slipped the camera around

his neck and grasped her upper arms, holding her upright. "It's okay, Sophie, take it easy."

His words echoed through the fog in her head, his voice soothing. But nothing could calm her pumping heart.

The video of her, posted on a social media site for all her world to see, with a message she did not deliver, hijacked her brain. A streak of pain shot through her, and she covered her heart with her hand.

"Give me the memory card…give it to me." She kept saying it over and over, an almost mantra, as tears slid down her cheeks and she clawed at his chest. She was losing control and couldn't stop herself.

Max spun her away from the side of the boat and edged her across the deck, away from gawking eyes and open mouths.

"Sophie, calm down." He gently shook her shoulders and stared into her eyes, obviously attempting to reach into the depths of her haunted mind.

She couldn't breathe. Gasping for air, she felt dizzy and faint and sick all at the same time.

"Breathe slowly," he encouraged. "In…out. In…out."

She followed his instructions as he sat her down and stayed close, all the while counseling her with soothing words.

"I'll delete any photos of you. Don't worry. I'll give you the memory card so you can check."

Closing her eyes, she concentrated on her chest expanding and contracting, slowing it down, getting it under control. It took a while, but finally, her panic dissipated. She opened her eyes.

And there was Max, just inches away, rubbing her

back, gazing at her, his brown eyes melting into hers, his full lips serious with concern.

She wanted to lean into him. Feel his arms wrapped around her, his strength seeping into her. Block out the rest of the world—the video, the parents, the headmaster, the board—and of course the prying eyes of her friends in the water, surely wondering what demon had entered her body.

"Are you okay?" His caring words curled around her.

She sighed, wishing she could just disappear. "I'm okay."

Lowering her head, Sophie tried to conceal the humiliation now replacing her panic. "Why don't you go snorkeling? I'll stay here and hide."

"You don't have to hide, Sophie."

He took her hand and rubbed her knuckles with his thumb. A gesture so easy and natural it shouldn't have made her heart bounce. But it did.

"It's obvious you're still in a lot of pain over the video. I never meant to panic you."

Her face heated as embarrassment washed through her. "I know. I know. I can't believe I reacted that way."

"The best thing to do is to get in the water and see the sights. It will take your mind off...things. And it won't give the rest of them a chance to talk about you."

He was right. But she couldn't take that first step. Rooted to the spot on deck, she looked at him, pleading understanding with her eyes. "I can't."

"Yes. You can. You're strong, Sophie. Look at you. You've only been here for two months, and you've learned so much. Even though you thought you never would. You even managed to snag the job of acting director." His chuckle lightened the mood. "So don't tell me you can't."

"That's not what you said to me the other night in your tent."

He exhaled. "You haven't quite mastered camping yet, but you will."

He slid his arm around her waist and pulled her up with him before steering her toward the other side of the boat. She stood there for only a moment, then jumped in. He came in right behind her with two sets of snorkels, masks, and fins.

"Here," he said, handing her a set. "You can sit on the ladder to put your fins on."

With no choice but to participate, she followed him over to the gang. But even though they all splashed and laughed and included her in their revelry, the reality of her situation hit her hard.

Despite everything she had accomplished here, she was allowing a malicious deed to plague her. The respect she was building day by day from teaching, learning the marine activities, and running the school could evaporate in an instant if she fell apart. She had to deal with the video issue. Now.

Because if she didn't, it would follow her everywhere.

Chapter Fifteen

What had gotten into her?

Sophie paced her eight-by-ten living room slash kitchen with barely enough space to take three steps in one direction.

It wasn't like Max was planning to alter her image and put it on social media. He'd just been taking fun pictures of colleagues having a great time.

How could she have reacted that way? She vowed to give the memory card back to him. But not now. Not tonight. She needed time to get her head together and ensure she wouldn't act like a deranged lunatic again. She obviously had her work cut out for her.

But at least she had taken the first step. She'd called Headmaster Ryan and told him her suspicions about Greg Nelson. No more hanging back and waiting for someone else to come up with his name as the number one suspect. She'd actually gone even further. She demanded that Greg not only be questioned immediately, but that his computer and cell phone be confiscated and sent to a forensic technician to analyze. Her meltdown had some benefit.

A knock at the door temporarily postponed her self-analysis. She stopped in her tracks and held her breath, contemplating whether to pretend she wasn't there. But no use putting off the inevitable. She'd have to face her co-workers again sooner or later.

After crossing to the door, she opened it slowly, biding for time before facing her caller.

"Max!"

He stood in shadow on the top step, his jaw set, the planes of his chiseled face taking her breath away.

"You don't look very happy to see me." A confused but concerned look covered his face.

"It's not that," she quickly assured him. "I just wasn't expecting anyone." *And I certainly wasn't expecting you*—the one person who had unwittingly caused her breakdown, then had to deal with it.

His eyes flashed in the darkness. "You wanted to hide out some more, is that it?"

*Something like that.* "Of course not." She added conviction to her tone.

Although she had tried to bury the humiliation deep within, her unhinged scene on the boat earlier that day left her ashamed and more than a little embarrassed. She just couldn't face her friends tonight, even though she'd made a valiant effort to mingle in the water that afternoon while brushing her tirade under the rug.

They had all been wonderful, pretending she hadn't gone off the deep end over Max taking a picture of her. And Max had been the most wonderful of all, soothing, caring, understanding—even giving her the memory card as soon as they got off the boat.

He pushed past her and entered the living room, carrying a pizza box and a bottle of wine.

"You went into town to get pizza?"

"Since you didn't show for dinner, I assumed you'd be hungry so..." He held out the box as if it were a present, and her spirit soared at his gorgeous smile.

She took the pizza and placed it on the kitchen table.

"I love pizza. Thanks." Why was he being so nice? Especially after she'd embroiled him in that lovely scene on the boat.

"No problem. I figured you needed sustenance to continue your battles." He winked, acknowledging his teasing statement.

"Most of my battles are with you." She turned away, hiding her smile.

"We are worthy opponents. Perhaps we should drink to that. Got a corkscrew?"

She glanced over her shoulder and saw him holding up the wine bottle. "I might. Let me check."

She moved toward the kitchen drawer, his intense gaze following her. Thankfully, she'd dressed in her newer shorts and a halter top instead of her button-down blouse and those long shorts he loved so much. Fate must have stepped in for a change.

She produced the corkscrew and two wineglasses. "Actually, I'm glad you stopped by. I wanted to give you back your memory card. It's hard to explain what came over me." Heat crept over her skin. "Luckily, it was you at the other end of my hysterics. At least you know my story. I shudder to think what the others must have thought."

"I told them you were feeling seasick. That you told me you didn't want your picture taken just before you were about to puke. That I went ahead anyway."

She held back a snort. *Nice.* Yet a warm, safe feeling spread through her. He had her back and blamed himself for her mania. "Did they believe you?"

"Of course. I can be very convincing when I want to be."

She knew that firsthand. He had been so persuasive

about his marketing ideas that, even though he snubbed her after their intimate night on the beach, she considered his plan anyway.

"Thanks for giving my hysteria a logical reason." A bewildering host of emotions washed through her.

He took plates from her cabinet and set the table, finding napkins and silverware to finish the job. He was capable of pushing every button she had, causing her to erupt during what should have been harmless encounters, yet he could be considerate and thoughtful. She pictured him on the catamaran, stroking her, calming her, understanding her craziness about being photographed. Then she rewound to their night on the beach when he had kissed her—free falling as she melted into him.

So why was their relationship so volatile?

"Have a seat, mademoiselle." He bowed, then pulled out her chair.

She sat, hoping the glass of wine sitting before her would clarify her confusion.

He served her a slice of pizza with a flourish and asked, "Other than the obvious problems you've had with me, how do you like it here?"

Offering banal conversation to fill the void, to sidestep the trauma of the day, was a perfect accompaniment to their dinner. Grateful, she dove in. "The people are wonderful. Kristin has been a real friend, helping with everything. She's a great sounding board. So reasonable. So fair." She took a bite of pizza, savoring the gooey cheese and thin crust. "Sue's been incredibly helpful too." She lowered her lids, trying to decide whether to raise the subject of Maddie, but Max took care of that.

"You and Maddie haven't clicked. What's going on between you two?"

Sophie shrugged. "I don't know. It's not that she's mean to me. She just doesn't like me much. I got the impression she doesn't trust me."

He arched an eyebrow. "Maybe she doesn't. She found out you were suspended."

"What?" She almost choked on her pizza. "Who did she hear that from?"

"Cassie somebody. She works at Valen. Maddie knows her from college and gave her a call to find out your story."

Fire burned through her veins as resentment coursed through her blood. "Why would Maddie go behind my back? Why is she playing detective?"

Max's intense gaze never left her face, as if he too were performing some sort of analysis of her reaction. "She didn't believe that you took a sabbatical right before you were to become chair of the English department. Just like I didn't believe you."

Her back stiffened. "Well now you know the reason. And apparently Maddie does too." Defensiveness colored her tone.

"Why didn't you tell me you had dated Greg Nelson? He is the guy you suspect took the video, right?"

Was that accusation in his eyes?

Oxygen failed to reach her brain, and dizziness swarmed her head. Max sat back in his chair, as if challenging her to give him a good answer.

"Yes, he is the guy I suspect. But we did not date. We just hung out together once in a while. Dinner, a movie here and there. Although, eventually he wanted it to be more."

"That sounds like dating to me."

"In my mind, we were just friends. Our relationship was based on companionship, collegiality. There was no holding of hands, no kissing. No expectation of being each other's plus one. We split bills or paid our own way. Very platonic. But then he told me he wanted more than friendship. I didn't." She shrugged. "He got angry and accused me of being the queen of cool. Only caring about getting ahead—running up the ladder of success to become headmaster. That I would regret it someday. I assumed he meant that I'd be alone, not that he would do something to ruin my career."

She shook her head. "After that, we only interacted as colleagues."

He eased forward and picked up his pizza, seemingly accepting her truth. "Do you think your rejection of him spurred him on to take a video of you and edit it? If he cared about you and you blew him off, then his hurt pride could have been the catalyst to destroy your reputation."

Sophie held on to her belief. "No. When I told him I wasn't interested in dating, he acted like I wasn't worth knowing. If he's the one who did it, which I do believe to be true, it was because he wanted to be chair of the English department. He'd been at Valen a year longer than me and felt he deserved it more than me."

Max sighed in what seemed like frustration. "You may have blinders on, and I'm not sure why." He looked straight into her eyes. "You should have told me about him. Cassie told Maddie he knew you well. That the two of you dated. By keeping your relationship with him from me, or whatever it was, it's apparent you don't trust me enough to share your whole story. And I can't trust you to tell me the entire truth."

A stab to her heart killed the defensiveness she'd thrown up to protect herself. All she felt now was the pain of his statement. Trust. Such a powerful principle.

"Is that why you were so horrible to me on our camping trip?"

"I was hurt. And because you didn't share that bit of information, I could only wonder about your relationship with Nelson and how serious it must have been for him to try to ruin your career."

Trust was a huge issue for Max. It was the last thing she wanted to violate between them. She reached across the table and covered his hand with hers. "I am so sorry. But please understand that from my point of view, there was nothing to tell. It was an insignificant friendship that ended when he wanted more."

He held her gaze. Then a shadow darkened his features. "If only we could leave the past where it belongs."

His serious and philosophical words signaled a returning skepticism over her explanation. That along with his glum look didn't bode well for their own relationship. Maybe she wasn't cut out to be part of a couple, for finding love. When he first arrived tonight bearing pizza, wine, and good humor, she had thought maybe, just maybe, she and Max could get back to where they'd been that night on the beach. But her initial euphoria over his unexpected visit disintegrated into the muggy air with his distrust over her relationship with Greg. She remained silent while imaginary ants crawled over her skin, waiting for him to continue.

"I've thought long and hard about your advice to exchange one promise for another. To let go of my self-imposed penance where women are concerned. I would love nothing more than to look forward to the future—with the institute and with my personal life." He paused as if searching for the right words. "I thought you could be the one to pull me out of the past and into the future." Sadness dulled his eyes.

The crawling ants attacked, and her body tensed. "You're no longer willing to let me?" Sorrow squeezed her heart.

He exhaled. "I'm conflicted." Confusion replaced the sadness in his eyes. "We are extremely different in so many respects, and we both have enough baggage to fill an ocean liner. I know, intellectually, we should steer clear of each other."

He paused, and she held her breath, waiting for him to seal her fate.

"But I can't seem to do that. You've branded me."

His words seared her heart and stole her soul. "I'm...I'm so relieved to hear you're not severing whatever it is we have between us. Because I can't stop thinking about you." No matter how hard she'd tried to douse her feelings for him, they reemerged as if hot spots in a stubborn fire.

His smile emerged. "I'm happy to hear that." He reached for her hand, and sparkling fireworks detonated at his touch.

After a moment, he released her hand and edged back, but at least their emotional gap had been bridged. His smile turned somber. "I want to thank you for pushing me to deal with my past."

"I'm glad you've forgiven yourself." The weight that had settled over her at the beginning of this conversation disappeared, and elation took its place.

His beautiful eyes held gratitude.

"No more brooding Max?" Her teasing question brought out a chuckle.

"I don't know about that." He took her hand and raised it to his lips.

His romantic gesture erased her smile and sent shivers through her blood. Brown eyes, the color of mocha, drew her under his spell.

"I'm sorry about the way I treated you camping the other night."

She swallowed. Her innate reaction would be to point out his rudeness, but given their tenuous bond, she nodded her forgiveness. Especially since she now knew the reason for his horrific behavior.

Then she rasped, "You were wonderful today."

"I know what it's like to be haunted by the past." Tension worked his jaw. "What are you going to do about your demons?"

Sophie traced the design on her napkin. "I already took a step in that direction. I called Headmaster Ryan earlier tonight and told him my suspicions. I also laid out specific things I wanted the board to review."

"Congratulations." The smallest of smiles inched over his lips.

"Not sure that calls for any high fives. Unless they're able to come up with proof of my suspicions."

She had been proud of herself for diving headfirst into the investigation. At least the disaster from today had resulted in a positive move.

She continued. "While we're on a roll of dealing with thorny topics, there's something I need to discuss with you. It's about your request for marketing funds to update the school's website." She hated raising this controversial subject, but it had to be dealt with. "I agree that this place needs more effective marketing. But Sue made it clear that Andy is not behind your idea. I don't think it's my place, as acting director, to make such a huge policy change." She bit her lip. "At least not yet. Your proposal needs more information."

"I expected as much. Andy shoots it down every time I present it. But I want you to know I'm not giving up. I'm following your recommendation and working on an in-depth marketing proposal. I'm laying everything out on paper, complete with ideas, costs, different platforms, and how they would work together to put Sunrise Island School on the map. I'm including information about the forthcoming research institute, but I'll understand if my plan is too ambitious by adding that piece of it." Excitement over the process poured from his entire body. "You were right. I can't lay all of this work in your or Andy's lap. I have to do it and, in the end, hope for approval. I definitely have my work cut out for me."

Joy over his new direction buoyed her spirits. "I'd be happy to review any concrete proposal you come up with. When you have your detailed plan in writing, bring it to me, and if it's a great proposal, I'll talk to Andy and see what I can do to persuade him." She ventured a look at Max.

He nodded. "I understand. No guarantees. That would be great if you'd take a look at it once it's complete. You might have other ideas to add to it."

Hope shone on his face. His eyes sought hers, and while she wanted to avoid his intense gaze, she just couldn't do it. He pulled her in and sent somersaulting signals to her heart.

"Sophie, I never meant to make you feel like I was

using you. Or trying to find a way to get around Andy. I just feel very strongly about my ideas and thought if I could convince you of their merits, we could get it done. Together."

*We.* It sounded so perfect. She let the word swim around in her consciousness for a while before responding.

When she didn't answer, he continued. "I'd like to go ahead with my idea of taking photographs and writing the copy for the website. That way, if my request is eventually approved, we can jump right in." He paused, searching her expression for her take. "Unless you tell me it's pointless."

He swallowed, and she watched his Adam's apple move up and down in his throat.

"Sophie?"

Her eyes shot up to his, and she forced herself to focus on the issue presented. Clearing her throat, she sat up straighter in her chair and started shredding her napkin. "Sure, you can do the work. As long as you understand that I'll need to see the entire marketing proposal, along with the projected budgets for the various projects suggested in it. If it's comprehensive and rises to the level of importance as all the other requests for funds, I'll speak to Andy."

Although they were facing an uphill battle, she was up for the challenge. "I personally think it's a great idea. I've always been a proponent of marketing. And you're right. This school is a well-kept secret. Not good for its future or that of your research institute." She looked directly at him before continuing. "You know, Max, I'm certain that before long, Andy will give you the go-ahead for your institute. It's a brilliant concept and so relevant.

Your passion for it is key. It will assure success."

She attempted a smile, hoping to underscore her certainty about the institute, without holding out any misleading promise for his future request. Her discussion with Kristin had hammered it home that all requests deserved equal consideration, despite the fact she'd like nothing better than to be a "we" with Max.

Sophie pushed her plate back. "It's just a matter of putting all your ducks in a row. And gaining allies."

"Are you an ally?" he asked, a twinkle in his eye.

"If your forthcoming proposal convinces me, then yes."

"Fair enough." He grinned.

He had to feel discouraged she was putting him off, but he hid it well. Her admiration for him quadrupled. He was a determined, focused advocate for his plan, and even though she was not giving him the news he wanted to hear, he took it like a trooper.

"Have you thought about getting Ben and Dan on your bandwagon for the research institute?" Perhaps steering the conversation toward his passion project would help them both. "Ben would be terrific at pulling together the statistics you'll need to support your ideas. Not just with Andy, but later when applying for grants. And Dan could help with the logistics of the whole thing. Like how you'd deal with the students helping with research as well as the teachers you'll want to attract during the summer months. How many can you accommodate every semester? What will be the impact on the rest of the school? Or should the institute be totally separate?"

Sophie's wheels turned, spitting out questions and ideas that would need a strainer to contain if she didn't stop. She itched for a pad of paper to start writing them all down—but this was Max's project, not hers. And she wouldn't be here long enough to get involved with it.

She caught him staring at her, with awe or incomprehensibility, she wasn't sure.

"You really do know how to get this thing off the ground, don't you?"

"Of course." She raised an eyebrow. "Do you really think I'm just spouting off random ideas?"

"No…no." He shook his head vehemently. "I simply didn't understand how much you knew about putting something like this together. I mean, I know you created your Summer Teaching Academy. I don't know why I didn't think you could do the same for my research institute. I guess I figured you had to be involved in environmental studies to fully grasp the concept."

His jaw tightened, a sign Sophie had come to know as annoyance. Only this time it was directed at himself. She hid a smile. The great Max Heaton had turned his venom inward.

"Are you accusing me of not caring about the environment?" She could no longer contain her amusement.

"You're amazing." He grinned as his deep voice curled around her, oozing charm and something much more. Something she couldn't quite put her finger on. But it penetrated her being and sent unnerving quivers to the far reaches of her extremities.

She needed breathing room, physically as well as emotionally, so she stood and started clearing the table.

He helped by wrapping up the leftover pizza and storing that, along with the remaining wine, in her refrigerator.

"Not to get too personal if you don't want to," he started, "but when was the last time you were involved in a relationship?"

His abrupt change of subject threw her off, but considering their previous conversation about her friendship with Greg Nelson, she shouldn't be too surprised.

"The first two years I was at Valen, I dated a Princeton math professor."

"Why didn't it last?"

"He wanted me to move in with him. While I loved getting together on the weekends when I could, I was happy living my life independently. I was busy with my classes and then doing all the work I needed to do to get the Summer Teaching Academy off the ground. My focus was elsewhere—and not on strengthening our bond." She shrugged. "He realized after a while that things weren't going to change anytime soon. So he broke up with me."

"Hmmm."

"What does that mean?"

"Nothing." Max took her hands in his and connected with her eyes. "I better get going. I have an early class in the morning."

Disappointment that the night was ending wended through her, but she had to be very careful where he was concerned. She pulled back, cloaking her heart in self-preservation.

"Thank you for being there for me today." She lowered her lids. "And for the pizza."

"You're welcome. See you around." He headed for the door but must have reconsidered because he turned toward her.

After covering the distance between them, he took her hands in his and pulled her toward him.

Her insides shook with a combination of anxiety and excitement while her skin tingled with desire. Desire she knew she should tamp down but couldn't. She'd been here before. She raised her eyes to his, seeking his meaning, but melted at the yearning she saw on his expressive face. Her need intensified as he lowered his lips and covered her mouth with such tenderness that she ached for more.

He tasted like red wine and heat, and she ran the tip of her tongue over his lips, eliciting a groan, before he opened his mouth and devoured hers.

Her arms inched up his chest and moved around his neck, as a small voice in the back of her brain whispered to back off. She didn't want to fall under his spell again before feeling more secure about their relationship. And she certainly didn't want to find herself reliving the moment if things between them didn't work out.

Although these prickly thoughts tried to distract her, they were no match for Max's passionate kiss. She felt herself spinning in his web, blocking off all further negative contemplation.

His hands stroked her back, each vertebra burning with heat as his fingers moved to the next. Her body responded by inching closer to him, his hard chest against her softer curves, his strong arms encircling her, his hips pressing into her with the undeniable bulge that proved desire.

She ached to feel his hot skin against hers, the palm of his hand caressing every inch of her inflamed being. She moved her hand from around his neck, across his shoulder, and down his chest, feeling the muscles jump as she lightly teased a response from him. Her fingers slipped beneath the hem of his shirt and traveled the same course they had just taken, but this time over skin and muscle and fire.

His sharp inhalation spurred her on, and her hand wandered over his torso, then back down to his waist where she played with the button on his cargo shorts. Every nerve in his abdomen tensed and contracted with her fleeting touches, and she delighted in her sexual power.

But the feeling was short-lived.

Max backed her against the wall and took hold of her hands, entwining his fingers through hers, raising her arms up over her head in a dominant mating dance as he continued kissing her mouth, then her neck, coaxing a groan from deep within. While his one hand captured both of her wrists, his other trailed down her cheek, to her neck, to her shoulder, then across her chest, sending her into space with each new stroke. She arched toward him, begging for him to mold his hand around her breast, for his fingers to tease and circle its peak. And he did. Expertly.

He disengaged his other hand from her wrists and slid it down the inside of her arm, tickling every nerve his fingers came into contact with. But no giggle emerged. All she could do was kiss him deeper and harder and longer, weaving her tongue with his until his breath mingled with hers.

His hand fell to the nape of her neck where her halter top was tied.

And then it wasn't.

The silky material fell away, and the cool, surrounding air whispered over her lace-covered breasts, causing her nipples to stand at attention. He dipped his head and took the peak into his mouth before sliding the material away and laving her with his expert tongue. His teasing movements sent flickers of heat and fire to her core, zapping all of her strength and energy and spinning her into a boneless mass of ecstasy.

As her knees started to buckle, he swept her up into his arms and carried her to her bed, then laid her gently on the covers. She watched him through heavy lids as he removed his T-shirt, pulling it up over muscled chest and shoulders, rumpling his hair in the process. Very sexy.

Long, tanned fingers unbuttoned his shorts before yanking the zipper down and freeing himself of the rest of his clothing. His erection evidenced his desire, and her own juices gathered between her legs, silently demanding him to fill her up and stop the ache of pure need.

His hot gaze settled on the clothing still partially covering her, and he quickly removed all impediments while his fingers scorched every pore as they flickered over her skin.

Sliding next to her on the bed, he whispered against her ear as his hand lazily blazed a trail down her torso. "You are so beautiful."

Those glorious words, intermingled with the wisp of his breath against her lobe, sparked even more heat than the combustible fire he had already started in the pit of her belly. She reached around his neck and pulled him on top of her, needing to feel his strong, hard length against her. Needing to connect in a primal way.

Then she opened herself up to him, casting aside all doubt, all trepidation. And she allowed the present to envelop and surround her, as she surrendered to Max.

Chapter Sixteen

Sunlight found its way through a crack in the blinds, and Max squinted at the alarm clock sitting on the end table. Six fifteen. He instinctively slid his arm around Sophie's waist, drawing her warm body closer until she was tucked against him.

He nuzzled into her neck and breathed in her sweet flowery scent, closing his eyes to make her fragrance more powerful. Max wanted to remember this morning and the calm, blissful feeling that surrounded him, making him want to stay here in this cocoon for a very long time.

This morning's elation was the direct result of last night's rapture. Sophie had been amazing. Soft, warm, sexy, erotic. And open. Someone he could trust.

He wanted her again. But he should get out of her cabin before everyone else was up and about. As acting director, she might not want to flaunt the fact that he'd stayed the night. A smile curved his lips. Unless she didn't have a problem with it.

Sophie stirred in his arms, and he held her tighter, savoring the brush of her skin against his. "Wake up, sleepyhead," he crooned, kissing the back of her head. Her chestnut hair spilled over the pillow and felt like silk against his cheek.

"What time is it?" she asked, her voice heavy with sleep.

"After six."

She sprang up out of his arms and peered at the clock. "Oh no. I have to meet Kristin at seven." Disappointment echoed through her statement. Good. She didn't want to leave him.

"I'm sure she won't mind if you don't show up one day. Stay in bed." He used what he liked to think of as his sexy, come-on voice and reached for her, but she ducked out of his grasp with a teasing smile.

"Yes, she will mind. I ditched her once before, and I could tell she was really hurt that I hadn't bothered to cancel. I can't do that to her again."

She slid out of bed and stood there for a second, totally naked, totally sensual. With not an inhibition in sight. His libido kicked into high gear. Maybe he could change her plans for this morning.

But as quickly as the thought flitted through his mind, Sophie turned and headed for the bathroom.

The full force of the shower spray echoed through the small cabin before the curtain squeaked over the metal bar in an open and closed motion. She talked over the noise. "Kristin's been so nice to teach me to swim and kayak. Today we're supposed to photograph something for her class. I forget what."

He chuckled. Ever the environmentalist.

Max turned on his back, sighed, then stared at the ceiling. He was usually up and out by now too. He loved this time of morning on the water, before it got too hot. But today, he would have preferred getting hot with Sophie.

He reluctantly got out of bed and pulled on his shorts and T-shirt. "I better get going," he called over the steady stream. "If I see Kristin, I'll tell her you're on your way."

"No," she shouted, popping her head around the shower curtain. "You don't want her to know that we spent the night together, do you?"

He shrugged, then smiled at the alarm on her face. "Why not? Are you ashamed you were with me?"

"Of course not," she sputtered, looking adorable with her hair plastered to her head as it dripped on the bathroom floor. "It's just that this is a very small community. We need to think this through. Figure out what we want to say...or do...if anything."

He chuckled at her apparent confusion over what to make of their night together. And if he were in her spot as acting director, he wouldn't have known how to present it either.

"How about if I join you in there and help you figure it out?" That plan sounded very promising to him, and if Sophie hadn't ducked back behind the curtain and turned off the water, he just might have done it.

"Hand me a towel, will you?" she asked, her arm sticking out of the shower but no other body parts visible.

"I don't know. I kinda like seeing you naked."

"Max!" It was a cross between a laugh and a wail. "I'm going to be late."

"Really?" He kept his voice calm and noncommittal.

He grabbed the towel from a rack across the small bathroom. "Here you go." He stood in the doorway but refused to go closer. She would have to come to him.

She laughed. "I never knew you to be such a game player." Then she slid the curtain back and walked slowly and very sexily toward him. She had an incredible body: long, lean, regal. Mischief danced in her eyes, but her mouth had lost all trace of mirth. "So you want to play, do you?" Her voice was low and husky.

"Do I ever." His heart nearly beat out of his chest at the prospect.

He dropped the towel on the floor and took her into his arms. The imprint from her wet body traced itself onto his dry clothes. He lowered his mouth to hers and drank her in, all playfulness lost in the heat of passion.

Her hands pushed against his chest, and she backed him into her bedroom. His blood pumped testosterone to every extremity. Sophie stopped for a moment beside the nightstand and picked up the phone without moving her gaze from his. Then she punched in a few numbers.

"Hi, Kristin. It's me." Her gaze bored into his. "Something's come up this morning, and I can't make it. I'm really sorry. Talk to you later… Thanks. Bye."

Short and sweet and sexy as hell. She replaced the phone in the cradle, tossed him a condom, then pushed him onto the bed before collapsing on top of him, never breaking their connection. She straddled him while pulling his T-shirt up over his head, then planted kisses on his chest, sending lightning bolts ricocheting through his system. His hands reached out and encircled her waist, feeling the soft, silky skin beneath his fingers, as her hips pushed against his, grinding against the bulge in his pants. He could hardly breathe.

His pelvis moved up to meet hers, but his shorts interfered with the exquisite pleasure he'd surely feel if they'd just disappear. Yet he didn't want to stop her from driving every nerve in his body into orbit.

She sat over him, her breasts full, her nipples hard, her eyes closed, her luscious lips slightly open as she now moved to her own rhythm. Her hands glided across his chest and over his shoulders, then down his arms, until she found his fingers. She raised them to her breasts, showing him what she wanted.

An ache, so sweet yet so powerful, rose in his chest and threatened to suffocate him. Could this intense feeling be solely from physical pleasure? Impossible. Much more than his body participated in this luxurious, sweet seduction.

His hands moved over her, feeling the roundness of her curves, the tightness of her muscles. He reveled in the response of her nipples as they pebbled against his fingertips—her moan reverberating in her throat.

It damn near did him in.

He moved his hands to her hips and lifted her over to his side, then ripped his shorts off as quickly as a superhero. After lifting her back on top of him, he pushed himself into the wet, warm paradise between her legs. Her heat engulfed him and sent cascading sparks to every cell in his body.

Slowing the rhythm, he inhaled, attempting to keep his pulse from thrusting into overdrive. But that proved impossible. He was with the most incredible woman he had ever been with—a woman who had no idea she was the sexiest creature on earth. A woman who had been used to hiding her curves and beauty behind baggy clothes and a doctorate degree. A woman who believed in him.

"Open your eyes," he pleaded, aching to see into her.

She did, and her brilliant blue irises sparkled with intensity as she held his gaze. Her lips were swollen from his kisses and her cheeks pink from exertion.

Absolutely beautiful.

She picked up the pace, moving over him with exquisite pleasure. He watched her teeth bite her lower lip, her eyes close involuntarily, her body tense and then melt around him as she experienced the ultimate delight.

And then he met her. No longer holding back, no longer observing. He held her hips and thrust into her in hard, fast bursts. The wave began slowly, rising up and up until it could reach the sky, before curling, then crashing down all around him in a euphoric release.

He gripped her hips as he spun out of control—every nerve in his body reacting to the pleasure that she gave him.

And then it was quiet.

Sophie lay on top of him, her heart beating against his, her face burrowed into his neck. He never wanted to move from this spot. For the first time in ten years, his painful past seemed a dull and fading memory, and he had no intention of disturbing it from its eternal resting place.

\*\*\*\*

Back in his cabin, Max sat before his laptop, unfocused on the words before him as he replayed the intimate scene from the night before.

He had planned to leave, then decided against it. Just taking her hand in his had detonated cherry bombs throughout his system. Their connection was palpable. And intense.

A smile broke out.

Produced by Sophie.

She was one complicated woman. Sassy, smart, driven. And hurting. At least her meltdown yesterday had compelled her to take a positive step in the investigation. With any luck, Greg Nelson would be identified as the culprit, and Sophie would regain her rightful place as chair of the English department at

Valen. Demons be gone.

Thankfully, he'd been able to talk her down yesterday and push her to participate. If he hadn't, embarrassment would have kept her on the boat and everyone whispering about the cause.

But the real breakthrough came last night.

The final sword had been sheathed, and he'd stated his feelings for her. As did she.

Yet niggling at him were the pitfalls, always pitfalls. She was as bad as he was in the dating department. The one relationship she had over five years ago was overshadowed by her drive to succeed—a weekend respite when she had time. And the other she'd relegated to the friendship category, even if Nelson didn't.

Neither one a blueprint for a true connection.

Was Sophie capable of commitment? Was he?

Max was ready to try. He had fallen for her—the woman who brought out the worst and the best in him. Now that he'd given himself permission to commit, the person he chose was leaving at the end of the semester.

Unless he could change her mind.

The one thing that might turn her head would be involvement in his project. Her eyes sparkled, and enthusiasm oozed from her pores when tossing out marketing ideas for the school as well as his research institute.

He opened up the document for his marketing proposal. The sooner he finished it, the sooner he could share it with Sophie and get her onboard.

The way to this woman's heart was through an academic venture.

And he intended to make it a joint venture.

\*\*\*\*

Sophie's week sped by with classes, field trips, and administrative duties. All around her, the teachers and students were buzzing about the Blue Sky Games, which were scheduled for Friday. With a day off from classes, the participants played assorted team games, which began at nine and went until three. The winning team got bragging rights for the rest of the semester, along with a tacky tin trophy.

Happy to have the day off from teaching, she planned to catch up on budget requests and assorted other paperwork. Sophie sat at the teachers' table with a hearty breakfast of bacon, eggs, and toast, which should get her through the day without having to break for lunch.

Kristin sat next to her with a similar plate of food. "Aren't you excited about today?" Her tone gushed enthusiasm.

"Why? Because I could get my work done without interruption? I guess so."

"No! Because of the games. This is your first experience. And it's so much fun."

"I'm not joining the games. I have too much work to do."

Max's voice broke in. "Every teacher joins the games. There are no exceptions or excuses. Haven't you read the rules in Andy's manual?"

She chuckled. That couldn't be true. Andy would assuredly be holed up in his office on a free day such as this. "Nope. Didn't see that rule, so it must not be in writing and therefore not enforceable."

"If necessary, I'll call Andy right now and let him inform you of your duty." A teasing smile dominated his mouth, but his tone held no such escape.

"Seriously?"

"Seriously."

Just then, Dan walked to the front of the dining pavilion and got everyone to quiet down. "Okay, I've chosen the team captains. Once I call your name, stand over by the railing. Then each in turn will choose a colleague, who will be the co-captain. I've already assigned the students to Teams A, B, C, or D, which letters align with the order in which I call you. Ready?"

A general shout of approval burst from the entire pavilion, excitement running high.

Dan continued. "The team captains are Maddie, Kristin, Max, and Sue."

The four of them followed Dan's directions and stood by the railing in front of their team letter.

Maddie chose Ben, Kristin chose Dan, Max chose Sophie, and Sue chose Keith. Now she'd never get out of it.

Dan instructed the students, who had each been assigned a letter, to go to their captains, and he provided each team with an agenda containing the ordered list of activities. "The co-captains will keep track of the points assigned for each activity and bring them to me at the end of the games. I will then determine the winner and announce the winning team at our ceremony. Best of luck to all of you."

Sophie sidled up to Max as he led his team to the beach. "Are you sure you wouldn't prefer that I bow out? I may be a hinderance to your team."

"Nice try, Kearns. But there's no getting out of this." He added a friendly smile. "Don't worry. It'll be fun."

"That's what Kristin said." Yet what Sophie considered fun and what her esteemed colleagues at

Sunrise Island School considered fun were worlds apart.

Max gathered his team around him in a circle. "Our first event is the water balloon toss. We start at the first markers, which are about six feet apart. Half of you on one side, half on the other. With each successful throw, both partners move back a foot. The first round has one point associated with it if the balloon doesn't break. The second round, two points, et cetera. Don't toss your balloon until I blow the whistle. Each set of partners should keep their own score and report it to Sophie at the end. The balloons are in that red bucket—one to each couple."

The students hustled over to get their balloons, laughter and joy following in their wake.

"Sophie, you're with me."

"I don't get to pick my partner?"

Max's slow grin sent the butterflies in her stomach crashing into each other.

"I need to keep an eye on you so you don't defect." His mischievous eyes sparkled.

Now that she was tethered to the games, she intended to have the fun that was promised. "I'll toss the balloon first." She picked out a huge pink balloon and hefted its bulk from hand to hand, getting a feel for it.

With their team divided in half, Max blew the whistle, and the first toss was made.

She looked down the line. "No burst balloons yet. We're off to a good start."

They proceeded to the next round and the next, but by the fourth round, water was spurting and spraying everywhere. She and Max were still in the game, though.

It was Max's turn to throw, and Sophie's confidence waned. He blew his whistle, and the balloon came at her like the missile it was intended to be. It caught her shoulder and burst with a pop with water soaking her shirt and arms.

"Hey. You did that on purpose. You weren't even aiming for my hands."

His laughter rang out. "No? I thought I was." He could barely get the words out.

She slitted her eyes at him, walked over to the bucket, picked up an extra-large balloon, and threw it. Water cascaded over the front of his T-shirt. The kids entered the war, and water balloons were bursting and spraying everywhere. Laughter and squeals rang in the air around them until the last balloon was broken.

Max blew his whistle. "Now that we used up all the balloons for the rest of the teams, we'll have to go back to the dining pavilion and replace them." He picked up the empty bucket and led them to their chore, which they accomplished in record time.

"Hey, Mr. Heaton, what's next?" asked Brad, one of the students on their team.

"Volleyball. We're playing against the A team at ten."

Now there was a game she wasn't too shabby at. "Do you play six or two at a time?" Sophie asked.

"Six. I'll make substitutions throughout the game so everyone gets a chance." He looked at her as if she'd made a comment.

"What?" she asked.

"I'm waiting for you to tell me you don't know how to play. You've said that before every activity you've done here from day one." He smirked. "Except for the water balloon toss."

She smirked back. "I happen to know how to play

volleyball. I was on my college team."

"Get out!" His surprise was almost comical.

She shouldn't have said anything. What if she was terrible? "I haven't played since then, so I may be a little rusty."

"Not a problem." He nudged her playfully with his elbow. "I'm just glad I don't have to explain the rules to you."

"I thought you liked having the upper hand and making me feel inadequate." As soon as the words were out of her mouth, she regretted them. Today was a fun, frivolous day and one she did not want to ruin with cutting remarks.

He stopped and turned to face her. "I promise I will never do that to you again." His jaw tightened, and his serious eyes held hers. "I am truly sorry for the way I treated you."

She bit her lip. "I didn't mean to bring up the past. Let's go win this volleyball game."

He nodded, but the elusive smile she loved so much didn't appear.

They met Maddie's team at the net, which was set up on the beach, and Max chose his first six players, which included her. Being in territory in which she was comfortable felt good.

The game started with the requisite amount of trash talk between the students, who all knew each other well. The game came back easily to her, and whenever she was in the front line and the opportunity arose, she spiked the ball to win the point. The cheering and jeering on both sides were loud and kept the spirit of the game high. While Max substituted players to give everyone a chance to play, he never took her out.

And they won all three games.

"You were our ringer. Great job." Max's smile was back and in full glory.

"Thanks. If we could just play volleyball all day, I'd be in great shape. But dare I ask what's next?"

"Kayak races. All the teams participate at eleven thirty."

"Two person kayaks, I hope." Although she'd become proficient at the activity through her morning ritual with Kristin, she didn't feel strong enough to compete on her own.

"Yes, it is. You can be my partner."

She liked the sound of that, not only for the race but personally.

The event turned out to be a relay race, and she and Max were taking the last leg. She cheered her teammates on, yelling and screaming with the rest of them, until it was their turn.

Kristin's team was in the lead going in, but Max's smooth, strong strokes invigorated her to put in every last drop of energy she had. Once they made the turn, they pulled out ahead of the others and stayed there until the bitter end.

Victory!

Which was all the more sweet having gotten there with Max.

Their team came running into the water to celebrate with them, and within seconds she and Max were pulled from the boat and doused in the Gulf, joining in the revelry.

But there was no rest for the weary. Next they had a dodgeball competition, which they did not win, and cornhole where they tallied their points but wouldn't know where they stood against the other teams until Dan calculated the scores. The last event was a scavenger hunt where they found only twelve of the twenty items on the list.

At two fifty, Sophie took her team's scores to Dan, and he and Sue tallied up the conglomeration of points.

Sophie sat on the sand with her group, and Max joined her. "What did you think of your first Blue Sky Games?"

"I've never had this much fun in my entire life." She hadn't stopped smiling or laughing the entire day, and her face hurt—along with her body.

"Aren't you glad you joined in instead of working in the office all day?"

"Absolutely. If it wasn't required, I might have snuck off."

"Andy knew what he was doing when he created this day. It's a great way to bond with the students and put aside responsibilities."

She stretched out her legs and raised her face to the sun, taking in its warmth. This school was one very special place, and if it hadn't been for her suspension, she would never have experienced it. Sometimes things work out for the best.

All of a sudden, the students started clapping and hooting. Sophie opened her eyes to see Dan standing amongst them.

"The time has come to announce the winning team of the Blue Sky Games." He paused for effect, and the ruckus grew loud. Then he held up his hand to quiet the masses. "The winner is Team C—Max and Sophie's team."

Their group bounced up from the beach and cheered.

Max took Sophie's hand and pulled her to where Dan stood with the trophy. Max took it, then handed it to Sophie. It was lighter than the pink water balloon, but oh so satisfying.

Max made a little speech. "I want to thank the academy, I mean Sunrise Island School, for giving us the opportunity to come together and play in the spirit of fun competition. To our team, thank you for your effort today, not only in your prowess in the events but in cheering your teammates on." He held up the trophy. "Each one of you will keep the trophy for a few days to remind you of your fortitude and spirit. The first person to get possession of this very expensive, very unique trophy is my co-captain, Ms. Sophie Kearns."

He gifted her with his smile as he slid his arm around her shoulders, bringing her close.

Then he whispered in her ear, causing a riot of sensation to float from her neck to her toes. "You were unbelievable today. You fit in spectacularly."

Tingles and sparkles ran amok through her system and lit up her heart.

All because of those glorious words that Max rained upon her.

Chapter Seventeen

The ringing phone at eight thirty a.m. on Monday interrupted Sophie's morning routine, and she scowled at the intrusion, wishing to daydream instead. After winning the Blue Sky championship trophy on Friday afternoon, she'd participated in one celebration after another over the weekend. While she didn't have much alone time with Max, their connection was unmistakable, and she reveled in the thrill every time she saw him.

"Hello," she answered, a thread of annoyance pulling through her at the unwelcome disruption.

"Sophie? This is Headmaster Ryan."

The air stood still, and she dared to breathe.

"Sophie? Are you there?"

"Y-yes. I'm here."

"I have some news for you. Sorry to call so early, but I wanted you to be the first to know."

She swallowed and squeezed the phone at the same time she squeezed her eyes shut. When she called Headmaster Ryan to tell him her theory, she'd felt like she was taking her power back, and she didn't want that sense destroyed.

He continued. "I guess the pressure was just too great. Once you shared your hunch with me, it all fell into place. I had a little chat with Nelson after we confiscated his school computer and cell phone, and he confessed without us having to hire a forensic technician."

"That's good." It came out in an almost whisper. She cleared her throat. "I...I don't know what to say." Hearing the result, out loud—confirmed. She could hardly speak.

"I know taking a sabbatical was difficult for you," the headmaster began, not mentioning the fact it was a suspension and not a sabbatical. When she didn't respond, he filled the dead air between them. "And the investigation was dragging on. But once you shared your suspicions and we took Nelson's computer and cell phone, he saw the writing on the wall." Pride in his handling of the matter reverberated through the phone line.

Her thoughts were so jangled, so incoherent that she felt as if she were in a daze. She sat down at the kitchen table and held her head in her hand. She should hate Greg. Feel intense anger. He had done her such harm. But she only felt pity. How could he want a job so badly that he'd resort to surreptitiously taking a video of her and editing it with the intention of ruining her reputation?

"So come on back. We need you here."

Her head spun as she focused on the date. March twentieth. Andy was still in the hospital. She had planned to stay until mid-May—the end of the term.

"I have a commitment here until May twelfth. I can't come back until then."

"You're working there?" Incredulity peppered his voice. "I thought you were visiting Andy. Relaxing in the sun."

"No. I couldn't just sit around idle. He needed a lit teacher. So I signed on to work for the term. I'm also the acting director."

She filled him in on the details of Andy's boating accident, his injuries, and his request that she help him out by running the school in his absence.

"I'm so sorry to hear of Andy's misfortune. I do hope he'll be all right." Headmaster Ryan had not only respected Andy while he'd been at Valen, but he'd truly liked him. Genuine concern filtered through the line.

"He'll be fine. It will just take time."

"Will he be well enough to run the school for the summer term?" Did she detect a note of panic in his voice?

"Hopefully, he'll be well on his way to recovery by then. Even if he's not a hundred percent, he should be able to work at least part-time."

"You're getting excellent hands-on experience down there. Leave it to you to turn a sow's ear into a silk purse." He chuckled. "You always were an overachieving wonder. I admire you for that."

Sophie shifted in her chair as a nagging discomfort filtered through her at his praise. She should be basking in it, not wriggling away from it.

The headmaster continued. "This will help you immensely when you take over as chair of the English department upon your return. It could even help you in your quest to obtain my job when I retire." He chuckled as if his timeline had been pushed out a few more years.

So the position as chair was hers. And possibly the job as headmaster in the future. Where was the happiness, the joy that should be bursting from her pores? Had this whole event taken such a toll on her that she could no longer feel emotion?

Worse than that, cynicism crept in. Headmaster

Ryan's current pride in her ability and congenial tone had been conspicuously missing from his demeanor when the famous video surfaced on social media. And although she wanted it to feel like old times, with the headmaster as her benevolent boss and mentor, she struggled to feel the warmth.

"Thank you for the good news."

Sophie willed the tension to drain from her body. This whole, nauseating ordeal had finally come to an end. And a gratifying one at that.

"Well then, I guess we won't see you until mid-May." Headmaster Ryan's disappointment rang through loud and clear. "Please give my best to Andy."

She hung up and sat there staring at the wall for a long time. She had finally been vindicated. Her plan to return to Valen with head held high to claim her prize had materialized. Where was the satisfaction, the triumph? Of course, she felt relief. But there was no overwhelming elation. What was wrong with her?

*Maybe you don't want to go back.* The words echoed in her mind. She denied her subconscious. Ridiculous.

But she knew why that errant thought popped into her head. She knew as clearly as if he had been standing right before her. Max. Somewhere between all his noisy taunts and brooding silences, she had come to know a caring, sensitive, gifted man who sent her blood sizzling through her veins every time she caught sight of him.

And the other night he had said he couldn't seem to steer clear of her. That she'd branded him. She wanted to luxuriate in those words. But deep down, she knew a relationship with him would never work. She and Max came from two different worlds, and she would be returning to hers in less than two months. With that realization, an ache so big it threatened to cut off her air supply took hold and rendered her motionless.

She glanced at the clock. Eight forty. She had a class in twenty minutes and mountains of paperwork waiting for her on Andy's desk. She had no choice but to pull herself together.

After combing through her drawer, she donned a pair of shorts and a tank top, threw her hair up into a messy bun, and went on her way—the spring in her step from a great weekend conspicuously missing. The call that should have had her bouncing on clouds had the opposite effect.

And now she just felt drained.

\*\*\*\*

Sophie was knee deep in reviewing budget requests for class trips, equipment, and a myriad of other money-eating issues. Several of the grants Sunrise Island School received were for specific purposes, and the monies had to be spent for the right purpose by certain dates. The spreadsheets were detailed and getting more complicated as the weeks went on.

Max stepped into the office after lunch. "You skipped breakfast, and you just missed lunch. What have you been eating?"

She smiled. "I have some protein bars in my drawer. I did intend to make it to breakfast this morning, but I got detained with a phone call from Headmaster Ryan. He had good news."

"Really? Is it what I think it is?" He arched a brow in question.

"Greg Nelson confessed to taking and editing the video. When his computer and cell phone were confiscated so they could be analyzed by a forensic technician, he caved, obviously knowing he'd be caught."

"That's great news." He studied her. "Why aren't you happier?"

She inhaled, then shrugged. She couldn't vocalize the thought that had flown through her brain this morning. That she didn't want to leave. It would just lead to a conversation about why, and pinning her future on a relationship with Max was just absurd.

"You're not going back to Valen early, are you?" Distress circled his question.

At least he didn't want her to leave yet.

"No." She shook her head vehemently. "Not until May, when the term is over. When I anticipated returning."

"Oh." His tone was hollow. Just like she felt.

He placed a thick binder he'd been holding on her desk. "While you're still here, do you have some time to go over a few holes I have in my marketing proposal? With all your experience, I thought if we could discuss the open issues, it would solidify my ideas and I would get it done sooner." He looked at her pile-strewn desk. "But if you're too busy, I understand."

"No. I'd love to talk about your plan. It's much more interesting than what I've been doing. Have a seat."

That day started their daily meetings to work together on Max's proposal. Sometimes they would stay in the office, some days they would take a walk on the beach, and others they would kayak. It wasn't all shop talk. They laughed, they teased each other, and they got to know each other even more than she thought possible.

After a few weeks, while he was escorting her back to her cabin following a late night in the office, she stopped in her tracks. "Are you making up issues in your proposal just so we can keep working on it together?" She couldn't contain her smile.

"You got me. That, and to be totally honest and up front, I figured the more invested you became in it, the more likely you'd be to throw some money into it."

"Very smart, Mr. Heaton. But you know, I—"

"Yes, yes, I know." He held up his palm. "You have to treat everyone's proposal equally." His smile broke free. "But maybe you'll treat mine more equally."

She laughed with him. But this time, as they stood under the stars at the end of the Keys, he was no longer a manic-depressive stranger teasing her about her clothing choices.

This time, he was the person she was falling in love with.

Chapter Eighteen

"Hey, Andy. Don't you like your room?" Sophie had finally tracked him down in what appeared to be an exercise area at the rehab facility.

"I hate it." He spoke through clenched teeth, putting one foot in front of the other while using a walker.

She had to agree that the medicinal odor blended with ammonia had her nose scrunched the minute she'd stepped into the sterile environment of St. Elizabeth's Rehabilitation Center. The walls were painted a dull shade of builder's white, and the tile floor—white with gray specks—just looked dirty. Although colorful paintings and an occasional artificial green plant attempted to spice up the decor, the weight of depression hung over her as she moved through the halls in search of her friend.

She strode closer to Andy, but he hardly afforded her a glance. Beads of perspiration dotted his forehead as he focused on the matter at hand—walking.

"Your doctor thinks you're making remarkable progress." Kristin had been keeping her up to date.

"Doing the exercises is the only thing I have control over. Hopefully, it will get me out of this awful place sooner."

"You just got here two weeks ago. Are you sure you're not overdoing it?"

He stopped in his tracks and glared at her. "Are you

trying to keep me away so you can keep your job as director?"

That stung. Although Kristin had warned Sophie that Andy's moods were foul, especially since he'd stopped taking his pain medication, she hadn't expected such a biting comment directed at her. Obviously, the pain, along with his maniacal quest to push his body ten times harder than recommended, all added to his irritation. But he had a goal. To get back to Sunrise Island School in record time.

She responded to his accusation. "Of course not. The job is too hard. I can't wait for you to come back and take over."

"Well, well. The great Sophie Kearns has run into a job that is difficult for her." He studied her while slanting his head. "I thought I'd never see the day."

"Very funny, Andy. If you weren't in such a bad mood, I'd think you were teasing me. But seeing that scowl on your face and hearing the unpleasantness in your voice has me wondering." She walked up and down the room next to him, shortening her steps to conform with his.

When he didn't answer, she jumped right in with the reason for her visit. "I wanted to discuss something with you. About the school, of course."

She raised three requests for funds from different teachers for special projects. One was Max's new request for marketing funds. Sophie tried to tamp down her enthusiasm for the project but found it difficult. It was by far the best use she could see for the money, and if she hadn't been so afraid of her bias, she'd already have approved it. But in order to appear fair, she colored the other projects with the same amount of energy.

When finished, she looked at Andy to gauge his reaction. No nodding of his head. No verbal communication. Only his quiet determination to walk. Was he even listening?

Marching in front of him, she stood there so he couldn't get by. "Andy. What do you think? Do any of these three projects deserve funding?"

Finally, he looked at her, and she saw the most amazing expression.

Indifference.

She angled her head, as if to see it from a different perspective. But he spoke loudly and slowly as if to make sure she understood.

"I don't care, Sophie. Whatever you think. You're the acting director. Just do your job. And if you can't do it, get someone else to."

That was it. Said with no emotion whatsoever.

He then moved his walker to the right to get around her and continued his methodical movements up and down the room.

Incredible.

She stood there for a while. Should she try a different tack? Beg him to at least give his thoughts on the subject? But from the rigid set of his shoulders and the grim look on his face, she knew it wouldn't do any good.

"So that's it?"

"That's it. Say hello to everyone for me."

Sophie nodded and left.

What had become of Andy? Where did her friend go? From the time Sunrise Island School was a seed in his imagination until the day of his boating accident, he'd been involved in every decision, every plan that touched his institution. He'd spent hours weighing, discussing, evaluating, and dissecting whatever issue came before him. How could he just let her, an almost total stranger to the school, make these decisions without his input?

As each mile passed on her way back, her initial bafflement turned to shock, then anxiety. How could Andy put her in this position and then turn his back on her? These decisions were important for the future of the school. Only having been in charge for a little over two months, she didn't have enough experience to make them.

The knot in her stomach had quadrupled by the time she arrived back. Each day now, for the past two weeks, she'd dreaded a little more the job that awaited her in Andy's office. The joy she'd felt at the initial honor he had bestowed upon her had turned into anxiety and foreboding. The administrative decisions were making her crazy, and the perennial quest to deal with budget issues had her wringing her hands and gnashing her teeth. The pressure had become worse when she realized the fiscal year was coming to an end, and all grant money had to be disbursed before closing the books, or they would lose it.

Normally, a challenge of this magnitude would have her blood pumping and her mind buzzing as she analyzed programs and pored over paperwork. But recently, she found herself looking out the window, wishing she were with the students going on the next field trip or discussing what new experiment they'd done that day.

It also didn't help that Max's request made the most sense. She knew his marketing plan would make a huge difference for the school—and eventually his institute. It excited her. It was a plan whose bandwagon she was willing to jump on. Yet Andy's prior decision, to go slow, should guide her more than her own opinion. Besides, she was more than a little prejudiced where Max was concerned.

She had given Andy the opportunity to make his opinions known. To tell her what he wanted. But he'd refused. Not only had he refused, but he'd dropped it back in her lap.

She would have blamed his bizarre behavior on the drugs clouding his mind, if he had been taking any. Could it be that a debilitating accident could change a person's focus a hundred eighty degrees?

As she pulled into the long, gravel driveway of the school, Sophie's analysis led in a direction that surprised even her.

She had a huge decision to make. And it had little to do with the issues she'd just raised with Andy.

****

Not until three did Sophie run into Max on the patio by the classrooms.

"Hey." His brilliant smile flashed. "I missed you today. Where've you been?"

Her heart turned over at the very sight of him, and his words caressed her soul.

She swallowed, almost choking on the lump forming in her throat. She had to tell him of her decision—but not yet. "I went to see Andy this morning."

"How is he?" His brown eyes, flecked with amber from the sun, showed concern. When she didn't immediately respond, he asked, "Is everything okay?"

"No. I mean yes," she quickly amended. "He's working really hard to walk. He's so determined and focused." She paused. "I tried to talk to him about some issues at the school, but he wasn't interested."

She glanced at Max to see his reaction, but it hadn't changed from concern to surprise as she'd expected. He brought his fingers up to stroke her cheek, a gesture so out of character yet so telling of their changed relationship that she wanted to cry. How would she have the strength to tell him what she needed to?

"Don't worry, Sophie. You're doing a great job in Andy's absence." Max's calm acceptance of her position as director was a far different sentiment than his earlier take on her promotion.

"I don't feel like I am." She sat at one of the tables, and he sat down next to her, his thigh pressed against hers. Heat immediately seeped through her skin, and she flushed straight up to her face.

"Maybe I could help."

His penetrating gaze forced her to shift in her seat.

"What's the problem?"

"There are so many requests for funds. All valid. All worthy. There's just not enough money to go around." She sighed.

"Sophie, if you're worried that you can't approve my request for marketing funds, don't be. I understand the problems with the budget. I also realize that you feel obligated to follow Andy's blueprint." He smiled, but disappointment was clearly etched in his eyes. "I've been rejected before. But I'll keep coming back until it happens. If it's not on your watch, that's okay." He took her hand in his and stroked her fingers with his thumb.

The lump in her throat grew. She had to bite the bullet and tell him. Now. "I made a decision today." She held her breath, then released it slowly.

"What is it?" Resignation marked his features.

He had just given her a huge gift by trying to take the worry away from her. Yet this was going to be much worse than she'd initially thought. Her stomach clenched in rebellion.

"I'm resigning as temporary director."

There. She said it.

"What?" The look on Max's face transformed from bewilderment to disbelief to question. Then a seeming understanding descended, setting his jaw and turning his warm eyes sad. "Are you going back to Valen early?"

"No."

"Then why are you resigning?" Confusion furrowed his brow.

When she didn't answer immediately, he continued. "I don't get it." He rubbed his palm up and down on his thigh. "You're staying on. You wanted the experience to help you reach your future goal. Why would you step down now?"

The forty-million-dollar question that she'd wrestled with since she left Andy. "Because I don't like working with budgets or weighing requests or trying to figure out whose idea is more worthy. I thought I would. But I find myself longing to be in the classroom more, teaching the kids. Spending time coming up with exciting ideas for lit projects. Going on field trips."

She hated to admit defeat, but the daily grind of administration had definitely gotten to her. And when Andy stated, without so much as giving his opinion, that it was all up to her, realization had set in. She could never be a full-time administrator. She loved to teach. She should do what she loved.

"That doesn't surprise me. Ever since our first talk

on the beach, it became clear that teaching was your passion."

He leaned his back against the table, the tension in his face relaxing a bit. But she didn't want to lure him into this false sense of relief, or allow him to think for one second that her decision might be a blessing in disguise for him.

She needed to get out the next part of her pronouncement before she could no longer breathe. The anxiety growing in the pit of her stomach expanded, threatening to rise up into her throat and choke her.

"I'm appointing Kristin as temporary director."

She bit her lip and glanced at Max, anticipating a thunderstorm.

A cloud shadowed his features, but his voice remained even. "Why did you choose Kristin?" His jaw clenched. Not a good sign. Maybe even worse than a thunderstorm.

His questioning stare was unavoidable. "I believe she's the best person for the job. She's been here a while. She knows what's going on. And she doesn't have an agenda, other than what's best for the school."

"And I do?" Now, the anger escaped. The expected reaction.

"Come on, Max. You desperately want a research institute. And your path to it is through your marketing plan. Everyone here knows your goal. You can't be unbiased."

"Thanks for the vote of confidence." He stared straight ahead, his voice tight.

"I'm sorry. I really am. But I had to do what I thought was right for the school. And Kristin may approve your marketing plan once she reviews it. If that goes through, it's just a matter of time before your research institute gets approved."

"It may have gotten approved a lot sooner if you'd appointed me," he lashed out.

"See? That's what I mean. You wouldn't be able to see any other proposals in a better light. You're so focused on your institute and how you can get there that you'd be blind to other requests for funds." She tried to smile, to soften the blow. But it didn't work.

His face converted into a mask. "I thought we were getting to know each other. I thought we trusted each other. At least I trusted you. I guess I misread you."

The knife to her heart twisted with each statement, and nausea churned in her gut. "Max...please understand... Don't..." she pleaded, searching for the words that would somehow fix this—to make him see. She could be trusted. He didn't misread anything. This was a business decision. She reached out to touch his hand, needing to connect with him, hoping the bond would calm his spirit. But he pulled away and stood up, his icy eyes freezing her to the core.

Then he turned and walked away.

Chapter Nineteen

Why would Sophie choose Kristin over him?

Max paddled his kayak through the mangroves late that afternoon, the bunched muscles in his shoulders tense. He had hoped a communion with nature would calm him down and perhaps even take his mind off Sophie. And her decision. Who was he kidding?

With each stroke of the paddle, he mumbled under his breath, all the while gritting his teeth. How could she have given Kristin the job that clearly should have been his?

The viselike pain around his chest forced him to ease up on the paddle. He drifted for a while as he unfurled his hands from their grip. Although he'd been at it for at least an hour, he didn't feel one bit better. Leaning his head back, he took in a breath and slowly let it out.

It didn't diminish his resentment. She should have chosen him. He had poured his heart and soul into this school for the past year and a half. It had gotten into his blood. He understood its spirit. And it wouldn't have been a burden for him.

How dare she accuse him of being biased. How could she even utter such a statement? He had done everything in his power to make her job easier where he was concerned. When she told him she didn't think his request for funds to update the website would be approved since Andy hadn't been onboard, he'd told her he understood and hadn't fought her. When she was upset about the photographs he took of her on the catamaran, he'd deleted them and given her the memory card to prove it. When she advised him to garner allies by reaching out to others at the school for help and support, he had. And he'd thought she was his biggest supporter—helping him every day for the past few weeks as they worked side by side to make his proposed marketing plan as detailed and thorough as it could be. At every turn, he had taken her advice to heart and stepped back from his controlling ways. And what had he gotten in return? A slap in the face.

He gazed out over the water, so calm, so bright, as the sun arced downward in its westward trek. He needed to channel that calm before he even considered going back to shore.

Paddling again, he burned through his energy. His mission to get away from his thoughts a total failure.

Because what was bothering him even more—even more than the fact that she'd made a hurtful decision—was that she still planned to go back to Valen at the end of the term.

For the past few weeks, they had shared so much of themselves with each other. Slowly, they had given up pieces of their pasts, as if a gift. Whenever they could spend the night together, after making love—whether knock-down, drag-out sex or languid, erotic coupling—they talked for hours, tearing down even more barriers and letting each other in. No relationship in the past had even come close—when he'd felt so connected, so elated. She had given herself totally to him. And he had done the same.

Just this morning, before she went to visit Andy, she

had stepped out of the shower, teasing, sexy, wanting. As much as he'd wanted her. She had shown him in every kiss, every touch, every moan, every word.

Their connection had been intense and lighthearted at the same time. Just perfect. At least in his mind.

He shook his head to erase the images.

She obviously thought more of him as a bed partner than as a leader. And as such, only for as long as it was convenient for her.

Obviously, their relationship meant nothing to her. Not enough to appoint him as acting director and certainly not enough to make her stay.

He should have known. Or at least seen it coming. The last relationship she had had been five years ago, and it'd consisted of weekend dates with no thought from her to take it to the next level. And she hadn't even considered Greg Nelson's interest in her. Her real relationship was with her career. She'd proven she was worthy by getting a job as a teacher at Valen, after the school hadn't accepted her as a scholarship student. She would soon be chair of the English department, and her next goal, the headmaster's office, would assuredly occur. If she even still wanted it. Sophie was a force, and if she set her mind on something, it was going to happen. What a fool he'd been to think he could have changed her career goal by engaging her in his life's plan.

A searing pain shot through his chest. His head hurt, his throat hurt, his eyes hurt. His soul hurt. And there seemed to be nothing he could do to stop the agony.

\*\*\*\*

Sophie skipped dinner. How could she sit across the table from Max, pretending everything was fine between them? As if her heart wasn't breaking at the thought of losing him after just finding him.

Nausea had assaulted her stomach ever since he left her on the bench this afternoon. She'd known her choice would hurt him, but she'd irrationally thought her explanation would somehow make him understand. It hadn't. It hadn't come close.

The pain in his eyes had said it all. The words had driven it home. She had hurt him to the core, and that knowledge strangled her heart and pummeled her soul.

Dragging her feet along the beach, she let the sand squish between her toes. *Please, Max, please show up.* She needed to talk to him—alone—away from prying eyes and open ears. Maybe the right words would magically spout forth and make it all better.

Without thinking, she ended up at the spot where they had been not all that long ago. Where they had kissed under the stars. And much more. Just the thought sent shivers through her blood.

A noise broke into her thoughts, and she spun on her heel. Max. But as soon as he saw her, he turned away.

"Max, wait."

He kept walking.

She ran to catch up. "We can't just ignore each other. This place is too small."

He kept walking.

"Max, please…"

Her words bounced off his stiff back, unable to invade his system. She watched him go, refusing to acknowledge her. She looked out to the horizon. Why wouldn't he even talk to her? But she knew why.

Didn't he know she was hurting too?

She inhaled the tangy air and closed her eyes, hoping to purge the bone-deep misery that ate away at her. But nothing could heal her now. Only Max. And he had made it perfectly clear she was not on his healing list.

After what seemed like hours, she headed back toward her cabin but took a detour.

"Kristin?" She peered through the screen door, her throat aching, her eyes stinging. "Can I come in?"

"Sure." Kristin sat at her desk with a textbook and some photographs before her. "I was just planning tomorrow's lesson. Although I know I should be in Andy's office working. I'm not sure you did me a favor." She laughed, putting aside her book.

Sophie moved into the room. "I'm sorry. I know it's a tough job. Any help I can give you, please ask." Her voice sounded tired and maybe even a little insincere, so she tried harder. "It wasn't my intent to dump this on you and disappear."

"Don't worry. I have no qualms about taking you up on your offer." Kristin stood up and stretched. "So what's up?" She studied her closer. "You look upset."

Sophie flopped on the couch and pressed her lips together, wondering where to start. "I made a huge mistake with Max. He won't even talk to me now."

"That doesn't seem like a new problem. You and Max are always disagreeing."

"We were. But this past month has been amazing. We talked through our issues and started working together. I've been helping him with his marketing proposal. And…we kind of got together—relationship wise. Things between us were so good."

Kristin's mouth broke into a huge smile of approval. "Oh, Sophie. That's wonderful. I'm so happy for you. And Max. So what's the problem?"

"I gave the job of acting director to you."

Kristin walked over to the couch and sat next to her. "Oh." She nodded, obviously understanding where this was going. "I was wondering how he'd feel about that. Knowing he'd offered to take over for Andy before."

"He's furious. Even though I explained the reason." Sophie laid her aching head against the back of the couch and stared at the ceiling. "I really hurt him. He thinks I don't trust him."

Kristin chewed on her lip. "That's not a good place to be with Max. Trust is a big thing with him."

"I know. In hindsight, I should have discussed it with him before blurting out my decision. Maybe even before appointing you. It would have allowed him to come to the conclusion that he should be focusing on his marketing plan and research institute, not taking up all his time running the school." Sophie put her face in her hands and rubbed her forehead. "I know my decision was the right one. I just didn't go about it correctly." She sighed, trying to exhale the anxiety that pressed on her lungs. "And here I was supposed to be the one in charge, the one who deals logically and reasonably with people. I knew Max would want the job." She shook her head. "I just didn't handle this right at all."

Kristin put her arm over her shoulders. "We all make mistakes in judgment. We all learn from them. You can't be expected to deal with every situation perfectly."

Sophie turned to look at Kristin. "If Max was just any teacher here, I could rationalize this as a mistake that I'd learn from. I would apologize for my tactlessness and move past it. But he means so much more to me." She tried to swallow the clog expanding in her throat, attempting to strangle her. "Up until today, he'd been so empathetic about the pressure I'd been under in dealing with all the requests for funds from all the teachers. Even telling me that if I couldn't support his request for marketing funds, he'd understand." She sighed. "I'm such a fool."

"Are you in love with him?" Kristin's question was so out of the blue it nearly knocked Sophie off the couch.

"Of course not." She would have added a laugh to prove her denial if she wasn't so miserable—and if she didn't think she might have been outright lying to her best friend. "Anyway, he hates me."

"I'm sure once he cools down, he'll come around." Kristin squeezed Sophie's shoulder.

She doubted it. "This afternoon, when I told him my decision and why, he acted as if I'd stabbed him in the gut." She pictured his mask-like face and his curt response before he'd gotten up and left. "I tried to talk to him earlier on the beach. But he just walked away." Sophie got up and paced the floor. "Max helped me so much in dealing with the whole video episode. He encouraged me to tell Headmaster Ryan about my suspicions. To stand up and fight. To not allow that skunk, Greg Nelson, to take my position and get away with it." She sighed. "He was right. It was great advice and it worked." She paused and looked at Kristin, wishing she could talk to Max like this.

"It sounds like you and Max have been leaning on each other for support. A far cry from your first month here."

"That first month. Ugh. Most of it was spent arguing or apologizing." She recalled those days when she'd questioned her sanity for coming down here. "There was something about each of us that infuriated the other. I've never had so many arguments with one person over so short a period of time as I've had with Max."

"Someone once told me that opposites attract." A smile played around the edges of Kristin's mouth.

"Ha." Sophie remembered the adage she had quoted to Kristin about Maddie and Max. "If we were any more opposite, we'd have repelled each other to the opposite poles of the Earth. Thankfully, we've managed to stay in the same hemisphere."

"What are you going to do?"

Sophie sighed. "I don't know. I should probably just put my nose to the grindstone, work hard with the kids, try to learn as much as I can about the environment here, and get through the next few weeks without causing any more problems. I can't believe there's only a month left before the end of the term."

Kristin nodded, playing with a loose thread on her shorts. "Don't you think you should try to talk to Max again?"

Sophie stared at the wall, contemplating. "I guess. Although, frankly, I don't know what I could say to make this any better, even if he finally does listen."

"I know Max really well. He came here to get away from the pain of losing his brother. He hasn't dated seriously in the entire year and a half he's been here. And not for want of women trying. I've been out with him and the others on a Saturday night, and he could have gone home with any number of gorgeous ladies."

"If you're trying to make me feel worse, you're succeeding."

"I'm not. I'm trying to tell you that you must be pretty special to Max if he's spending time with you. And not just time, but pieces of himself."

A knock on the door interrupted them. "Kristin, it's me. Can I come in?"

Max's deep voice floated through the screen and sent Sophie's heart pounding against her ribs. Kristin jumped up off the couch, motioning for Sophie to go into her bedroom.

"I can't hide," she whispered frantically, wanting instead to disappear. "I'll leave, unless I can get him to talk to me."

Kristin went to the door. "Hi, Max. Come on in." She stepped aside to let him in.

But once his gaze fell on Sophie, he stopped in his tracks. "I didn't know you had company." His voice was gruff, hostile. "I'll talk to you later." He started back out the door.

"Wait, Max, please," called Sophie.

He stopped and turned, looking cool and calm, but his eyes betrayed his outward composure.

"Will you please talk to me? We need to discuss this." Her heart raced as she searched for the words that would make him stay.

"You've already told me the plan. There's nothing to discuss." His dispassionate statement sent a clear message. She was dismissed from his life. "Kristin, I'll see you later." He turned and left without a backward glance.

Tears sprang to Sophie's eyes, and an involuntary sound escaped her mouth. Fingers of intense heat squeezed her throat, suffocating her.

"I have to go," she croaked, barely able to see as she brushed past Kristin.

She had to get to the security of her own cabin where she could give in to her misery, unobserved by anyone.

Chapter Twenty

The next few weeks ambled by with routine, polite conversation, and dedicated work. Sophie did what she'd set out to do. But her heart was heavy with the pain of losing Max.

He had steered her to a path that was liberating and empowering by convincing her to lay her suspicions out there and deal with the problem head-on. Not only had he helped her with the video issue, but his words had replayed in her head before she made the decision to give up the job as acting director—since it was Max who'd questioned her career goal in administration when he discovered how much she loved to teach. She longed to talk to him again, to spend time with him, sharing more of themselves. But it was not to be. She slid into a depression that rivaled the despair she'd felt when she first was suspended.

It was late in the afternoon, and her walk on the beach was meant to clear her mind before dinner. But it wandered from subject to subject, looking for closure on any one of the problems crowding it.

Her friends here had been great. So helpful. So encouraging. Whether anyone other than Kristin knew about her brief affair with Max, she didn't know. If yes, no one had let on. They'd been as friendly and cordial as before, and even though Sophie had initially tried to stay at arm's length, it was no use. They were a family, despite the fact she was leaving in a few weeks to go back to Valen.

But to do what? Before the video fiasco, she had been nominated to become chair of the English department. And Headmaster Ryan had assured her of the position in their last conversation. But now she wasn't so sure that's what she wanted. She wasn't sure about anything anymore.

Her heart sank at the prospect of returning to Princeton in mid-May. Although the flowers and trees would be blooming, and the weather would be warming up, she'd be inside working on her Summer Teaching Academy—alone in the confines of her eight-by-eight-foot office.

She looked around. The Gulf was a brilliant blue in late afternoons, and the breeze carried a mist of salt water. Birds trolled for food along the surface of the undulating sea as they gracefully glided through the air. Palm trees swayed in unison, looking like a perfectly choreographed dance.

But it wasn't just the beauty of her surroundings. It was the students, the teachers, the courses, the activities. When she first arrived, she'd never thought she could get used to this. Not only did she, but she found herself loving it.

How would she ever be able to leave it all behind?

But, then again, how could she stay? Things were so dire between her and Max, and the staff was so small, that any tension between two teachers definitely affected everyone else. And she couldn't live like that. As it was now, he either avoided her, ignored her, or dismissed her.

She headed back toward her classroom to pick up some books. Tonight, she'd work on her notes for tomorrow. That would, at least temporarily, take her mind off her troubles.

When she exited the classroom building, a bee buzzed near her ear, and she swooped out of the way. And bumped right into Max.

"Sorry." She caught his gaze, and her heart somersaulted while kicking into her ribs. She held her books to her chest for support, nearly cutting off the circulation in her fingers.

Initially, he looked as stunned as she felt. But then he got his bearings.

"Just like you to be afraid of a bee."

His cutting statement ignited something within, and she turned on him. "You are the most frustrating human I know. If I'm afraid of a bee, that's my problem. Not yours to comment on. I am sick to death of your treatment of me. You've already dismissed me as not worthy of discussion with you, so why don't you stick to your own rule and never say another word to me again?"

She was ready to stalk off, ready to act as dismissive as she'd accused him of, but the great Max decided to speak. To her.

And his words nearly took the breath from her lungs.

"You hurt me, Sophie."

They stopped her in her tracks, and she raised her eyes to his, seeing the raw pain etched there.

He continued. "I thought we had broken down the barriers between us. I thought I was falling in love with you. But you treated me like one of the rank and file. Not talking to me, but talking at me. After you'd already made a huge decision that mattered to me. It affected you. And it affected me. I deserved more."

She wanted desperately to reach for his face, to

stroke it, to ease the tension in his jaw, but their rift prevented her from breaching his space. The noose that had slipped around her neck tightened.

She ached at his words. *I thought I was falling in love with you.* A clear indication that the emotion had died with the past. She cleared her throat and searched for the right words to say. To make him understand.

"I know I didn't handle our conversation well that day. You're right. I should have discussed it with you. Before making a decision. At the time, it didn't occur to me. Andy had given me strict instructions to take charge and make a decision on the requests for funds or appoint someone else who would. I guess I took it to heart." She closed her eyes for a second, gathering up strength for what she needed to say. "I am so sorry. I didn't mean to hurt you."

She wanted to tell him that she was hurting too. That she had fallen in love with him too. Yet the words stuck in her throat.

"But you did." He turned to leave, dismissing her. Again.

"How can you just walk away?" She heard her strangled voice plead, her tone escalate. "Why don't you understand?"

He stopped. "What I see…what I saw was a woman who had been turning my world upside down, telling me that my feelings didn't matter. That you had made a decision. And I would just have to live with it. Yet your decision was based on a perceived prejudice for my own project. After I had done everything in my power to take my request for funds out of your hands. So you wouldn't agonize over it. I thought you believed in me—in my ideas. I trusted you. But you turned that trust around and threw it in my face. Well, you know what, Sophie? I am living with your decision. But I don't have to agree with you." He paused. "I guess it doesn't really matter. You'll be leaving in a few weeks. It was never meant to be. We don't share the same interests or the same goals. You don't fit in here—never did, never will. I don't know what I was thinking."

With that, he turned and left her there, fighting against a pain so great that it sliced through her being and threatened to sink her to her knees.

\*\*\*\*

"I need to speak to you. Now." An irrational statement for six in the morning, but Sophie didn't care. Since she hadn't slept the entire night, how could anyone expect reason to prevail?

She stood outside the screen door of Max's cabin, barely containing her anxiety. Her face burned as adrenaline ran through her body like a freight train. She'd be better served if this conversation could take place within his inner sanctum, but he stood on the other side of the screen, arms crossed over his chest, with an irritatingly amused look on his face.

"And what could you possibly have to say?" he asked with a smirk worthy of his demeaning tone.

"How can you say I don't fit in? For the past few months, I've done everything that everyone else has done around here, even though it was all new to me. I even learned how to scuba dive!"

"A real outdoors woman if I've ever seen one." Sarcasm permeated his voice.

"I am. I've learned how to pitch a tent and pack my backpack for camping. I learned what berries are edible, and I know how to fish. As well as clean them, no thanks to you. I can kayak, swim, and snorkel, and I even started learning the identity of different types of birds around here."

She was very proud of all her accomplishments.

"You couldn't survive for one night camping without encountering some disaster. And we both know it. Your true colors came through on our last camping trip together." He was definitely smirking now.

"Well, you're such a...a...great outdoorsman." She tried to affect a sneer to go along with her pathetic statement.

"Is that all you can come up with?" He rolled his eyes. "Is that your great comeback?" Laughter erupted, and it actually reached his eyes.

If he wasn't making her so angry, she would have triumphed in the fact she had finally broken through his cold, icy facade.

"I'll prove it to you," she challenged, not knowing where that came from.

"And how do you propose to do that?"

"We'll both go to Big Pine Key and separate. Overnight. I'll show you that I can take care of myself."

"Fine." The smirk was finally gone. "This afternoon. Meet me at three o'clock with everything you need. We'll see how much you've learned."

Victory was within her grasp. She had broken down the barrier. At least temporarily.

"You're on. See you at three."

Chapter Twenty-One

What was the point of this little test anyway? Max sighed as he sat on a log in Big Pine Key, pitching twigs toward the trunk of a sand pine.

Big deal. She could camp. So what? He didn't need for her to prove it.

A few hours alone in the woods and he already regretted his taunting words. Instead of sitting here like a fool, he should be spending the night under the stars with her, talking for hours as they once had. Kissing her, ravaging her. Loving her.

Why had he egged her on? Max examined the real reason for this insane test. He'd bared his soul and exposed himself to her yesterday. Blurted out that she'd hurt him. That he'd fallen in love with her.

In his mind, he had to retreat from his vulnerable confession and lash out at her where it hurt. That she didn't fit in. He'd reverted to his old persona. Better for him, better for her.

And when she'd shown up on his doorstep, spouting off her accomplishments, he couldn't help himself. Pushing her buttons was his specialty. Challenging her, his forte. Although, in point of fact, she'd issued the challenge, not him. And it seemed the perfect way to prove his point and cover up his vulnerability.

*Smart thinking*. He hit his forehead.

Glancing at his watch, he groaned. Only eight thirty.

The sun had set and long shadows surrounded him as he searched for more twigs. The lonely night stretched before him, agonizing in its length. What was Sophie doing? Was she feeling the same dread as he?

His bitterness over her decision to appoint Kristin had subsided, and even though she'd hurt him, he had to acknowledge she'd been under a tremendous amount of pressure when she made the decision she thought best. His reaction was based on emotion, her decision on reason. Even if he didn't agree with her reason.

He stomped his foot. He was through with this nonsense. Why torture himself any longer? He wanted to spend time with her, talk to her. Why not enjoy each other's company for the little time they had together before she left the school for good?

With his resolve now firmly in place, he decided on his plan of action. He would find her, accept her apology, and put the past behind them. Hopefully, she'd agree. But he'd worry about that when he got there.

Finding her shouldn't be a problem if she'd walked due east from their appointed spot, a crooked, scruffy, little tree that stood alone in a clearing. From that point, they'd agreed to walk fifteen minutes in the opposite direction from each other before pitching their tents.

After grabbing his flashlight, he began his hike. A jolt of excitement coursed through his system. Within half an hour, he'd be with Sophie.

But ten minutes into his hike, his flashlight went dead. Not a real problem, except he'd left new batteries in his backpack at the tent. Disregarding a basic camping rule wasn't like him. He'd either have to turn around and lose precious time or keep going in the dark.

Max looked toward the sky and swore at the cloud-hidden moon. The barely visible, uneven path would slow him down, but his feet kept heading toward Sophie, not wanting to waste another minute. Even the dry pine branches hanging from broken limbs, which hit him in the face on more than one occasion, didn't keep him from staying the course. He'd made a decision.

But in the blink of an eye, his foot caught on a tree root, pitching him forward. Trying to gain his balance, he flailed his arms, seeking purchase, before he toppled to the ground, his foot at an odd angle beneath him. A searing pain shot through his ankle. *Ugh!*

He sat holding his breath and squeezing his eyes shut against the throbbing agony attacking his right foot. Minutes ticked by without relief. But he couldn't just sit here. So he pushed himself up onto his left leg and supported himself against a tree before placing his right foot down, gingerly at first, then testing it with more weight.

Zing! An acute pang traveled up his leg. He waited for a few minutes before trying again. He couldn't give up. He had a goal, and it was within reach. But no way could he hop all the way to find Sophie. Especially in the treacherous dark.

With each test, the pain ricocheted through him. Finally, he gave it up. He wouldn't be moving anytime soon. He'd have to spend the night here and figure out his next move at daybreak.

How stupid! And here he had given Sophie a hard time about the rules. He knew better. He knew to carry extra batteries. As a matter of fact, why hadn't he brought his backpack with him? He'd been in such a hurry to see her that all common sense had flown right out of his head. Now look where he was. Alone in the woods, without provisions or shelter, and with a possible broken ankle to suffer through.

All without Sophie.

Could this get any worse?

Yes. It could.

He had ten more hours of pure torture before the sun would rise. The ground was hard and uneven, the night air cool and damp. He had his sweatshirt but no sleeping bag, which would have been a luxury at this point. He knew if he tried to walk on his foot, he could damage it more. Besides, the excruciating pain didn't have the decency of waning, even when he kept it perfectly still.

With little sleep and hours on end of dwelling on his problems, sunrise did little to lift his spirits. He still couldn't walk. The only hope was that Sophie would find him in a few hours and call for help.

He'd better start praying.

****

Sophie looked at her watch. Seven fifty-five a.m. Only five more minutes and Max would meet her. They could leave this place behind, egos intact, and get on with their separate lives.

Disappointment flooded her system. What had she hoped to accomplish here anyway? Had she thought Max would come looking for her in the middle of the night, ready to accept her apology and acknowledge that she did fit in? Had she really expected him to cave in, and while he was at it, declare that his love for her had not diminished? Tell her that he wanted her to stay at Sunrise Island School and help him get his research institute off the ground?

Where had that Pollyanna thinking come from? A bittersweet feeling swept through her being. With as much as she'd scoffed at the idea of staying on when she'd first arrived, this place—and even more so, these people—had grown on her.

She had grown too.

No longer the buttoned-up intellect who'd preferred to spend her free time in the library, she'd reaped the benefits of the great outdoors and had loved every second of it—at least once she garnered some skills. But she couldn't change her mind about her future now. Not when her job was waiting for her back at Valen. When Max was barely speaking to her.

An hour passed while she mused, and still no Max. Where could he be? Had he forgotten a watch? Of course not. Not rules-follower Max. Maybe this was another one of his stupid tests. To see if she could keep calm in the woods at an unexpected turn of events.

Ire insinuated itself into her thoughts. He knew she had to be back at the school by eleven. One of her lit classes was performing vignettes from a few of the novels they'd read.

She'd been so proud of them when they came up with the idea of using literature to entertain the rest of the students and teachers as an end-of-semester treat. And they'd done it on their own, without her help. They'd wanted it to be a surprise to her too.

Perhaps she should go look for him.

Not wanting to venture too far from their meeting place, she began walking in the direction he had taken, calling his name every once in a while, in case he wasn't too far off. Annoyance turned to anger, and it filtered through her at the thought she'd be late. She yelled out his name.

"Sophie..." she heard, off in the distance.

"Max. Where are you?" She spun around, looking for him.

"Over here."

She squinted through the trees, and there he was. Sitting on the ground. Why was he just sitting there?

She tramped over tree roots and pushed branches out of her way with more force than necessary. "What are you doing?" Her annoyance pierced the air, and a bird overhead flew off. "You know I have to be back before eleven. You don't even have your camping stuff. What kind of game are you play—"

She stopped her tirade as she closed in on him. Something was wrong. Alarm shot through her, and she ran the last few feet. "Max, are you all right?"

"Not exactly." His voice sounded weak, tired. His face pale.

"What's wrong?" She threw her backpack down and knelt beside him.

"I might have broken my ankle last night."

"Last night! You've been lying here all night?"

How awful. Poor Max. And here she'd been thinking the worst. That he was setting her up.

She rummaged through her bag and gave him a bottle of water. As he downed that, she retrieved a protein bar, ripped off the wrapper, and handed it to him.

"You really did learn something about camping, didn't you?" He bit into the bar with a vengeance.

Sophie sat back on her heels, folded her arms over her chest, and arched her brow. "I didn't have one problem with my tent last night. I had the right food, and I brought ear plugs to keep the noise of those frightening animals out of my head. I did great." She couldn't help but grin. She had done it. "Which is more than I can say for you."

A slight blush crept across his face, but he covered up any embarrassment with his gruff words.

"Have any ibuprofen in there?" He pointed to her backpack.

"Of course." She took out the bottle and handed him two.

"You better give me two more." He held out his hand.

Sophie wiped the grin off her face. "I guess you're in a lot of pain."

He didn't respond, but as he shifted his body, she could see the misery etched on his face.

"Come on. Let me help you."

She crouched down next to him, and he put his arm around her shoulders. Using his left leg, he pushed himself up. She could tell he was trying valiantly not to cry out as she stood with him, encouraging him to lean on her.

"Let's get you to the car. It's not that far. I'll send someone from school to get our tents and backpacks later." The trip would be hard enough. No need to complicate it by lugging all their camping gear before getting him to the hospital.

"I can't believe this." He shook his head as self-recrimination echoed in his tone.

"Accidents happen. I'm just glad I found you." Thoughts of him lying there all night played out in her mind, and she cursed herself for being too stubborn to agree to bring cell phones or walkie-talkies. She had made the rules strict just to prove her knowledge and independence.

A grunt escaped her mouth.

"What?" he asked.

Not wanting to share her inner thoughts on the subject, she turned the question back to him. "Why were you walking around in the dark last night?" Had he been coming to see her? Maybe he'd decided he couldn't spend another minute without her. Butterflies collided in her stomach as she held her breath, waiting for the answer. Her fantasy come true.

A few seconds went by. "I had some energy to burn."

The butterflies dipped and died. She glanced sideways, but his eyes were downcast, not permitting her to see into them. She did observe an almost imperceptible tightening of his jaw.

"That's it?" she asked, silently begging for more.

He just shrugged.

Her heart sank. So much for fantasy.

Chapter Twenty-Two

Max felt like a complete fool. He'd made a stupid mistake, fractured his ankle, and missed an opportunity to spend the night talking with Sophie. One more example of how he'd misjudged a situation, which led to a disastrous outcome.

He sat in the x-ray room of the local hospital, drumming his fingers on the arm of the wheelchair. Ten minutes ago, the nurse had told him she'd be right back to take him to his next destination. Obviously, her definition of time and his were completely different. Sophie must be climbing the walls by now, most likely pacing the halls outside the ER, cursing him. He knew the time. After eleven. He punched the arm of the wheelchair, an ineffective vent.

He'd blown it. Not only last night but this morning. He should have told her his plan—that he'd been on his way to find her. But pure embarrassment kept him mute. Except, of course, for his grunts and groans. *Ach!* Worse yet, he'd made her miss her lit class's presentation. He put his head in his hands and massaged his forehead.

The ache in his skull, along with his foot, throbbed. But greater than that was the pain in his chest over blowing it with Sophie. He'd missed his opportunity to tell her how he felt. And now he knew he'd keep it to himself. What had seemed like the perfect idea while sitting in the woods alone at night now seemed like pure insanity in the light of day. Especially in the fluorescent glow of a hospital room.

He exhaled long and hard, then closed his eyes.

She really was incredible. She'd helped him confront the past and given him great advice about his future. And even though he'd accused her of not believing in him—deep down, he knew otherwise. She had spurred him on to put all his energy into a marketing plan and compiling data for his research institute. Along with her mantra to gain allies in the process.

She was right. About everything.

He'd just have to leave it at that.

\*\*\*\*

Sophie walked around her small cabin, looking for things to tidy up. She fluffed the sad, flat pillows on the couch, moved the utilitarian kitchen chairs an inch or two, and generally wasted time. Dead tired from a night in the woods and a day at the hospital, she wanted to sleep but couldn't.

She had finally proven her worth. She had rescued Max. But disappointment hung heavily on her shoulders.

Although Max had been grateful for her help and the endless hours she'd spent with him in the emergency room, when they'd finally arrived back at the school, his gratefulness hadn't translated into undying love—or even warmth. As a matter of fact, he'd seemed more distant than ever.

Perhaps the others gushing over her students' production had upped his guilt over making her miss the performance. At least the dark cloud hanging over her where Max was concerned couldn't dampen the elation that overtook her every time one of the staff praised her for her influence over her students' production.

Teaching them confidence, creativity, and teamwork. That was what it was all about. Not rising to the top, only to be stuck in some somber office buried in administrative tasks.

While Max had seen her true calling, it had taken her longer to seize upon her essence.

She'd hoped to share her epiphany with Max. Maybe then he would encourage her to stay on at Sunrise Island School. They could work as a team as they had been, developing marketing ideas that Andy would love, and she could also help Max with his grant proposals for the research institute. All while teaching literature and living in paradise.

When had her sole focus changed? Clearly, sometime between leaving Valen and her overnight stay in the woods. Perhaps she had been bitten by some crazy bug. Or perhaps she had just become a different person.

She flexed her arm and checked her bicep. Impressive.

Sophie toyed with the idea of going to Kristin and accepting her offer for the summer term. She could run her Summer Teaching Academy from Sunrise Island, through her assistant. But she knew her happiness here depended on her relationship with Max. And right now, they had no relationship.

As each day passed, she dreaded her return to Valen more and more. Once, she'd thought of her position there as her dream job, but now she questioned that commitment. She even questioned her life goal. What did she really want?

While exploring her options, Sophie made the most of her time on the island: sunrises, sunsets, the beach, the ocean, the Gulf, swimming, kayaking, snorkeling, and even fishing. For every event, she took a mental snapshot, wanting to hold on to the beauty of this place, and the experience, for the rest of her life.

Surprisingly, no one mentioned her upcoming exodus, but of course they all knew. It was such a small community.

"Hey, Sophie," asked Maddie one morning at breakfast during her last week there, "do you have any vacation planned once this semester ends?"

She chuckled. "I never go on vacation. I run the Summer Teaching Academy for six weeks in July and August. I'll be holed up in my office before it starts, preparing for it. Once it's over, I'll be figuring out how I can make it even better for next year. Then I'll work on my plans for the new school year at Valen."

Ben looked dumbstruck. "What do you mean? Aren't you staying for the summer term? Sara's not coming back until September, if she decides to come back at all. By then, we figured you'd fall in love with this place even more than you already have and stay. For good."

The rest of the table quieted down at his query, and everyone looked at her, waiting for her answer. Everyone except Max, who homed in on his dinner.

Sadness descended over her. "I have a job… This place isn't… I'm not quite…" Her throat constricted, making her voice rasp. She couldn't find the words to explain her situation, and the more she tried the more emotional she became. "I have to leave," she choked, struggling not to spill her guts and possibly her tears.

"So you're going back to Valen?" asked Maddie, her blue eyes wide with surprise. "We all thought you fit in so well here—that you'd want to stay. And the kids adore you. You were such an inspiration to them."

Were those words really coming out of Maddie's mouth?

"I do love it here," Sophie admitted. "But I can't stay." She glanced at Max, and his eyes held hers, but she couldn't read them.

"Of course you can," broke in Ben. "I'm sure Kristin would love to have you stay on."

Kristin nodded. "You know that, Sophie. I already told you." Her words were soft, comforting. But Kristin knew the real reason for her decision.

"We could use you around here," added Dan, picking up his activity roster. "You finally learned how to camp, and Max here is of no use to us right now." He clapped Max on the back. "Sorry, buddy, but until you get that boot cast off, you're flagged."

Max grimaced but kept his silence. The brooding loner was back. If only she knew what he was brooding about now.

Everyone started talking to her at once, cajoling, teasing, and downright begging. It was wonderful. Warmth and friendship collided and filled her with joy. She finally fit in—in a totally different environment than she was used to—and it had taken only four months. A full-blown smile inched over her lips. Her new friends wanted her to stay.

Except for Max.

Her smile faded.

"Thanks guys. You're going to make me cry." Tears stung the backs of her eyes. "This has been a great opportunity, and I loved meeting all of you. You've been wonderful to me." She avoided looking at Max. "I've learned so much, and you've all been so patient." The tears started leaking down her cheeks, and there was no stopping them now. "I know I'll miss you."

With all the difficulties and missteps she had encountered, she wouldn't have traded this experience for the world.

"You should stay." Maddie's voice was soft, encouraging. Not at all like the cool, calculating, city woman she often portrayed.

"I would if I could," Sophie managed to choke out. She rose from the table, not able to participate in this conversation any longer. "I have to prepare for class tomorrow. I'll see you all later."

She turned and left, unable to utter another word. She heard the murmurs behind her and guessed they had more to add to the conversation, but it didn't really matter.

She had two days left.

And then she'd be gone.

\*\*\*\*

Sophie bit her lip and knocked on the screen door. In those few seconds before he answered, she thought about fleeing. This was not a good idea.

Then it was too late.

"Sophie. What are you doing here?" Surprise hung just below the surface of Max's words.

Not exactly the reception she'd wanted. Although she did anticipate it.

"I'm leaving tomorrow, and I thought we should clear the air tonight." She tried to keep her tone upbeat, even.

"There's nothing to clear."

He talked through the screen, his arms outstretched with his hands resting on each side of the doorframe, missing a shirt. He looked amazing—sexy, even with a cast—his muscled body lean and tan, his hair streaked with gold, his brown eyes flecked with light.

She opened the door and pushed her way past him.

"Since you're not inviting me in, I'm inviting myself. I don't want to have this conversation through the door." Anxiety pumped through her veins. He was baiting her. Again. And from past experience, she knew she would soon be arguing with him—not something she wanted to do in the presence of bypassers.

He looked amused, a small smile tugging at his lips. "What conversation would that be?" He turned and followed her with his eyes.

Inhaling for fortification, she braved on. "I'm not sure what you and I had together, but I do know it was powerful. At least to me." She paced back and forth in front of his couch, not daring to look at him, just needing to get this out. "I know I hurt you by not appointing you in my place as acting director. I already explained that decision. I apologized for not having talked to you first before I appointed Kristin. But that decision should not have ended our...our friendship." She stopped pacing and afforded Max a glance. "But I guess it just wasn't meant to be."

He nodded and moved away from the doorway, his jaw set, his eyes sad. "When are you leaving for Valen?"

At least his question engaged him in this conversation.

"I'm going back to Princeton on Friday, but I've decided not to return to Valen in September." Her heart pounded in her chest at the words, finally said aloud. "I'll be living out of a hotel for a while since I had school housing. I'll run this summer's teaching academy and then close it down until I figure out my next move. I've made several calls and have some interviews at schools in the area. Hopefully, I'll get a job quickly." She sat down on the couch, suddenly drained of all energy.

Max moved away from the door and came to sit on a chair close to her. "Why aren't you going back to Valen?" His voice softened, and his eyes gentled.

For once, he didn't have a snappy comeback or rude remark.

She swallowed and tackled the question. "I don't want to go backward there. I was on track to become headmaster one day. But while I was here, in large part thanks to you, I realized it's no longer what I want. I want to teach—to make a difference in kids' lives. I also want to give myself some free time, which I intend to spend outdoors—doing something physical. There are a few lakes in the area where I can kayak or canoe. There are even dragon boat clubs." She laughed at the thought, and the weight of her revelation lifted her spirits. "This place has been amazing for me. I never thought I had it in me to become an outdoors person."

Max smiled. And even though it was tinged with sadness, it turned her inside out as it reached into her soul.

"That's great." Silence hung between them.

"Is that all you have to say?"

It couldn't be. It never was. And now that she wanted to hear from him, he wasn't cooperating. All those other times when she would have preferred his silence, his stinging retorts had come spewing from his mouth. What was up with him today?

He rubbed his forehead with his thumb and fingers, taking his time to respond.

"You're a strong woman, Sophie." He looked directly into her eyes, and his intense gaze invaded her being. "You've been through tough times in the past four months, but you held on, persevering through difficult situations. For someone who didn't know the first thing about outdoor activities, you really came through—working at it until you learned the ropes."

He pulled his chair closer and took her hand in his, shocking her with the intimacy of his action. He stroked her palm with his thumb, sending shivers of pleasure up her arm and through her body. "I know this sounds strange, but I'm proud of you."

His words poured through her like strong brandy on a cold winter's day, sending a warm buzz through her system that made her want to shed all inhibitions and throw herself into his arms.

He continued. "I know you apologized to me before. I should have accepted it instead of acting like a stubborn mule. You've been an extraordinary sounding board concerning my research institute as well as the marketing that has to take place before it can become a reality. I intend to follow your advice."

If true, why wasn't he asking her to stay? Sophie pulled her hand out of his and turned her face to avoid his eyes. Then she shrugged, attempting to shed the confusion over his omission. "This was a mistake. I shouldn't have come here."

She started to get up, but Max reached for her hand and pulled her back down.

"Please, don't leave yet." Sorrow was written all over his expressive face.

Her heart wrenched. She didn't want to leave. Not today, not tomorrow, not ever. Somewhere between the arguments and disasters, the intimate conversations exploring each other's souls and working together on his proposal, she had fallen in love with Max.

Her eyes met his, and all resolve floated away. He leaned over and kissed her, so gently, so sweetly at first that she could hardly feel it. He moved his fingers up to her face and stroked it, deepening his kiss until all she could breathe was his breath.

His hands brushed over her arms, pulling her up with him until they were standing, not an inch between them. His arms encircling her, bringing her closer still, crushing her to him—mouth to mouth, tongue to tongue, heart to heart.

She could feel his heart beating against her chest, and she moved her hand over his flesh to cover it, to feel it better, all the while losing herself in his dizzying kisses, his erotic touches. He moved with her, as if in a dance, toward his bedroom, toward his bed. His fingers deftly slipped under the hem of her tank top and raised it over her head. Shivers streamed through her blood as his hands cupped her breasts while his fingers stroked her, making her ache. Such exquisite pain.

His palms moved over her midriff, and his fingers dipped below the waistband of her shorts, sending every nerve in her stomach into spasms of pure delight. He continued to tease and fondle until she instinctively wanted to rip off the rest of her clothing and take him inside of her. But whatever still functioned in her brain told her to take it slow. Enjoy every minute. Because tomorrow she would be gone.

At the thought, tears welled up in her eyes, and she heard herself cry out, "No."

"What's the matter, Sophie?" whispered Max

against her ear, sending more shivers to places she didn't know existed.

The tears streamed down her cheeks, and Max held her close to his chest, wiping them away with his thumb.

"Do you want me to stop?" True concern pierced his voice.

"No, Max, no. We...we'll never see each other again after tomorrow...after tonight." She tried to swallow the painful clog in her throat. "I'm sorry. I don't want to think. I just want to feel. Please make love to me."

She raised her mouth to his and kissed him with all the hunger, all the need she had stored inside of her. She loved him, but there was no point in telling him that. Yet the words bubbled up inside her throat and clamored to get out.

Instead, she kept them imprisoned inside her head. *I love you. I love you. I love you.*

She reached for the button on his shorts and pulled it open. Wanting him so badly, wanting to be connected to him, wanting to feel him inside her. To be one with him.

She quickly disposed of the unnecessary barrier, then started to work on hers. He grabbed her hand and stopped her.

"I want to do it," he said, his voice husky, his eyes hooded.

He stepped back and gazed at her, stroking her shoulders, her arms, her torso. Driving her crazy with desire. She bit her lip and closed her eyes, willing him to hurry. He unhooked her bra and let it fall on the floor beside them. Then he dragged her shorts and panties down her legs, as his fingers blazed a trail from her waist to her toes. She reveled in every touch, every flicker, until she felt him standing before her.

"Look at me," he said, lifting her chin with his forefinger.

She opened her eyes and stared into liquid chocolate, so soulful, so beautiful. The planes of his face were chiseled in shadow, and his lips were parted as if ready to speak.

But nothing came out. She reached up to stroke his cheek, then moved her fingers over his lips as if to unlock the secret.

Instead, he hugged her tight, then found her mouth with his and kissed her until passion repossessed them. He laid her on his bed, and soon she was where she needed to be. Connected to him by love.

At least for tonight.

Chapter Twenty-Three

Max limped along the beach, his bleak mood having nothing to do with the ache in his ankle. Only two weeks until the beginning of the summer term. He should be working on his research project or planning his lectures. Something. But with Sophie gone, he had no desire to do anything.

Just yesterday, he'd decided against accompanying the gang going to Maddie's family's house in Newport, Rhode Island, for a week before the summer semester started. Why ruin everyone else's celebration?

He inhaled the salt-infused air, hoping to tamp down the nauseous feeling invading his stomach. It didn't work. Sophie's face kept appearing before him: laughing, scowling, musing, smiling. She haunted him wherever he went, leaving him unsettled, restless. And sick.

Her visit the night before she left had initially given him hope that she'd changed her mind. When she told him she wasn't returning to Valen, he'd dared to believe she'd stay on the island. Stay with him. But that dream was annihilated in an instant. She was returning to Princeton.

She'd made her decision to live her life without him. He had to forget her, get used to the fact she was not coming back.

"Poor, sad Max." Kristin fell into step with him as

he limped along, having just had his cast removed. "What seems to be the problem? Did Andy read you the riot act for making Sophie leave?"

"What are you talking about?" He glanced at her as his jaw tightened. "I didn't make her leave. She left on her on accord." He kept walking, hoping to lose her. In this instance, misery did not love company.

"If that's what you want to believe…" She left her comment hanging, refusing to go away.

He sighed. "It's exactly what I believe." He thought back to their last conversation together. When he'd practically choked on his words so he wouldn't beg her to stay. "It wasn't meant to be. We're too different."

"Or maybe too much the same." Kristin sighed. "In my opinion, you're both stubborn."

Max would have chuckled at the insult if he hadn't been so gloomy. "I like you too." He ventured a glance at her, whose annoying grin inched over her lips.

"Why are you ignoring all of us? Why aren't you coming to Maddie's parents' house for the week?"

So that was the real reason for her intrusion. "I'm not in the mood."

"Could your mood be affected by the fact that Sophie's gone?"

"No," he lied, keeping his eyes straight and his words short. Kristin would get tired of this sooner or later.

"I don't believe you." She said it so tenderly, so quietly, that Max did a double take. She laid her hand on his arm with quiet comfort. "I think you fell in love with her."

"What makes you think that?" His tone was harsh. Even mean. But it didn't stop her.

"Because you've been wandering around like some lovesick puppy ever since she left. You've been avoiding meals. Jeez, you didn't even come sailing with us, and that's one of your favorite things to do. If that wasn't telling enough, you brushed us off the other night when we all went to Key West. We know you're moody as a general rule, but these past few weeks have taken the award."

He had nothing to say to that. So he didn't.

"Since you're not coming to Rhode Island, why don't you go visit her for the weekend?"

Her suggestion spiked his heartbeat.

"She said she wasn't doing anything other than working on her Summer Teaching Academy. It has to be depressing spending her days in a hotel. Alone."

A spark flashed through his system at the thought.

"I have an even better idea," she continued. "Why don't you go get her in Princeton and drive up to Newport to meet the rest of us? We all miss Sophie. And it might cheer her up to spend the week with her friends."

Kristin's idea began to take hold, and the ever-present knots in his stomach loosened just a bit. But then reality set in.

"No." He shook his head. She had said good-bye to him as if they'd never see each other again. Showing up at her hotel room to whisk her away for a week sounded more like a sappy plot in a romantic comedy. An idea better left for the actors in a made-for-TV movie.

"Have you spoken to her?" he asked.

"Of course. She's my friend."

"Did you ask her to go to Maddie's?"

"Yes."

This was like pulling teeth. "What did she say?"

"That she was too busy. Her standard answer."

"Then what makes you think my showing up to invite her would change her mind?"

The only good answer would be that Sophie said something to Kristin that led her to believe she loved Max and couldn't live without him.

She shrugged. "Maybe it won't. But at least the two of you would be in the same spot, away from here, and realize that you miss each other and want to be together."

Not the answer he needed to hear. "Sophie clearly doesn't want to be with me. She left. End of story."

"Oh, Max. Maybe it's time to listen to your heart instead of your head." Sadness streamed through her words.

She gave him a pitying look, then left him in peace.

But the peace he'd been seeking was now shattered by Kristin's sage but dangerous advice.

\*\*\*\*

Max sat outside with Andy at the rehab center after having convinced him to take a break from his physical therapy.

"What's up?" No-nonsense Andy got straight to the point.

"You need to get Sophie back." So much for Max's original plan to ease into the discussion.

"Why do you people keep coming to me with your problems?" Exasperation punctuated his words. "Go talk to Kristin."

"Kristin wants Sophie to return. I know it. But she's too close to her to interfere with her decision to leave."

"Sophie always intended to leave after the semester."

"That's because she was going back to Valen. But

now she's not."

Andy's eyes widened, and his mouth hung open. It would have been comical if the topic of discussion wasn't so serious. "She's not going back to Valen?" he finally sputtered. "Why?"

Max scrubbed his face, then massaged his forehead, hoping to ease the pounding in his skull. "It might have had something to do with a conversation she had with me. I noticed that she loved teaching, so I questioned her ultimate goal of becoming headmaster. I didn't understand why she would want to take over the administration of a school at the cost of doing what she's great at." He stared at the cracks in the concrete patio. "She took our conversation to heart and eventually realized that she didn't want what she thought she'd wanted. Her focus had changed." He squirmed in his chair, trying to get comfortable. "I believe stepping into your shoes as the director showed her the light. That's when she decided to give up the position of acting director and appointed Kristin." He sighed. "But in my opinion, there's a deeper reason. She loved it here and can't imagine working in a stuffy northeastern prep school again."

"Then why didn't she stay?"

That was the gut-wrenching question. While he'd refused to admit it out loud to Kristin, or anyone else at the school, the time had come to fess up and deal with the issue. "It might have been because of our relationship."

Andy's brow arched. "What relationship?"

"We were pretty close for a month or so. She was helping me with my marketing proposal and some other stuff." Like his personal demons—which he had no intention of sharing with Andy. Max stood and walked over to an unadorned fountain on the patio, staring at the trickling water. "When she appointed Kristin as acting director, I got angry with her. We were never the same after that."

Andy spoke to his back. "I know I've been out of the loop for a while, and maybe my mind isn't working as well as yours, but if you're the reason she's not going back to Valen, and you're the reason she left Sunrise Island, shouldn't you be the one to ask her to come back?"

Max caught the hint of sarcasm in Andy's voice. "I can't. It's too personal. But if you do it, maybe she'll consider. You know, tell her the school needs her." He paused, knowing he sounded pathetic. "Never mind." He came back and sat down. "As usual I'm trying to manipulate the situation to get what I want."

A smile crossed Andy's face. "You're pretty good at it. This is the first time, though, that you're admitting it."

Max nodded. "Sophie brought my flaws to my attention. She told me I should try to get allies who could then persuade as a group, rather than trying to control everything on my own."

"Sophie's a smart lady." Andy stroked his chin, seemingly deep in thought. "As a matter of fact, you made an ally out of her."

"How so?"

"She came to me with your marketing plan. Her enthusiasm for the project convinced me to let go of my old-fashioned strategies and enter the social media world starting this summer."

Blood pumped through his veins. Was Andy finally

coming around? "That wasn't *my* marketing plan. It was *ours*. Sophie's and mine. She helped me for weeks to make sure we covered every possible issue."

Andy smiled. "I figured, although she didn't take any of the credit. That's how it was with my grant applications. By the end, she knew every fact, every detail as if it were her project."

"She is pretty amazing." Max tried to wrap his head around Andy's change of heart and Sophie's support. He had no idea she'd been working behind the scenes to get Andy's blessing. Warmth spread through him. If he hadn't already been head over heels for her, this would have pushed him over. She had trusted in him enough to go to bat for him.

"Not only did she beat me over the head with your marketing plan, but she also talked very highly of your environmental research institute. We can discuss the specifics once I'm back, but why don't you start exploring grants?"

"Are you serious?" Shock took over his system before his grin turned into a full-fledged smile.

"Finally, some joy. Two minutes ago, you were as glum as an ogre."

"I'm speechless." What an understatement. He was in awe. But it just underscored the fact that he needed Sophie here. "I can't believe that after all this time I've been trying to convince you, it took Sophie to win you over."

Andy started to speak, but Max held up his hand.

"We need to do whatever it takes to get her back."

Andy nodded. "I agree. Sara telephoned the other day and decided not to return. I'll call Sophie and offer her the lit job here. I'd also like for her to work with you on the marketing plan. I got the impression that what was put down in writing was just the tip of the iceberg for her. And she's an ace when it comes to writing grant proposals. We can really use her down here." He dragged his fingers through his sandy, brown hair. "Better yet, why don't you deliver my offer to her personally? Since you two seem to have some issues to work out, maybe you'd better do that before making the offer." He stood up slowly and grabbed his cane from against the wall. "And don't blow it. I expect Sophie to be back here as soon as her Summer Teaching Academy ends."

Andy's gruff voice couldn't put a damper on the excitement coursing through Max's blood at the prospect of working side by side with Sophie on his research institute. He exhaled, and the weight of the world fell from his shoulders.

"Maybe you should take your own advice," ventured Max, knowing he was stepping precipitously close to thin ice.

"What's that supposed to mean?" Andy started walking slowly around the patio, relying on his cane to keep his balance.

"Get it together with Kristin."

Andy stopped in his tracks. He finally spoke, but not the denial Max expected to hear. "How'd you know I…" He looked Max squarely in eye, then shook his head. "It won't work. Besides, she's getting frustrated with me. Every time we gain some momentum, I back off. I just don't think it's a good idea for me to get involved with one of the teachers." He hung his head. "I'm here to run a school. To foster thinking and education and concern about the environment. I'm not here to indulge in whims that could end up with disastrous consequences."

Max's chuckle escaped. "You know, Andy, theoretically speaking, you're right. Your job is to run the school. But you're human. This is the real world, not some scientific experiment where you can set the variables the way you want them. You are allowed to have a social life. A love life."

"There are other places where I can meet women. There's Key West and Islamorada and every Key in between."

"So why isn't that working out for you, then? Why aren't you looking for love somewhere else?"

Andy sighed. "Because I don't want to." He looked pained as he stroked his forehead. "I'm crazy about Kristin."

"Then stop being a martyr and do something about it."

Andy sat down, dragged his hand through his hair, and tapped his foot. "I'll think about it."

That statement was closer to yes than no, so Max decided to let it simmer.

Andy kicked at his cane, then got up and went inside without so much as a good-bye, leaving Max sitting outside of the rehab center, wondering what good karma had just entered his world.

Chapter Twenty-Four

Sophie sat alone at a table in the middle of the hotel restaurant, waiting for her dinner companion. Channeling calm sophistication in her little black dress and emerald earrings, she knew she was in the driver's seat, and it felt good. She glanced at her watch and crossed her legs, cautiously anticipating what promised to be a very positive meeting.

She smoothed her hair back and checked the sleek chignon she'd accomplished before placing her hands in her lap and glancing around the room at the other diners. Businessmen, couples, would-be lovers? A bittersweet pang ran through her.

"Ms. Kearns?" asked a deep voice behind her.

She turned and saw the bespectacled chair of the English department at Princeton University, escorted by the maître d'.

"Mr. Baylor." Sophie extended her hand, smiling broadly. "It's nice to see you again."

"Please call me Ned." A faint blush colored his pale face.

"Thanks. And you can call me Sophie."

Taking the seat across from her, Ned wore the uniform—a navy-blue blazer, khaki pants, and conservative, blue-striped tie. The familiar sight flooded her brain with memories of colleagues from Valen. Fond memories, except for Greg Nelson, but she had moved on. And she knew in her bones she had made the right choice in not returning to her comfort zone. She'd become a different person. Learning new things, stretching her boundaries. Ready for a clean slate.

"Sophie, we're thrilled you're interested in joining us. I know you've been hesitant to accept our offer, so I'm here to convince you that the university is the right place for you."

Ned certainly got straight to the point. No small talk, no wasted time. Impressive.

He continued. "I've been authorized to increase our salary offer by twenty thousand."

Her heart beat double time. Their previous offer had already topped her salary at Valen.

"And we'll make sure you have the funds necessary to continue your Summer Teaching Academy at Princeton." Ned peered at her expectantly, the hint of a smile on his lips as he waited for her acceptance.

They obviously wanted her very badly, and pride in her reputation flowed through her system. Pride and hesitation. *What was the problem?* With Princeton University behind her academy, there was no doubt it would be much bigger and better. And who wouldn't want more money? She should be jumping for joy at the offer.

"Sophie?" She heard her name through the fog in her head, but it hadn't come out of Ned's mouth.

She looked up. And there was Max!

Her breath hitched, and she blinked to clear her eyes. It couldn't be. But there he stood. Gorgeous Max. Looking oddly out of place in a light-blue, button-down dress shirt, navy trousers, and real shoes instead of sandals. His hair was neatly combed, and his clean-shaven face was set in its serious mode.

She took a few moments to get her bearings. And to calm her racing heart.

"Max." She jumped up, almost knocking her chair over, as she took his hands and brushed a clumsy kiss on his cheek. Then fear shot through her. "Is everything all right? Is Andy okay?" Why else would he be here?

"Everything's good." He smiled and squeezed her hand, sending comfort and something much more straight to her heart. "Andy's fine."

Her uncalled-for fear turned to confusion. "Then why are you here?" He hadn't even come by to wish her well the day she left Sunrise Island. That had hurt. She still felt the pain. Why would he go out of his way to see her in Princeton? Unless... She dared to hope. Had he come to his senses and decided he couldn't live without her? That he loved her?

She looked at his handsome face for clues. His smile faded with her question, and a shadow replaced the light in his eyes.

"I'm sorry. I didn't mean for it to come out that way."

"I'm on my way to spend a few days with some friends in Woods Hole. Thought I'd stop by and see you since it's on my way. Kristin told me where you were staying."

The nonchalant, casual visit had her even more confused. As if he lived in the neighborhood and just dropped by her hotel for a friendly drink. Not what she wanted. Not what she needed. She wanted him to declare his love for her, beg her to come back and work with him on his research institute. All in the middle of the hotel restaurant with Ned Baylor sitting three feet away.

"That's very nice of you, but..." But what? Did he have an ulterior motive? She needed to know more. She searched his eyes.

"I'd like to talk to you before I leave in the morning." His beautiful eyes held hers. "I see now is not a good time since you're on a..."

"This is a meeting." Interesting that he thought she was on a date. She smiled at the hint of jealousy in his unfinished sentence. "This is Ned Baylor from Princeton University." She turned to introduce them. "He's here to discuss an employment offer."

A cloud passed over Max's face. Or was that just wishful thinking?

"Ned, this is Max Heaton. A brilliant marine biologist who teaches at Sunrise Island School. He plans to start an environmental research institute there."

Ned shook his hand warmly. "Very impressive. I know of quite a few students, as well as teachers, who would love to participate once you're up and running."

Sophie glanced at Max to see his reaction, and the expected spark appeared.

"I'll be sure to get in touch with you...once I get the institute off the ground."

Ned nodded. "I'd heard of Sunrise Island School before, but Sophie filled me in on the specifics in our previous discussions. Sounds like a wonderful place."

"It is." Max beamed. "You should come down and take a look at it so you can see for yourself."

Sophie put her hand on Max's arm, feeling his hard strength, his warmth. But just that insignificant touch sent heat to her core. "Why don't you join us?" The words slipped out of her mouth unchecked. *Where had they come from?* She wanted to be alone with Max, not sitting here with him and Ned, discussing the job offer that would keep them apart.

"No, thanks," he declined, graciously. "I'm sure you two have a lot to discuss."

Sophie inwardly exhaled, grateful he hadn't accepted her rash invitation, and ecstatic he wasn't heading for Woods Hole before they had a chance to talk. She filed away the almost imperceptible tightening in his jaw and hint of disappointment in his tone, hoping to explore them later.

He turned to her, and his eyes held hers, pulling her into his world and taking her breath away.

"Stop by my room when you're done. I'm in 215." He touched her arm lightly as he leaned over.

His warm lips whispered a kiss against her cheek, and she inhaled his familiar scent—pine soap and ocean mist—despite him being hundreds of miles away from the Gulf. She closed her eyes to inundate her other senses.

"See you soon," she croaked, feeling a flush creep into her face at the yearning she was sure could be heard in those three little words.

Max moved away and broke the spell. He shook hands once again with Ned and headed toward the hotel lobby.

Sophie stood there, like a fool, watching his retreating back as a pain so acute shot through her heart and threatened to disable her.

She breathed in and swallowed.

She was so in love with Max.

\*\*\*\*

Max paced the width of his room, the carpet silencing his footsteps. Yet nothing could quiet the noise in his head or the hammer pounding away in his stomach. He had showered and dressed in tattered jeans and a black T-shirt, hoping that the comfort of his clothes would help calm his anxiety. It didn't work. Hadn't come close.

*Don't jump to conclusions. She may not have accepted the job.* He balled his fists and paced some more. But of course she would. Who wouldn't? It was Princeton University—one of the top universities in the country. The best of the best taught there, and Sophie was being offered a position with that esteemed club. She would be one of them.

He should have pulled her aside and told her about Andy's offer. At least it might have given her food for thought before she ultimately accepted the job at Princeton. Instead, he'd tried to act cool, indifferent almost, as if his heart weren't bursting at the sight of her. Fools did foolish things. What difference would it have made? It was too late.

A knock on his door stopped him in his tracks, and a chill ran through his blood at the thought of her news. But he propelled himself across the room, shaking the tension out of his arms as he approached. He took a calming breath, then opened the door slowly.

His gaze took in the vision. Beautiful Sophie, dressed for success. The sophisticated black crepe dress, high heels, and emeralds were a far cry from her shorts, tank tops, and sandals. His mouth went dry, and all thought flew out of his head. He wanted to take her in his arms and kiss her long elegant neck, capture her lips, breathe her in, and keep her in his heart forever.

"Hi." She broke through his fantasy. An uneasy smile played around her mouth, and he stood back to allow her entry. Why were they so uncomfortable with each other?

"Come on in." His voice tightened with anxiety.

She hesitantly moved past him and into the room. The lights were low, and soft music played in the background. A queen-sized bed stood on a platform in the middle of the room, making it impossible to miss. He shouldn't have invited her here. He should have suggested they meet in the bar. This was too intimate.

"It's great to see you." Sophie looked around the small space, perhaps thinking the same thing.

"You too." He finally smiled. "You look beautiful. Very classy."

She laughed. "Go ahead, say it. Very Princetonian."

His smile widened. "Much better than that." For the first time since he'd arrived, his taut nerves began to relax—just a bit.

His earnest compliment produced a flattering blush, and she brought her hand up to cover her heart. "Thank you." She lowered her eyes as if embarrassed.

"Would you like to sit?" He pulled out a chair from the desk and held it for her before taking a spot on the bed.

Silence hung in the air between them, and Sophie crossed her legs, sitting very straight, very formal, driving him back to his recent agitation.

"I guess you're wondering why I came here in person." He leaned his arms on his thighs, bringing his face closer to her.

"You said you were going to Woods Hole. Is there some other reason?"

Did she look hopeful? Of course not. What planet was he on? She inched forward, and he glanced at the carpet, wondering where to start.

"What is it?" she asked again, her voice soft, encouraging.

"I went to see Andy the other day. He's accepted our marketing plan and wants to start implementing it over the summer. He also said I could start looking for grants for the research institute."

A wide smile burst over her lips, and genuine joy sparkled in her eyes. "That's great, Max. I'm so happy for you."

"He wanted me to ask you to come back and teach. And work on the school's marketing efforts." His eyes shifted to the floor again, and he rubbed his hands against his legs. He wanted her to come back too. But he couldn't say it. Couldn't interfere with her dream. Couldn't make this hard on her. He needed to backpedal. For her sake. "Of course, he doesn't know you were offered a position at Princeton University. I'm sure he'll understand if you decide to stay here." Sure, Andy would. And Max would have to too. He got up and started pacing. "How'd it go with Ned? He seemed like a nice guy."

He struggled to make his voice even—to still the nerves jumping through his skin.

"It went very well. He offered me a great teaching position at an even greater salary. And they want me to transfer my Summer Teaching Academy there." Pride filled her words. "It's almost too good to be true."

Max pulled his fingers through his hair. He had to let her go. Ever since high school she'd wanted to prove to the powers that be at Valen that she was more than worthy, despite their decision not to grant her a scholarship. She'd worked hard, gotten a job there, started a teaching academy, and was offered the position as chair of the English department. Her goal had been to fit in. And she'd done that in spades. If not for the video fiasco, he would have never met her and she'd still be at Valen, clawing her way to the headmaster's office. Now she was even higher on the ladder of success, leaving Valen in the dust.

"Then of course, you'll accept it. Andy will be disappointed, but he'll be happy for you. I mean…Princeton. Who could blame you?" He dug his hands into his pockets and started pacing again. "And you deserve it, Sophie. You've worked hard to get where you are. Two schools bidding for you. Although Sunrise Island School can never match the salary you'll get here. It's hardly a contest. And the prestige. I feel silly for even raising the offer." The air stilled and closed in all around him.

He sat back on the bed, studying her. Sophie's forehead furrowed, as if she couldn't quite understand what he was saying. He'd been talking to fill the space they had created between themselves—trying to get out some semblance of a "congratulations" without letting her see the devastation that ripped at his very bones.

Then she stood. "Well, I guess that's that."

Slashes of red colored her cheeks, but no joy shone in her eyes. She should be ecstatic. She'd just been offered the job of a lifetime, and he, like a chump, was supporting her in her decision.

"Thanks for stopping by with Andy's offer. It was nice of you to go out of your way."

Although the words were right, the tone was off by a mile. Flat sarcasm instead of gratefulness seemed to be the undercurrent.

She continued. "You've had a long day. Me too. I need to get some rest. But before you leave tomorrow, I have information for you in my room concerning a few grants for your research institute. Why don't you stop by in the morning to pick it up? Room 323." She paused. "Better yet, why don't we meet in the restaurant for coffee at eight? I'll go over it with you there."

"Sure." He followed her to the door, numb from their exchange.

Sophie looked into his eyes. He lowered his lids to shield the overwhelming sadness he couldn't hide.

"Good night." Her voice was quiet, dejected.

Then she turned and strode down the hall.

A piercing pain shot through him. Then it splintered and maimed.

Chapter Twenty-Five

Max arrived at the restaurant a half hour early—restless, tired. And anxious. He ordered coffee and tried to focus on the morning news on his cell phone. But when he read the same paragraph three times without comprehension, he put it down and stared off into space.

His stomach jumped and spun. He'd made a decision. Despite the fact that Andy was handing him everything he wanted, he now knew he could never be happy without Sophie. He was going to leave Sunrise Island School and move up here. A euphoric rush flowed through his system, and a smile transformed his features. He'd just have to hope she'd be as happy with his decision as he was.

He couldn't wait to tell her. Should he blurt it out, build up to it, make her guess? He was almost giddy with happiness—the antithesis of the pain he'd felt at the thought of losing her.

He'd find a job in the area, and they'd be together. There were dozens of prep schools and colleges he could apply to. And although he'd have to re-establish himself at yet another institution, he'd be with Sophie. His research institute would have to be put on the back burner for a while. But it'd be worth it.

"Am I interrupting anything?" Sophie stood before him, looking tired but pulled together.

He rose while clearing his mind of all his crazy

thoughts. It wouldn't do to sound incoherent or scattered. He had to say this correctly.

"No, of course not. I was just reading the news." What a stupid thing to say, since his phone was face down on the table.

They both stood next to the table, and for a few seconds, he felt like an awkward teenager waiting for the right moment to ask Sophie to the prom.

He pulled out her chair and bit back a smile before seating himself.

Dressed in a yellow-and-blue floral dress with a matching blue sweater, she looked the part of a northeastern professor taking a summer holiday. Conservative but chic. Sophisticated but breezy. There was still a little bit of the island left in her. Including her cascading hair highlighted to perfection and toned arms and legs bronzed by the sun.

"You're in a good mood." She poured herself a cup of coffee from the carafe sitting on the table.

"Yes." But he wasn't ready to divulge his secret. "You look great. When you first came to the island, you used to dress so conservatively. Remember?" He thought of her too-long shorts and button-down cotton blouses.

"I believe you called me frumpy." The initial edge in her voice disappeared, and a grin escaped.

"You told me that was the way people dressed in Princeton. But you look freer than you did back then. It suits you."

"I decided to change my style when I changed my attitude. Thanks to you. I've become more independent, more my own person." She looked into his eyes. "Good advice, don't you think?" She arched her eyebrow and waited for his answer.

He wanted so badly to take her in his arms and kiss her until she couldn't breathe. Until he couldn't breathe.

"It's only good advice if I get the benefit of spending time with you. With you up here and me down there, I think it's terrible advice." He tried to keep the conversation light and teasing. At least until he told her of his decision.

His stomach bunched into a knot. Would she be happy? He inhaled to push down the angst. When he finally knew in his gut he couldn't live without her, it had been like a cosmic epiphany. And now nothing could stop him from going ahead with his plan. Unless, of course, Sophie hated it. A wave of fear reeled through him. No. He couldn't think that way. This was right in so many ways.

She seemingly ignored his clue and leaned over to pick up a redwell filled with papers that she'd set on the floor by her purse. From it she pulled several stacks, clipped together in four different groupings.

"In my spare time, I did some research for you. I found four grants I think would be perfect for your institute. I printed the applications as well as the criteria and highlighted the most important sections."

He swallowed hard, and his stomach fell. No! She couldn't have done this for him. He was going to give up his dream of the institute. At least for now. He had to. To be with her.

She held the first package toward him, and he slowly raised his hand to take it, as if any quick movement would hammer home what this meant. An unwanted change of plan.

He looked at the top of the first page. The Stewart Foundation. A few highlighted words jumped up at him.

*Innovative research. Environmental protection. Marine life.* He flipped through the stack of papers and saw not only highlighted material but notes written on the sides of almost every page in Sophie's handwriting. He looked up, feeling the blood drain from his face.

"When did you have time to do all this?"

"In between interviews. If I didn't find something to occupy my mind, I would have gone crazy. It was fun." She smiled, and her shining, brilliant eyes held his gaze. This couldn't be happening.

"I don't know what to say." He skimmed the other three packets she handed him. All with the same amount of detail. "But you didn't know that Andy was going to approve the institute. You might have done all this work for nothing." *Please say it was effortless. That it didn't take you hours on end to research it.*

"I knew he'd approve it sooner or later. And I was betting on sooner. That's why I devoted so much time to it. Besides, I know how to reach Andy. I intended to push him on it. Your plan is brilliant. And it will give even more credibility to his school."

She held up two other folders. "These are some marketing ideas. I was going to send all this to Andy by mail, but now that you're here, you can deliver it to him in person. I also put together an in-depth outline with eight different steps." She pointed to the appropriate pages. "You can add it to your ideas or not. Whatever you think. Once you're back there, feel free to call me, and the three of us can discuss it."

Why had she done this? It was ruining his plan. "Sophie, I hope I don't sound ungrateful or rude or...or stupid, but why would you do all this? You're leaving the school behind. Moving on."

Tumultuous thoughts ricocheted off his brain, causing pinpoints of pain, not only in his head but to his heart. He couldn't now tell her he was ready to give up his idea of the institute. He couldn't throw all this in her face. She believed in him. She'd gone through all this trouble to find the best foundations to apply to. She'd studied their requirements, their conditions. In order for her to come up with four, she must have reviewed fifty. And she developed more ideas to add to their marketing plan.

"You look shocked." Sophie's brow creased.

"I'm sorry." He reached over and squeezed her hand. "I am. You've done so much." He should say more. Thank her. But his agitated state of mind didn't allow it.

She bit her lip and tilted her head, as if trying to figure him out. "I happen to love that school. I know it sounds ridiculous, given my background and my initial inability to fit in. But after a few months there…" She shrugged. "It got under my skin."

Max bit back the remark that was dying to gush out of his mouth. *Then why don't you come back? Give up the offer from Princeton.* But he held it in. Because vying for equal time was his decision to leave Sunrise Island School to be close to her. But that decision had been turned on its ear. He couldn't do it now. Not after Sophie had invested all this time and effort in his project.

And then it hit him. While he was figuring out how they could stay together, she was working on them staying apart. It had obviously never even crossed her mind that the two of them should work things out. She had applied for jobs in the Princeton area, with no intention of ever coming back to Sunrise Island. And she was making sure that Max stayed where he was by handing him the roadmap to his future with the research institute.

She had moved on.

And he was sinking.

Fast.

Chapter Twenty-Six

Sophie's palms were sweating and her heart pounding. She waited alone in the director's office, sitting in front of his desk, her crossed leg bouncing uncontrollably.

"Sophie! I'm so glad you're here." His familiar voice entered the room before he did. The door closed with a click, and his footsteps, slow and deliberate, echoed across the floor.

She stood and turned toward him, a bright smile beaming on his face.

"Andy! It's so wonderful to be here." She entered his outstretched arms and hugged him. "How'd you convince your doctors to let you return so soon?"

"I promised to do my therapy here. I hired someone to work with me, because you know what would happen."

She laughed. "I know, I know. You'd get so caught up in running the school you'd forget."

"That's exactly it." He still used a cane, and his gait was uneven, but determination was written all over his face.

"You are one strong-willed guy. And you look great."

He chuckled as he maneuvered to the chair next to Sophie's. "You're a good liar. I know I could use some sun, and I've lost about twenty pounds, but honestly, I feel really good. I needed to get back here for my mental health. The rehab center was so depressing it was making me crazy. Now that I'm back, I can't seem to stop smiling." He sank into the chair. "I really missed this place."

She reclaimed her chair after positioning it to face his. Just seeing Andy allayed some of the anxiety pummeling her over returning to Sunrise Island.

"I'm glad you reconsidered." He massaged his thigh as he looked at her.

Did Max feel the same way? She hadn't talked to him since the day she'd seen him in the hotel restaurant three weeks ago. He had looked so stunned, so confused over the work she'd done to help him. His lukewarm thanks had her as muddled as he looked. And soon thereafter, he left, leaving her mystified, unsettled. And upset.

Until Andy had called, demanding to know what she had done to Max to make him so irascible. And why she hadn't accepted his offer.

It took a while for Andy to get it into her hard head that Max really wanted her to come back. He just didn't want to get in the way of her incredible offer from Princeton. But Andy had no such qualms. He'd used every bit of ammunition he had to make her choice clear, including the fact that she'd left her heart on Sunrise Island.

And not just because of Max, although he was a huge part of it. But because he was offering her a life that contained balance. She could teach, market, help get the environmental research institute off the ground, and do whatever else she wanted to do—including running her teaching academy from down here. And between those jobs, she could walk on the beach and kayak. And maybe even camp under the stars.

Andy wanted her there, and he had made it next to impossible for her to turn him down. Not that she intended to. The job was everything she could ask for. The only offer that righted her equilibrium and validated her existence.

At least once she dealt with Max.

She regarded her friend and smiled. He looked so much more relaxed than he usually did. His constantly creased brow contained less lines, his perpetually straight mouth held the hint of a smile, and his green eyes, generally glancing past whoever was talking to him, focused on her.

"You really do look good," she said, this time with emphasis. "Rested. Even happy." She didn't mean for it to sound so surprising, but that's how it came out.

Thankfully, he chuckled. "I know it's hard to believe. I always walked around here with a critical eye and a frown. No time to appreciate what I had, always striving to make it better. I'm working on my attitude. Once you come so close to dying, you see things differently." His eyes actually twinkled.

"The new attitude works!" She feared saying more at the risk of insulting him. So she changed the subject. "How's Kristin?" A grin threatened to escape, so she bit her lip, trying to keep it contained.

"Why do you ask?" His arched brow advised her he knew what she was after.

"I was just wondering if you two…" She let the suggestion hang in the air. He could fill in the blank.

He looked Sophie squarely in the eye. Then a slow grin turned into the most amazing smile. "I'm working on it. My negative attitude on nepotism here was so ingrained that it's taking some time to come to terms with such a drastic change. But after talking to Max and seeing how beneficial a real partnership could be, if it works, had me thinking that I shouldn't have rules about personal relationships. If they happen, they happen. If it doesn't work out, the two parties will have to be mature enough to figure out their next steps."

Sophie nodded, knowing that in part, he was talking to her. Where would she and Max end up? As friends? As lovers? As real partners in every sense of the word?

Andy broke into her thoughts. "Kristin did a great job as acting director after you jumped ship."

Her eyes shot up to his to see if he was angry over her defection. But the teasing gleam proved otherwise.

"Don't worry. I'm not mad at you. As a matter of fact, Kristin really took to the job, and I offered her the position of assistant director. It will free me up to work on your and Max's fabulous marketing ideas, and also give me time for a personal life." A sparkle glinted in his eyes.

Sophie smiled. "So it all turned out for the best."

"Except where you and Max are concerned. I don't know what you said to him when he flew up to Princeton to see you, but he won't even talk about you."

Her heart dropped into the pit of her stomach. "He doesn't know I'm coming back?"

Andy shook his head, and his grimace said it all. "I thought that conversation would best come from you." He stood up and grabbed his cane. "I need to discuss something with Dan. We'll talk later."

And with that he was gone.

\*\*\*\*

The time had come to deal with Max.

After several hours and twenty-one days since their last encounter, she couldn't stand it another second. The flitting butterflies in her gut turned into zooming vultures. She was scared.

Would he even consider reestablishing an emotional relationship with her? She hoped they wouldn't be relegated to the friend category. Or worse yet, friendly acquaintances. She wanted much more than that. But for now, she'd have to settle for whatever he was willing to give. And in time…

She knocked on his cabin door, a déjà vu from just three months ago. Offering up a silent prayer for help, she closed her eyes and held her breath.

"Sophie!" He filled the doorframe, looking incredibly handsome in a navy T-shirt and faded jeans. Shock marred his features. Not surprising since Andy hadn't paved the way for her. What a bum.

"May I come in?" Her voice squeaked, and she castigated herself to get it together. Be strong.

He stepped aside and opened the door.

She stopped short when she saw Maddie lounging on the couch, looking ever so comfortable and cozy, like she belonged there. Could it be that she was too late? Had Max and Maddie stepped up to the plate and tried out their chemistry, now that Max was open to a relationship?

"Hi, Maddie." Disappointment echoed in her voice. "I just got in and wanted to come by to say hello. Andy offered me a job here, and I decided to take it."

Maddie's smile brightened the room as she jumped off the couch and came to greet her. "Welcome back, Sophie. I'm so happy to hear that. The kids are really lucky to have a great lit teacher like you."

Her genuineness stunned Sophie. Even though Maddie had come around toward the end of the semester, Sophie had never underestimated their fragile relationship.

"Thanks." She ventured a look at Max.

The stunned—and perhaps guilty—expression on his face cemented her assumption that they were an item. Her spirits sank.

"I guess I'll leave you two. I need to unpack." The upbeat note in her voice belied her dejection. She reversed her steps, then turned and fled, an unseen fist clenching her heart.

She found her way to her cabin, all the while reprimanding herself for thinking—no, hoping—things would so easily fall into place. She had prayed that Max would be ecstatic to see her and all past problems would just slip away once they were back in each other's orbit. When had she become such a hopeless romantic? When had she started considering a man when making life decisions?

She banged through her door and pulled her suitcase, with much effort, into the bedroom. Opening it on the floor, she knelt beside it as tears of frustration and hopelessness leaked out of her eyes and down her face.

She threw her clothes from her suitcase to the bed, many of them missing and ending up on the floor. When she got to her shoes, she tossed them against the wall, not even caring whether she scuffed the paint or ruined the leather.

"Whoa," she heard, as if off in the distance. As if through a fog.

Then strong hands wrapped around her upper arms

and pulled her up from her place on the floor. He spun her around.

"What are you doing?" Max searched her eyes, no doubt questioning her sanity.

"I-I'm unpacking," she stuttered through hiccups, as the tension of the day tugged at her every cell.

Then he wrapped her in his arms and hugged her close. "Stop," he said gently. "Just stop."

He stroked her back and whispered soothing words, holding her head against his neck, letting the unrelenting tears soak his shirt, until she could finally breathe again. She burrowed into him, inhaling his scent, feeling his strength, not wanting to ever let go—because if she did, she might never feel him again. Slowly, the pent-up tension drained from her body, and she feared she'd collapse if he didn't keep holding her up.

After what seemed like an eternity, reason returned, and she knew she couldn't stay attached to him any longer. She had to face him.

After pulling away, she moved to sit on the bed amid the mess of tangled clothing.

"I'm sorry." She shook her head. "I'm sorry for this little scene. I'm sorry that I just barged in on you and Maddie. I'm sorry for steamrolling my ideas over you in Princeton, and I'm sorry for ignoring your feelings when I appointed Kristin in my place." She sighed heavily and placed her head in her hands. "Our whole relationship has been one apology after another. I'm such an idiot."

He knelt in front of her and took her hands away from her face, holding them in his. "I know." He looked at her, ever so serious.

Laughter bubbled up inside her and erupted from deep within. Then Max started laughing too. And before she knew it, she slid from the bed onto the floor next to him where they both fell into hysterics.

"You finally decided to come back," he choked out.

"Yes. I finally did." Her decision should have been based solely on the fact that she loved teaching here and wanted to continue the experience. While those things were true, she knew that deep down she had made the choice because she wanted to be with Max.

The laughter left his face, and his expression became almost somber. "What made you change your mind about taking the job at Princeton?"

"I fell in love with this place. And...I missed you."

There. She said it. Sort of.

A faint light twinkled in the depths of his soulful, brown eyes. But when he didn't respond, a stab of pain shot through her heart.

She broke the silence. "If you've moved on...if you're with Maddie now—"

He placed his fingers over her lips. "I didn't. I'm not."

He dragged them softly across her mouth, sending sensual shivers throughout her body. Then he leaned over her and replaced his fingers with his lips, brushing them over hers tenderly at first, then becoming more insistent, more demanding. She moved her hands around his neck, pulling him closer, threading her fingers through his soft hair. Reveling in the feel of him.

Even if only temporarily, he was here. With her. Even if this was him feeling sorry for her because of her meltdown, she didn't care.

She would treasure these moments forever, remembering...

He teased and tormented her with his mouth,

moving from her lips to her neck, to her ear. Delicious, luxurious tingles radiated down her arms, down her legs, until they covered every inch of her body. She squirmed under him, pressing herself against him, feeling his hardness, his desire, which inflamed hers.

He lifted his head and looked at her, his eyes heavy with yearning, his sensuous mouth parted.

He took in her bed, covered with strewn clothing, then he turned his head in the other direction where her suitcase was still partially packed and sitting just inches from them on the floor. Other pieces of apparel littered the rug around them.

Without saying a word, he bent his head and covered her mouth again, picking up where he had left off, apparently deciding that the floor was as good a place as any.

She moaned under his ardent kisses, his roaming hands—silently begging him to make love to her...to love her. He hadn't responded to her heartfelt words, other than to sweep her off her feet, but she wouldn't press, couldn't bring herself to even ask.

With his strong arms, he pushed himself off the floor, straddling her, as he removed his tee. She reached up instinctively to feel his bronzed chest and muscled forearms, all the while gazing into his passionate eyes. Lost in their intense depth.

Her fingers trailed to the button of his jeans and, once undone, tugged on the zipper. He slowly stood and removed them, looking like an impassioned statue of David. Reaching down, he held his hand to her, and she took it, rising in one fluid movement. Like a perfect dance partner, he moved into her space and encircled her with his arms, hugging her to him. She closed her eyes and inhaled, never wanting to forget the beachy scent that was all him.

Much too soon, he pulled away, standing before her, gloriously naked. "Unbutton your blouse," he said, his voice rough with need.

She started with the top button, then stopped, watching his smoldering eyes, his Adam's apple move in his throat.

"Another," he rasped, and she complied, drawing it out slowly, sensually.

"Keep going," he ordered, sending shivers of delicious expectation down her spine.

She did, and when she had undone the last button, she looked at him expectantly.

"Take it off."

She slid one side over her shoulder, then the other, allowing the material to slip down her arms and onto the floor. He reached out to touch her lace-covered cleavage, but she backed up, just out of reach. A hint of a smile crossed his lips.

"Take off your shorts."

She obliged, ever so slowly, ever so erotically, her sole purpose to make him crazy with desire. Her matching bikini panties were very tiny, purchased and worn for Max's sole pleasure. She had only hoped she would get this far with him. And miraculously, here he was, standing in her littered room, a Greek god to her seductress.

Fire sparked through his eyes, and as she watched him watch her, she brought her fingers to the clasp of her bra, playing with it but not unhooking it.

"Do you need help?" His husky voice had taken on a playful note.

"I think I do." She bit her lower lip in anticipation.

She took a step forward, and his hands reached out to stroke her through the delicate material. Her peaks hardened, pushing against the lace, begging for his hands to fondle and touch and inflame her from the outside in. He slipped a satin strap down her shoulder and kissed her where it had been, pulling the material away from her as his hand cupped her naked breast. A sound escaped her throat, and she leaned her head back, reveling in her ecstasy.

He moved his hands to her waist and pulled her hips to meet his—the hard presence of his need pressing against her stomach. His brown eyes darkened with passion before he dipped his head and flitted kisses over her chest—his hot, wet tongue laving her as he covered her nipple with his mouth—blinding her with needy pleasure. He kissed his way over to her other breast, his breath uneven, his hunger growing as desperately as hers.

When she could no longer stand, she pulled away, inhaling deeply. Then she swiped her arm across the bed, sending every piece of clothing down to the floor in a heap.

His chuckle warmed her soul, as did every other thing about him, and she pulled down the covers and invited him to join her. He lay down beside her, gazing so intently into her eyes that she couldn't speak. The connection drew her in and held her there, as if through an invisible thread. His fingers caressed her face, slowly tracing her cheek, her chin, her nose, her mouth. "So beautiful," he murmured, before his lips replaced his fingers with a soulful kiss that reached down into her heart.

He sheathed himself and moved on top of her, deepening his kiss, spinning her into a dizzying vortex. Within seconds he was inside her, his every movement sending sparks to every nerve, fire to every cell. He shifted forward and back, at first controlling his movements as if engaging her in a slow, sensual rhumba. Every inch of him hit nerve endings she didn't know she had, spreading a wild rush over her heated skin.

His thrusts got harder and faster as he gripped her hips, pushing them both higher and higher toward their ultimate pleasure. Her breath caught in her throat as her insides exploded, sending cascading fireworks throughout her system. He was right there with her, calling her name through the thundering roar in her head.

Ecstasy tore through her and invaded her senses, blocking out the real world, and just allowing this to be.

Chapter Twenty-Seven

After basking in her sexual haze for as long as she could before the questions began hammering at her again, she disentangled her arms from around Max and inched away.

He took her hands in his and stole her words. "We need to talk."

She nodded her agreement.

"When you came to my cabin, you said that you're back. You chose this place over Princeton? Are you out of your mind?" His warm chuckle advised her he was teasing, which took some of the angst out of the discussion to come.

"Maybe." She smiled as she pushed herself up onto her elbow and laid her head in her hand. "I was honored to have received the offer. Who wouldn't be?" She still felt the surge of self-satisfaction gained from the approval of such an esteemed institution. "But a few days after you left Princeton, Andy called. He was very persuasive."

She took in the shadow that crossed over his eyes. Was he thinking about his lukewarm delivery of the offer? He'd barely even said the words. Instead, he'd made it sound as if the job at Princeton was a foregone conclusion and Andy would understand.

"Of course." Max lowered his lids, avoiding her gaze.

She watched him, waiting to see if he would give anything away. He was great at hiding his feelings, but she needed a clue, at least a crumb, to let her know she had turned her life upside down for a good reason.

He finally responded. "I guess you needed to hear the offer from Andy. I'm glad it worked. I knew this place had gotten under your skin by the time you left. And it's a good place for you. You can teach and work on the other things you love so much. I know Andy was excited about our marketing ideas."

Max went on in that vein, talking all around her reasons for being here, without including one word about them.

She got out of bed and found a large T-shirt of hers in a pile on the floor, then pulled it over her head. This conversation needed to be moved to the kitchen or living room—somewhere other than her bed.

He rose and followed her after grabbing his jeans and stepping into them. She stood by the kitchen chair but was too fidgety to sit. Attempting to read his mind was useless, but she sure wished she had some sort of radar that could penetrate his brain and see what he was really thinking.

"Why the look?" His forehead creased.

She couldn't help her sigh. "The main reason I came back here was for you, Max. Do you think you could tell me how you feel about that? Honestly?" She couldn't believe she had put it out there. Her insides churned at the thought of his reaction.

He sat down in his chair, a strange look sliding over his face. "You mean you don't know?"

"Know what?" The frustration echoed in her voice. "I told you I missed you. Instead of responding, you silenced me with a kiss. Not that I didn't fall under your spell. It was incredible. But if you...care about me, I need to hear it. If you don't..." She paused, almost unable to get it out. "I need to hear that too."

"I came all the way to Princeton to see you, Sophie. I was devastated that I was too late. That you had an offer from the university. I couldn't stand in your way—although I wanted to beg you not to take that job. To come back. But I know you. You have a need to be successful at a top school. To prove to yourself and others that you're worthy. And Princeton University..." He let out a breath. "What could be more rewarding? At least in your world." He sat back and rocked on the legs of the chair before continuing. "If you had given me a sign, I would have given up my job here and moved there in a flash. I had intended to tell you over coffee that morning at the hotel that I was going to apply to schools in the northeast just to be near you. I was ready to spend the rest of my life with you, Sophie."

Her heart thumped in her chest, and her mouth turned as dry as the island sand. She was powerless to move. To speak. But she had to. "Why didn't you tell me?"

"When you pulled out your folders with all the work you had done on the grants and on marketing the research institute, I understood that you wanted me to go back to Sunrise Island and follow my dream. In that instant it hit me. You had done everything possible to assure we'd be apart. You were staying in Princeton, and I was returning to Sunrise Island. Decision made. And if there's one thing I know about you, Sophie, once you make up your mind about something, you are one stubborn woman."

"I would have agreed to come back to Sunrise Island

that night, if I'd thought you wanted me to. But you made the decision for me. Told me you'd explain my offer from Princeton to Andy."

His eyes flashed. "I didn't think in a million years you'd turn that down."

"You didn't give me a chance to tell you how I felt." Her voice quivered, and her hands shook. She looked away from him to protect herself. "I was so hurt that you didn't even try to talk me into coming back. I thought you must not want me to. You were just going through the motions. For Andy."

"Why would I have come all the way up to Princeton to see you if I didn't want you to come back?"

She shrugged. "You were on your way to Woods Hole. It wasn't that far off your route."

Max swore as he pushed his chair back, then got up and started pacing. None of them good signs.

"That was just a ruse to explain my crazy trip to Princeton." He exhaled. "We are so blind when it comes to our feelings for each other." His words held an undeniable truth.

She moved in front of him and touched his face, forcing him to look at her. The closeness they'd shared during those few months while working together, the hours spent talking, slogging through their issues, and then laboring over Max's projects had dissipated around them toward the end, and in their place grew uncertainty, even hostility.

She had to fix this. "Max. I came back here looking for you. Looking for us." She pleaded with her eyes, her whole body. She needed him to see the truth. "When you came to Princeton, neither of us communicated our true feelings. About each other or about what we wanted to happen. I was a mess back then. Living in a hotel. Looking for a job. You shocked me when you showed up." She paused, seeing the insecurity in his eyes. It was now or never. She had to tell him what she felt. Dropping her eyes momentarily, afraid that if she looked at him, she would lose her nerve, she threaded her fingers through his, praying the connection would fuel her confession. "I never wanted to leave Sunrise Island. The best weeks of my life were spent here with you." She raised her eyes, and her throat tightened, making it almost impossible for her to go on. "I love you." She lowered her lids, the weight of her admission, along with the fear it wouldn't be returned, pressing on her heart.

His warm fingers lifted her chin, forcing her to look into his eyes. Then he drew her into him, his arms surrounding her, hugging her tight. She buried her face against his neck and breathed him in, replenishing her soul with his scent.

"Sophie, I love you too." He kept her close, holding her tighter. "I want you in my life more than you can ever imagine. More than I can comprehend. You've touched me in places I thought were dead. You made me care about you, even though I tried my hardest to keep you at arm's length." He laughed as he stepped back to study her, and she couldn't help but laugh too, as the weight of her anxiety fell away with his words.

"We're not exactly a match made in heaven." She sobered at the thought.

"Maybe we weren't at first. But there's no one I'd rather be on cloud nine with than you."

All mirth left his face. She stared into the depths of his eyes, trying to gauge the gravity of his feelings.

"Sophie, I'm more serious than you may want to

know. When we first met, we had our own battles to fight, which got in our way. But you helped me work through my problems, and I know you can say the same for me. We're different people now." He stroked her cheek with his fingers, then dragged them across her lips, causing every nerve in her body to crave his touch.

"You're right. If it hadn't been for you, I would never have realized that I'd rather teach more than anything. It makes me so happy." She shook her head. "What I thought I'd wanted all along, I didn't."

"You mean to become a headmaster at Valen?"

"Yes." She turned her gaze to him, and streams of pure happiness trailed through her body.

He hadn't only pushed her to become proactive where her reputation was concerned, but he had also made her see there was more to life than following a path that had become ingrained within her. There was a whole wide world out there to experience, and she had only just begun with her ventures at Sunrise Island School. "My world was so small, so comfortable. So dull. But I didn't see that."

"I know how exciting scuba diving, fishing, and camping are, but I didn't think you felt the same way." His skepticism shone clearly in his eyes.

"I had my difficult moments." She laughed. "But when faced with the prospect of living in Princeton and burying my head in my books, I felt this strange longing to stay here…to get in a kayak at seven in the morning when the sun is rising and glide through the mangroves, to sit on the beach with you at dusk—reveling in the golden hour when the sky turns pink and orange and purple. I wanted to get back out there on a catamaran with the whole gang and go snorkeling—without the breakdown of course."

He didn't even crack a smile at her attempt at a joke. Instead, his handsome face took on a somber look as he searched her eyes. "Are you ready to move forward? To start a new life? With me?"

An answering grin moved across her lips.

His smile lit up the room, as well as her heart, before he took her in his arms and kissed her until he took her breath away.

She breathed a sigh of utter happiness and whispered the words they both needed to hear.

"I'm ready."

## Epilogue

*Seven Months Later*

"Hey, Kearns. Meet me on the beach at five thirty tonight." Max's smile bloomed with his familiar invitation.

"Okay, Heaton. I'll be there." She was sure her smile rivaled his.

Working side by side with Max over the last seven months had been a dream—sleeping with him every night, a fantasy. While they each had individual time teaching their classes and going on field trips, they also worked tirelessly together, applying for grants and planning for the environmental research institute, which was becoming a reality.

Every day she pinched herself over her luck in finding this new existence—she was truly living and working in paradise. If that edited video hadn't been posted, if she hadn't been suspended, she would never have known what she'd been missing in her life.

And now here she was, doing what she loved—teaching—but enhanced by so much more. A year ago, she had never experienced the joy of kayaking alone at dawn or hiking through the scrubby pines with a group of teens or snorkeling on the reef with the best of friends. And she had never taken the time to sit on a beach and experience the colors of the golden hour, right after the sun set, next to the man she adored.

She was one lucky woman.

The rest of the day sped by, as all her days seemed to, and she rushed back to her cabin at four thirty to get ready to meet Max on the beach. Today was the first anniversary of the day she'd arrived on Sunrise Island, and although that day, in particular, had been a rude awakening, she reveled in how far she had come since then.

She showered and slipped into her pretty new dress, pulled the sides of her hair up, and styled the rest in long, beachy waves. Then she headed out the door to meet her man.

All of their colleagues were already on the beach— the women in flowery sundresses and the men in pastel linen shirts and khaki pants. As she approached, Pachelbel's Canon in D began playing.

Everyone turned to look at her, but she only had eyes for Max. He stood at a floral archway, gazing at her with his soulful eyes holding love and promise and adventure. Tears dimmed her vision as she picked up the wildflower bouquet Kristin had left for her and headed up the makeshift aisle in the sand.

Ben had gotten ordained online and received his officiant's certification so he could marry them. Andy stood to Max's right, acting as his best man, and Kristin stood on the other side of the arch as Sophie's maid of honor. Maddie, Sue, Dan, and the rest of the teachers were there to bear witness to their solemn nuptials.

Within seconds, Sophie joined Max, who came to meet her halfway down the aisle. Chuckles erupted at his impatience, but only joy bubbled within her at his proof that he had no hesitation in entering into this union. And neither did she.

Although he surprised her on Christmas Eve when he got down on one knee and proposed in front of their pathetically decorated Christmas tree, the real shock had come when he said he wanted to marry her in a few weeks—on the anniversary of her coming to Sunrise Island—the day that had changed both of their lives.

So she'd bought a sleeveless white chiffon gown at a local boutique, which now floated around her legs in the breeze coming off the ocean. She had threaded Vinca blooms in her hair, which complemented the bouquet she now carried. And the love of her life had just met her on the beach, where they would exchange their vows to love, honor, and cherish each other as the sky turned pink, orange, purple, and red.

It was their golden hour.

### A word about the author...

Maria Imbalzano is an award-winning contemporary author who writes about strong, independent women and the men who fall in love with them. She recently retired from the practice of law, but legal issues have a way of showing up in many of her novels. When not writing, she loves to travel both abroad and in the states. Maria lives in central New Jersey with her husband—not far from her two daughters and granddaughters. For more information about her books, please visit her website at http://mariaimbalzano.com where you can also sign up for her newsletter.

Thank you for purchasing
this publication of The Wild Rose Press, Inc.

For questions or more information
contact us at
info@thewildrosepress.com.

The Wild Rose Press, Inc.
www.thewildrosepress.com